A FEW FOOLISH ONES

BY GLADYS HASTY CARROLL

AS THE EARTH TURNS

A FEW FOOLISH ONES

A FEW FOOLISH ONES

By

GLADYS HASTY CARROLL

New York - 1935

THE MACMILLAN COMPANY

Set up and electrotyped.
Published April, 1935.

PRINTED IN THE UNITED STATES OF AMERICA
NORWOOD PRESS LINOTYPE, INC.
NORWOOD, MASS., U.S.A.

"Foolish ones, Gus called the birds, these left behind when all the rest had flown off to some place where picking was easier than here. Tough little fellows; they dipped and soared as if it were summer, or bit and tore at the bushes in a frenzy of industry, or sat dully on an icy branch with foot tucked in among their feathers, depending on the kind of spirit they had. Foolish ones, perhaps, to hang on here, the few of them alone, just because this was the place where they had pricked the shell; but they seemed to be making out."

—A Few Foolish Ones

MORNING LIGHT

1870

page, 1

NOONTIME

1895

page, 51

EARLY EVENING

1920

page, 245

MORNING LIGHT

1870

IN 1870 York Road ran rich with life, the whole nine miles of it teeming, from the salt marsh up Grou'nut Hill and along the flats to Claypit, down into the sands past the school building, over Dockham's bridge and by the Selden Hill Dam, up Rolling Rock Hill and around the turn past Captain's eddy and the blind lane leading only to Mount Assabenbeduc, then on to Nubble Point where the meeting-house stood. Neither of its outlets was much used: neither that, at one end, where it joined the highway to the beach, to deep-sea fishing and longshore lobstering, nor that at the other where it merged with the road to Derwich Village, inland center connected by river with European and Oriental waters. This, though Maine, was neither a fishing nor a shipping community. The settlers were farming people, of sound English, Scotch, and Irish yeoman stock, and York Road kept itself to itself.

Broad, low houses with small, woodbine-covered windows poured smoke from central chimneys at noonday and flickered with candlelight at night. All day the maple-shaded yards were bright with children, hens, sheep, calves, and fenced-in flower gardens. Barns were full of cattle and hay and grain and harnesses. Tilled ground neighbored tilled ground with only walls of round field stones between. Bragdons, Grays, and Linscotts lived here, digging and driving, laughing and shouting, feeling afraid, glad, proud, eager, lazy, knitting, pounding, baking their bread, finding themselves in love, bearing their children with outcry, singing and praying and dying; the Blaines, Joys, and Dockhams, Allens, Cheneys, and Shoreys, Seldens and Elys and Hamiltons.

Many must cross the Road in going from house to barn; the cattle fed beside it all summer; children on their way home from school strewed it with ragweed seed. Men walked here behind oxen; girls going berrying; dogs scenting rabbits; babies tottering abroad; Aunt Let Ely to bring another Linscott into the world; a young man hauling lumber for a new house; an old woman carried along the Road to the edge of the woods to be laid beside her husband; horse sleds gliding over the snow with a load of crackers, tea, sugar, and salt cod for Asa Shorey, who kept store. Up and down, back and forth over the Road went the feet of the Bragdons, Grays, and Linscotts, Blaines, Joys, and Dockhams, and the rest. To glance out from a back kitchen window was ever to rest the eye upon a stretch of field and the deep woods from which it had been stolen and thereafter continually battled for against its natural master; but no one looked long toward the Road without seeing life. Even when for a brief space nothing passed, there remained in the subsoil a kind of pulsing left by what had already gone.

In the summer of this year religion took the Road. First, Evangelist J. S. Johnson came walking through from Derwich Village to the beach and stopped in at several places to talk and pray, learning the meeting-house had fallen into disuse through the intemperance and lack of interest of its members. A week later he came again, this time with his wife who had a big voice for singing. They ate and slept at the Grays' and at the Dockhams', by turns, and there were services every night in the church. The dutiful old and the curious young went to hear him. The men took silver coins from their chests, the women aired and pressed their shawls and bonnets until they had something fit to be seen in, and Elder Johnson brought them all to their knees. The old recalled, sometimes with sobs, what the Lord had done for them in the past. The young thought less of dancing the soles off their boots, and more of baptism. York Road underwent a reformation, and Elder Johnson, leaving, pronounced the remnants of the old church society qualified to organize a new.

A proper notice duly appeared, attested copies

of it posted for seven days in public and conspicuous places, one on the schoolhouse door, and one on a board nailed to the elm tree beside the meeting-house.

NOTICE

Derwich, July 27, 1870

To the members of the Temple Christian Society

You are hereby notified and legally warned to Assemble at the Meeting house at Nubble Point on Wednesday, the third day of August A D 1870 at seven of the clock in the evening then and there to act upon the articles to wit

1st To Choose a Moderator to preside at said meeting

2nd To Choose a Standing Committy

3rd To See what Action the Society will take in regard to hireing a minister to preach the Gospel at Nubble Point Meeting house

4th To Choose all other Necessary officers and pass any other vote or votes for the benefit of said Society not contrary to law

Given under our hands this 27 day of July in the year of our Lord one thousand eight hundred and seventy

James Gray
Moses Dockham } Standing Committy

"Seems mighty strange for goin' to meetin' to get to be the fashion," said Roxanna Gray, sitting with her sister Sarey on the schoolhouse step, resting for a bit on their way to the church and reading the notice again.

It had been much read during its seven days. Nowhere else along the roadsides was there anything new to see. Its words spoke loud and clear through the midsummer stillness of pine tree and oak, witch grass and sweet fern and yarrow. Every crease of the paper and every curl of the writing was familiar to the girls as they studied it.

"Father's prayed so long for everybody I didn't suppose they'd ever start a-prayin' for theirselves," said Roxanna. She took out her handkerchief to polish her new buttoned boots, and crimped the bow of her bonnet strings more saucily under her ear. "It makes a great time, though, don't it? With all the folks it ain't like just father a-scoldin' and a-takin' on to the Lord. Old Mose Dockham, don't he make a piece of work? All he can think on is a-signin' of that pledge, now he ain't been drunk himself sence he put his name to it. I lay he'll talk again tonight if 'tis a business meetin'. He's got an awful tongue in his head."

Sarey sat looking at the notice, her face lifted and turned sideways. Her bonnet was off and lay on her lap. Her hair, combed sleek and braided, was thick and honey-colored, her mouth soft and uncertain. She was sixteen, but her body remained flat and childish, her arms thin and blue-veined under the bunched material of her blue calico dress. Her eyes would have been called beautiful in a world where that word was used; large, full, and purplish blue, inquiring and sorrowful.

"You ain't payin' me a mite of attention," Roxanna said. She added suddenly, "You've still got Gus Bragdon on your mind."

Every night of Elder Johnson's week of meetings James and Mindwell Gray had driven him and his wife home, whether to their own house or to Dockhams', proud to be one of the few along the Road who drove a horse and owned a wagon. Every night Roxanna and Sarey had set out after them on foot, sedately and alone, to be met at Assabenbeduc Lane by two or more of the young fellows who had sat on the fence as the girls came down the church steps and then hurried by a short cut through the woods to be at the appointed place before them. Once there had been Berias Blaine for Roxanna, twice Trumann Selden, once Orrin Cheney, and twice the two Shorey boys and Amos Hamilton making a merry group to surround her, for Roxanna was eighteen and dark, ready with her laughter and spicy in her talk, old enough to have been married a year or two but still not promised. Every night for Sarey of the sleek hair and soft mouth it had been the same one, Gus, the youngest Bragdon. They were always so quiet the others scarcely knew they were along; but still they had talked a little together, and all their words had counted, as Roxanna understood now. Last night in bed Sarey had confided to her that Gus would like it if Sarey would come to live in the new house he thought of building.

"You've still got Gus Bragdon on your mind," Roxanna said. She heaved a short, impatient breath. "Seems like I never see such a little fool. Listenin' at your age to talk of tyin' up to somebody that don't think of nothin' but what an old man might. Can't you see if you wait you'll get where you can take a little good out of livin'? We'll be old enough to rights to have our own say about where we'll go and what we'll be a-doin' of. We want to do a little dancin', don't we? We want to git us each a piece of plaid silk and make it up, and have our hair cut short and curled. We might even light out and git us jobs down to Great Works Mill and live to a boardin' house. Sho, Sarey, after all I've told you, what chances there is and how great you're favored, I snum if you hadn't 'bout as soon as not take up with one that clips his own hair and pegs his shoes hisself. Great lummockin' cutter, every step he takes sounds like you hit the ground with a plank."

"I don't know," Sarey answered painfully, hanging her head and twisting her fingers. "Gus is most likely well enough. I ain't so awful favored. Nothin' like you now, Roxan. 'Tain't likely anybody to Great Works would pay no attention to me."

"Plague take you, Sarey," Roxanna said, springing up. "You beat all. What do you have to be so meachin' for? Won't nobody think nothin' of you if you don't think nothin' of yourself."

They padded soberly through the sands, not looking at each other.

"One thing I will say," Roxanna broke out as they came in sight of the meeting-house. "Father'll make it hot for you if he ever hears of this. You know what he'd say to you havin' anything to do with fellows, and you know what he thinks of Bragdons' folks that's all for gettin' holt of worldly possessions. The way they do ain't his way any more'n 'tis mine. He says they may be honest but they ain't pious, and nobody trades with them but gits themselves trimmed. He'll tell you that and more besides it if ever *he* hears of your goin's-on with Gus, and it'll be no skin off my back. You hark what I say, Sarey, if you go ag'inst me on this. You'll find out what 'tis to fend for yourself to home. I won't lift a finger to save you. Now you mark my words! . . . Why, father'd sooner you'd take up with anybody on the Road but the Linscott tribe . . . Hello, Lovice! Ain't it fine tonight?"

Sarey climbed the church steps without lifting her head, moving miserably a little behind Roxanna and Lovice Joy, Polly Selden and Adeline

Cheney, who clung together and paused outside the door to finish their talk and laughter before going in. They were early. No one else had arrived, and the lamps had not been lit.

"Let's stay out here till the rest come," Lovice said.

They sat in the warm twilight, the four of them, and Sarey a little apart. The pink flowers of smartweed blossomed about Sarey's feet. She reached down and broke off a leaf. Yes, it was smartweed and would sting her tongue if she bit it. Lady's finger looked the same except that its leaves had a dark spot in the center, and lady's finger had no burning taste. Gus Bragdon had taught her so years before, when she first went to school and he was one of the big boys who came to study only when it stormed so hard that they could not work in the fields or in the woods.

"They've both got pink blooms," Gus had said. "Where the difference is, is in the leaves."

"Did you hear about Keturah Linscott?" Adeline asked between her teeth. "Aunt Let Ely went over there this mornin'. Ma mistrusts her young one is comin' along."

"She does?" Polly whispered. "Oh, Ad, shouldn't you s'pose Ket's hopin' it'll die?"

"No, *I* don't s'pose any such thing," snapped Roxanna. "Them Linscotts had as soon have young ones without fathers as with 'em. Don't make no difference. Mother says them Linscotts is as near to the beasts of the field as any cutters with souls could be."

"Oh, don't you imagine it's awful for her, though?" asked Lovice, stirring self-consciously. "Havin' it, I mean? Why, she ain't near so old as Sarey."

Sarey quivered, knowing well enough the trial which lay ahead of even the most virtuous married woman, and tried not to listen. The smartweed flowers made her think of thoroughwort. Pink thoroughwort was no good, Gus had told her. It was the white-blooming his mother brewed for a spring tonic. The Grays bought their medicines from the shelves in Asa Cheney's store, but Sarey knew now from Gus that it was better and more saving for a woman to make her own.

Back along the Road others were coming to the meeting. At the first place where a fish peddler would call as he drove a cartload of fresh-caught haddock and clams inland in the early morning, Aaron Bragdon waited at the door for his wife, Hannah, to get her aprons off. His square fist held the reins of the horse firmly, and he sat, broad and stooped, well toward the center of the wagon seat.

"There's some as thought I shouldn't reap nothin' here but rock and brine," thought Aaron, for his three-cornered field and trim apple orchard faced the salt marsh. "Well, I guess they won't none of my dozen young ones do no better than I've done. Onless 'tis Gus."

Hannah came out, hurrying, bent and worn with work, and climbed up beside him. Aaron grunted to the horse, and they drove out of the yard into the Road.

Their sons Charles and Edward and their daughters Leteshy, Kate, and Hattie had gone on ahead. Other sons, Silas, Ruel, and Albert, and two more daughters, Sarah Jane and Thirza, would be setting out with families of their own from houses here and there along the Road. Gus, too, might come, their youngest son, from his place up Assabenbeduc Lane, but this was not so certain, for it looked like rain tomorrow; mares' tails lashed the sky; and Gus was a lone hand at his haying. Only one child of Aaron and Hannah, Jefferson, their second boy, was too far away for the meeting; Jeff had come home from Gettysburg in a box.

Other families also crowded the way, most of them on foot but one or two with wagons. Enoch Blaine walked with Catherine Shorey, for they would be married after harvest, a gay couple, laughing at the gibes of those who passed them. It was new for a Blaine to have traffic with the church; it must be Catherine had used persuasion on him. The Blaines were all for fiddling and dancing, running off and then coming home with taller stories to tell than a sensible man could take much stock in, but well enough to hear.

Betsy Joy and her girls came out from their house, but Albert stayed behind to keep an eye on Isaac. The Joys always had a care for him, different from the Seldens who sometimes went away for days and left Aunt Sal Peters alone in the attic, crazy as a loon, tearing off her clothes and going without shoes until she got a sliver in her foot clear to the bone. Old Isaac was quiet tonight. Those on their way to the meeting could see him peering out through the barred window of his room in the west end of the house. Sometimes he bellowed like a polecat in a trap, but tonight he was quiet, and Albert, who had stayed to watch him, sat comfortably on the door rock, lifting his hand in greeting to each passer-by.

No one went churchward from the Linscotts'. It was not to be expected. They stood about their two-room shack a little back from the Road, a group of men with short, thick bodies, a litter of children scrambling and squealing, a woman or two. It was a sight to make good wives hope they had locked their doors, and farmers to fear for what lay in the ground ready for the taking.

"I do love trematers," Tim Linscott, father of the Linscott tribe, often muttered feelingly through his whiskers. But he never grew tomatoes. It was Silas Bragdon who grew them and soon found he could not risk leaving them to ripen on the vines. In the fall rows of the luscious fruit reddening on Siley's window sills made Tim's mouth water; he sometimes stood still in the road to stare at them. "Oh, my God," he would say slowly, shaking his matted, mangy beard, "my soul and my God, I do love trematers!"

James and Mindwell Gray, driving a thin, hoary mare down the steep hill from their house to the Road, were figures a little apart from the rest. James was old, over seventy, and sat tall and thin with his lash whip in his hand, his suit and hat and tie greenish black, his countenance hollow and solemn. Mindwell was young, not more than forty, with ample bosom and lap for mothering the world, but wearing on her smooth, pink face a rapt expression which set her forever apart from worldly things. These were the two who had harbored the evangelist when he first came, these the two who had been faithful with desertion all about them, and spent years in praying for neighbors not interested to pray for themselves.

"God be praised," muttered James as they rode. "God be praised. God be thanked. Praise be to His holy name."

Mindwell's full throat swelled with music she hoped to pour out to the Lord before the evening should be over. He would be coming soon now, she thought. He would walk again upon the earth and claim His own. Mindwell came of Adventist stock.

A mile and a half over Assabenbeduc Lane, as Roxanna and Sarey sat by the schoolhouse talking, a young man was shoeing an ox. The beast hung patiently in his sling, one foot securely fastened to a block, snuffing as he watched the fire which burned in the forge. The blacksmith, quiet and intent, crouched to draw a curved strip of iron from the flames, his movement slow, his hands steady in the sharp heat, his features turned livid by the light; crisp, pale hair, eyes of a thin blue like frost on a window with night beyond it, a face mild in shape and bony feature but with an expression of powerful immobility, as if to say one might talk but talk meant nothing; all was settled in a man's mind. He rose to lay the strip of iron on the anvil and stood beating upon it with a hammer, not a large man but broad-backed with long, heavy arms, wearing a sleeveless leather jacket over his checkered shirt, a leather apron over his blue, homespun pants, and boots with pegs which had left marks on the dirt floor of the shed.

This shed, moved from one of his brothers' places, and the fine new barn were the only buildings Gus had here as yet, but they were a good many for one not far past twenty-one, and he would build him a house when he saw the need. For himself the hay was good enough to sleep on and the forge fire would fry a fish from the brook whenever he could not go home to his father's. Lately he went there less and less; he had his work to think of.

For the reason that Gus was the sixth son Aaron had seen to manhood, no property which Aaron had accumulated along the Road remained to be given to him. The sixth portion was the twenty-acre strip behind the Blaine pasture, land the first Bragdon settler had cleared and fenced and built his cabin on. To make it up to Gus, Aaron gave him three wood lots, while the older boys had only two apiece and none of theirs was so well grown as one of his.

Gus was satisfied. A patch good enough for the first Gus was good enough for him. In those early days this whole section through to the sea was the Blaine Grant, owned by men known to Charles I, gentlemen, sea captains, with windows in their houses, china on their tables, and veils and flowers for their women when they married. The first Gus was neither gentleman nor adventurer, no acquaintance of the King, but a yeoman farmer from the north of England who paid for his passage with labor for the Blaines, then rented and later bought this strip of land. He was a worker. He knew how to clear his ground by cutting down the trees in June when fresh leaves clung to their branches, burning them early the next year when the soil was still protected by its own damp, digging up the roots to be interlaced and used for fencing. He had plowed with a wooden mattock and put in his seed at the proper season, carefully, frugally, on the right elevation, with regard for the signs which were all about him of the wetness or dryness, heat or chill lying in the months ahead. He did not dance and sing like the Blaines, nor did he live like the Linscotts, who even then squatted on the commons roundabout, a pack of good-natured rogues and wastrels. Gus Bragdon worked, his eyelids drooping at the corners from much close figuring. And in time most of what had been the Blaine Grant fell into Bragdon hands, and still there had been more Bragdons to go afield all through York County and spread into the north of Maine. The first Gus, looking ahead, had been satisfied here; another Gus, eight generations later, felt no less so; he, too, was a worker.

His hands gripped the ox's foreleg. His hammer drove the nails with quick, firm blows. His shears snipped away, unhesitating, a border of hoof the steer would be better without.

"Ye'll do," he said at last. "Down with ye."

The block was removed. The sling slid low on its pulleys. The ox stepped out gingerly and plodded away to his stall beside his mate, next to the cows. Hay came into the row of mangers by forkfuls. Creatures never went hungry in a Bragdon barn, nor cold, nor dirty, nor sick. Do without fondling, they might, and did, and work hard by day; but at night they took their ease. It was so in Bragdon houses as well as in Bragdon barns.

Gus stripped to his underwear and boots and washed in water the oxen had left from their drinking. His hands plunged deep, and he flung the water over his face and neck down to where brown skin met the white, cleaning his ears with his forefingers and slicking his hair smooth. A blue suit, a light shirt, and a plaid scarf tie hung waiting in the harness closet. He put them on with thick fingers, and stepped about rather as the ox had done in his new shoes; but starting out across his land, he soon forgot what he wore.

These were his twenty acres: his rise of ground, fit place to put a house; his meadow and pasture, his brook and walnut grove and big red oaks. A strip bounded on the west by a marsh and on the east by a river. As things were, he must cross the river by footbridge in summer, on the ice in winter, and by raft in the highwater months; but some day he would have more than a right of way across the Blaine pasture. Some day he would own from here to York Road, lay him a carriage bed, and build him a bridge fit to bear up a yoke of oxen any day in the year.

This winter he would work on the Navy Yard,

boarding with his mother, and walking the five miles to and from Kittery night and morning, passing his own place to do the chores. Wages were paid in money at the Yard. Gus often worked there in the quiet months, earning a few years ago the cost of schoolbooks and flannel shirts, now that of brick and nails and the milling of lumber with which to build a house.

"Evening, Gus. Nice evening."

It was Thoc Blaine's voice. Gus could scarcely see him for the dark, but he was now at the end of the lane, passing the Blaine place, the only two-story house along the Road. He knew the gentle, smiling Blaine voice and the Blaine step, deliberate but neat, on the spongy turf.

"Yeus. Fine."

"Stop in on your way back. We'll have some music, like enough."

"Well. I might."

Gus was not much for dancing, but he had scoured sand off the flat rocks of Mount Assabenbeduc now and again at Fourth of July picnics. He remembered these occasions in brief triumph.

A lantern swinging ahead, carried by another also bound to the meeting, glinted and squeaked. Gus followed it up the little path to the church steps, his footsteps falling heavily among the pink blossoms and burning leaves of Sarey's smartweed.

2

"I rise to nominate Asa Cheney moderator of this meetin'."

"Second the motion."

"All them in favor of Asa Cheney servin' as moderator of this meetin'—"

"*Aye.*"

"Them opposed? . . . Brothers and sisters, your motion is carried. Brother Cheney will serve as moderator of this meetin', and may the Lord bless him in this office."

James Gray closed the big Bible over which he had bent to make his opening prayer, and laid it on a shelf inside the pulpit, as if he feared a store-keeper might forget its sanctity in the stress of business. His eyes, full and blue like Sarey's but dull with age, dwelt somberly on the stout and smiling Asa as they met on the platform steps.

"For His Name's sake, Brother Cheney."

"Amen, Elder. Amen to that."

The meeting-house would seat a congregation of a hundred and was nearly full. Above the straight backs of the pine pews reared the uneven rows of heads, bare on one side of the room, bonneted on the other. Mindwell and her daughters occupied the front pew of the women's side, and Lovice Joy and Moses Dockham's wife and daughters with them, placed there by the evangelist to lead the singing. Hannah Bragdon and her daughters might sit where they liked, for there was no music in the Bragdon family, but Leteshy, the oldest, must be near enough the platform to hear distinctly, for she was clerk pro tem, writing in a notebook with mottled red and black covers all that took place. It was likely to be a Bragdon for writing or figuring. The Grays and Dockhams could sing, and the Blaines fiddle and dance and tell yarns; but a Bragdon must survey the road and superintend the school and keep whatever record was kept of business transactions. It was the way, a good way, of operating the community, to place each one where he was of most use and give him both the responsibility and the rewards fitted to his position.

"The first matter of business to come before this meetin' is the 'lection to membership in this Society of them as took the first step in Elder Johnson's meetin's two weeks back," said Asa. "These is the names. Catherine Shorey, Enoch Blaine—"

"God bless 'em."

"Yea. Praise His Name."

"Leteshy, Kate, and Hattie Bragdon—"

"Amen!"

"Betsy and Lovice Joy, and Sarey Gray—"

"His handmaidens. Yea. Keep the oil in the lamps, for the bridegroom cometh!"

"Trumann Selden, Augustus Bragdon, and Orrin Joy—"

"Yea. God be praised."

Moses Dockham and James Gray had the front pew of the men's side to themselves, for they were the deacons of the old church, and must give their voices to the meeting, not only to sing but to keep contact with the Lord. They remained one at each end of the seat, a great space between them, both thin and old, James tall, Mose little and red-cheeked, one still as marble except for his mouth uttering words, the other eager, restless, fidgety, as if he could scarcely wait his turn. Behind them Aaron Bragdon and his sons had ranged themselves solidly, their arms folded, attentive but hardly participating. They knew little of these things and said nothing except an occasional amen. Gus in his store suit and scarf tie sat if anything more solidly than the rest, looking out with level eyes upon the meeting as it moved about him. He saw Sarey turn her timid gaze upon him through her eyelashes, but he gave no sign. This was the church.

The Society voted that Leteshy Bragdon, now she was a member, should continue her duties as clerk for the ensuing year.

Leteshy rose and was sworn, and, sitting down, wrote in her book, "Officers chosen:—Asa Cheney, Moderator. Leteshy Bragdon, clerk and sworn." Later she added to this list: "Moses Dockham, Shem Joy, and Lyman Allen chosen Standing Committee for the ensueing year. Aaron A. Bragdon chosen collector and treasurer and duly sworn."

And later:

"Shem Joy and Enoch Blaine chosen Sextons to give strangers seats when they meet with us.

"Augustus Bragdon takes Care of the Meeting House for the Ensueing year for one Dollar per month.

"As long as he is physicaly able, Elder James Gray will bring God's message to us in the Meeting house every Sabbath afternoon for such a sum of money as can be raised and collected by subscription, and his winter's wood."

It was growing late, nearly nine o'clock. The behavior of the boys in the back pews was not quite what it had been an hour before; they took thought of the churchyard fence, a good place to sit while the girls went past. The doors stood wide to the warm night, letting in midges which flew against the lamps, letting in, too, the smell of hay and ripening wild fruit, garden flowers and weeds and river water. Aunt Let Ely, who had come in after the meeting was well begun, fell asleep in her corner. The women exchanged nods; she had been up all night, of course, with that Keturah Linscott, and like enough had to sit today breaking her poor old back to twotch up a blanket into something to cover the young one's nakedness; time and again over there she had not found even a clean blanket as the need came, and now made a habit of taking a few squares of something with her when she was called. The children grew drowsy from watching lightning bugs outside the closed windows. The men began to think of morning and the chores.

"Now if there is no further business to come before the Society," Asa said, and paused, looking at James and Moses.

James stood up.

"It would be a matter for wonder," said he slowly. His deep, accusing eyes travelled from one face to another. "I say, my brothers and sisters, it would be a matter for wonder if we could sit so long in the House of our Father and then go away from it with never a word spoke in praise of Him. We come here and talk of what will be done, and who shall have the doing of it, but nothing of faith, nothing of fear of Him who casts the thunderbolts, nothing of love for our Lord Jesus Christ."

The Elder's voice crept upwards and outwards from his low beginning. His eyes seared everything they touched, the men and women whose thoughts had wandered, the midwife who had slept, the fooling boys, the drowsy children.

"Don't it come to your mind that it is many

hours till we come together here for our Sunday meeting? Don't it grip you to your marrows what it will be for you if in that time it comes your turn to stand before your Maker? You draw the picture for yourself. There you are before your Lord, and St. Peter waiting. What can *you* say? When did you last declare Him? Them as are not for Him are agin Him. That was what He said. Have you denied Him? Are you denying Him tonight? Oh, my brothers and sisters, here is your opportunity. What has He done for you? What does He mean to you? Will you declare the Lord Jesus Christ?"

No one any longer slept or was sleepy. Though the doors still stood open, night and summer and all the chores of house and barn were suddenly shut out of the crowded room. The light from the lamps did not reach the corners, and Jesus filled the shadows. He could not be touched, but the majesty of Him, the power and terror and beauty of Him stood tall in every pew.

"I will," cried Betsy Joy, springing to her feet. "I will declare Him. He was the One they crucified for us. Oh, blessed Jesus! We have sinned and we have backslid, but He remaineth with us. He is the Great Forgiver! Praise His name, praise His blessed name!"

Gnarled and old at forty she dropped on her knees, her face hidden in her bonnet.

"I was the ninety-and-ninth," said Lyman Allen. "He come and got me."

"All that is good cometh from Him," Catherine Shorey said, seventeen years old, with ribbons instead of strings on her bonnet, she who would marry Enoch Blaine at harvest.

"I would speak His name," said Hannah Bragdon in a monotone, looking at the wall. "There has been times I couldn't a got through alone. He ain't forsook me."

Sarey stood, very slender and pale, her voice breaking.

"I ain't never known Him until this late," she said. "It seems a long time I been without Him. Now—I've found Him—I won't never let Him go."

Her father's eyes travelled from her, as she sat down and bowed her smooth head, to Roxanna who was looking at her hands. Roxanna, it seemed, had still not found Him. Roxanna was the mote in the Elder's own eye, for she would ever laugh and play, and sometimes was tricky. Sarey gave no one any trouble. Sarey was all woman, quick to tears and easy molded, safe enough under her father's hand. It was strange what a difference could be in sisters, one hard and gleaming like an icicle in the sun, the other soft and sweet as candy warm from the stove.

"Anyone else?" the Elder asked.

"It's in me to say," declared Mose, leaping up, "it seems to me we show ourselves too full of weakness. What use be we to the Lord but as an army? It's as soldiers we've signed up, soldiers of the Lord. Here in this room at Elder Johnson's meetin's we put our names to a pledge we wouldn't touch no liquor. I put my name there. You put your name there, Brother Gray. Many of us has put our names there, but we ain't all. Some of us is a-holdin' back. Some of us is *a-holdin' back on the Lord.*

"Here is our pledge. A handsome paper, ain't it? Brother Cheney, I'm a-goin' to ask you to hang it right up there where all can see."

Asa took the paper and fastened it with pins to the wall behind the pulpit. The letters of the words were clear and plain, filled in with color, red and blue, and edged around with gold:

I DO SOLEMNLY PROMISE, WITH THE HELP OF GOD, TO ABSTAIN FROM ALL INTOXICATING DRINK, INCLUDING BEER, WINE, AND CIDER.

"A handsome paper, ain't it?" Moses Dockham asked proudly. "My name is signed to it. I been a heavy drinker in the past. That ain't no news to you folks here. You seen me settin' in my kitchen passin' around the mugs of cider from my pitcher brung up from the cellar. You seen me on Saturday afternoons a-comin' home from market with the whisky in me. But all that is changed now, brothers and sisters. I have jined the army of the Lord. Other ones' names is there. James Gray's, and Mindwell's and their daughters; every Bragdon's name is there, and Betsy Joy's—but I want to ask ye, is *your* name there? . . . Is your name there? . . . If it ain't, ain't this the time to step up and write it in? . . . Ain't this the time?"

Asa crept down on creaking shoes and sat by Lyman Allen.

Through the hush Mindwell Gray's voice led the others into song.

"The Lord cometh. His day is close at hand. Sign up for His army. Sing of your love. '*Yield not to temptation, for yielding is sin . . .*' "

Jesus moved aside to let the boys and the children out of the pews and up the aisles to write their names with pencil in the space allotted, but He was there when they came back, and stood again near them, nearer than before. The air was heavy with the silent sound of the golden buttons and epaulets and spurs of His uniform. When Abraham Ely, who had been as great a drinker as ever Mose Dockham was, made his way up to sign, Jesus went with him every step, an arm across Abraham's shoulders.

"Anyone else to sign?" asked Mose.

"Anyone else to sing His praise?" asked the Elder.

The group had grown steadily more and more fused. It was no longer an embarrassment for one to speak before the rest.

"I've seen Him hold the hands of the sick and the dyin'—"

"Once in the berry woods He come to me—"

"All joy is from Him, all rest, and takin' thought, and goodness—"

"We must be strong to do His will."

"His mind is ever on us."

"There is no Hell for them as believe in Him, no fires and no everlastin' torture, but light and life forever and a mansion in the skies—"

"Them as has gone before we shall see again if we but do His will. He has promised—"

"If ye but obey His commandments, He has said—"

"—and do His will."

"Do His will and ye shall be—"

But from outside an alien sound was beating in upon the meeting, familiar enough at other times along York Road but strange and terrible to ears tuned to the low voice of worship.

"Waiting there at the gates to Heaven—"

"I'm old Jeddy Linscott! I'm old Jeddy Linscott!"

"May the Lord watch—"

"*—lick anybody—*"

"A place to the right hand of the Lord—"

"I pray I may be worthy—"

"*Dam' sneakin' skunks!*"

"Thy rod and thy staff—"

"*—old Jeddy Linscott!*"

It was no use. The worshipers lifted their heads reluctantly, their eyes filmed from the dimness of the place where they had been with Jesus; not this place, some other one; Jesus was not here. This was the meeting-house on Nubble Point, and a gang of the Linscotts, ugly with drink, were "on the warpath," singing and shouting their way down the road. Nor were they going past, but turning up the church path and stumbling over the steps.

"I'll show 'em. Let me in there. I'll show 'em. I'm old Jeddy Linscott. I'm old Jeddy Linscott, and I can lick anybody on this road. Dam' sneakin' skunks. I'll show 'em."

Jeddy himself appeared in the door, two or three of his boys in the shadows at his shoulders. Jeddy was long-bodied and short-legged, a man of sixty or more, son of old Tim who "loved trematers so." He was bareheaded, his hair hanging over his forehead and down his neck; barefooted, splay-footed, spanking across the floorboards; in shirt sleeves, his buttons off and the hide of him showing plain. He had been crying; his face was streaked, his shirt front wet; and his voice still thick with sobs, also with hiccoughs which had come out of the earthenware jug which he carried, as a man might carry a pig, under his arm. It was no way to appear in a church, but when did a Linscott ever know anything?

"So here ye be!" he cried. "So here ye set, the lot of ye. It ain't no matter to ye if she's dead. Ye'd jest as lieves we'd all be dead. It ain't no matter to ye about a neighbor's girl, what happens to her, be it? Ye can keep up your singin' and your fun here jest the same. It ain't no matter to ye—but she's dead! She's dead, I tell ye! My Ketury's dead!"

The Elder was standing now. He raised his hand.

"Jedediah! . . . Jedediah, I see you're in great trouble. Great trouble. Put down your jug, and come in, and—let us pray!"

Jeddy heeded the sound of his name, but before the Elder finished speaking, his mind had wandered; he did not hear.

"She was the best one of 'em all," he was saying gently. "Ketury was. Why, it wa'n't no time ago she was a-steppin' of it out to one great rate, there in the kitchen floor, when I played on my jew's harp. I never see no young one like her. She's smart, Ketury is. Why, she can make flowers grow and bloom whereverabouts she wants 'em. Wa'n't never ary other woman 't our house that could handle 'em so. It's just the same, too, with the cutters in the barn. Ketury, she always can go in around 'em. They wouldn't one of our cutters hurt Ketury *no more!* I've known her harness up old Moll, the meanest-feelin' old rapscallion of a horse—"

"Jedediah!" the Elder said again. "Your talk ain't fittin' for this place. Hark now. Keturah's dead, you say. Put down your jug and come in then, and we'll say her a prayer for you."

This time Jeddy heard plain. He did not put down his jug but he scuffed suddenly farther into the room and stood at the corner of the platform. The pride and tenderness that had filled his face drained out of it.

"Yeah, you're right. You're right. I was forgettin'. Ketury's dead. She won't plant her flowers nor harness up old Moll hereafter. Nothin' but a young one, she wa'n't. A little racin' young one. And somebody on this road got her. Somebody, like enough, that's settin' here now, a-singin' and a-prayin', he got her. And we, we never said nothin'. We never put up no fight. We ain't asked nobody to pay nothin' nor marry nobody. Linscotts can take care of what's theirn; maybe we ain't much, but we don't ask nothin' of nobody. We never put up no fight, and you know it. Ketury got her young one, and we'll take care of it. Nobody needs to worry about Ketury's young one. That'll be looked after right to home . . .

"He's an awful takin' little feller, too. He ain't bigger'n nothin', but them eyes of his is jest as bright—"

Jeddy was going gentle again. His sons pressed up against him, Bill and Hamesh, Joel and Ezra, all taller than Jeddy, their faces leaner and harder. They had been drinking too, but not so much as he, only enough to toughen them; as if Linscotts needed toughening. They stood together.

"That's right we're lettin' of it drop about the young one," Hamesh said. His voice was young and hoarse. "It would've all been let pass if Ketury had got through. But she hain't; she's dead. And somebody here is goin' to pay for it. I don't know who it is, nor I ain't a-carin', but somebody here is a-comin' out and git what we got to give him."

"It looked so awful easy," Ezra sneered. "She wa'n't nothin' but a Linscott. 'Twa'n't no matter what come of her. 'Twa'n't as if she'd been a Bragdon or a Dockham or a Gray—"

"Ain't no need of so much mouth," said Bill. "One of you come outdoors here and see what Santa Claus brought you."

The oil in the lamps was burning low. The air of the room lay thick with smoke and fear and threat and the smell of the Linscotts.

The Elder was not afraid. He stepped out into

the aisle, his breathing heavy. Standing with the Linscotts, he looked taller and thinner than ever, and very old.

"You boys," he said, "have got yourselves out of hand. You must quiet down. The Lord will not have such talk in His house. Take out your jug and come back and sit down and we will pray for you."

"Set down yourself and do your own prayin'," said Bill. He looked past the Elder at the rows of seated men. "Who's comin' out? . . . Because somebody's comin', or ye all will. There'll be a way of gettin' ye out of here."

"I mind Ketury rid old Moll bareback one day," said Jeddy. He leaned against the corner of the platform, rocking his jug in his arms and staring at it. "She set light as a feather, her hair a-blowin' out—"

At a nod from Bill, Joel, who was none too bright, took paper and matches from his pocket and began heaping small white scraps upon the carpet by the pulpit.

"I brung a-long a leetle kuro-seen," grinned Joel. "It's aw-ful good ter git her goin' smart."

"Jedediah, the Lord will not have—"

"Set down," said Bill.

Joel scratched a match on his teeth. The yellow light flashed over his grinning face and dropped out of sight between his cupped hands. He slid to his knees before the platform, the crusted soles of his feet turned upwards.

Four or five men started from their seats.

"Set down," said Bill. "One's enough. If any more comes down this aisle, I'll knock every one on 'em flat in their tracks. This ain't no free-for-all tonight."

The aisle was narrow. Only one man at a time could pass. Bill's fist was hard and accustomed, and the other Linscotts behind him had the freedom of the spare floor. Enoch Blaine, Trumann Selden, Orrin Joy, Ruel Bragdon, and Lyman Allen sat down again, uneasily. Jeddy still hugged his cider jug. Joel's match slid under the little pile of papers and flamed up. Joel, stepping back, grinning, pulled from inside his coat a greasy bottle with a goose quill in the top. Oil would sputter from it like a summer shower when he held it up and shook it; slow, soft drops. Hamesh and Ezra stood near their father but not looking at him, looking at Bill. And Bill stood by James Gray's and Moses Dockham's pew, waiting for whoever should come down the narrow aisle. The lightning bugs dipped and soared outside the windows, but nobody saw them, nor knew that it was growing cooler and the whippoorwills beginning to hop and sing.

"Put that bottle down, Joe," said Gus Bragdon's voice.

Heads turned sharply toward him where he sat beside his father. Sarey's hand flew to her mouth.

All the evening he had been there, the same man as when he had come in, one who would join the church because he understood it was the place for those who read their Bibles. The business meeting had neither impressed nor embarrassed him, hearing his name read out and praised. He had not been frightened by the Elder's threats of damnation, nor persuaded into giving testimony. He had not seen Jesus. All the evening, while the meeting rose and fell about him, he had remained Gus Bragdon, youngest son of Aaron, owner of a twenty-acre strip behind the Blaine pasture. Sarey he had kept an eye on without seeming to, noticing how her color came and went with her feelings, how full her mouth, how smooth her hair, how her eyelashes lifted when she stole a glance at him. The first sound of the Linscotts coming past the end of his lane had reached him, and all their shouting and burst of song on their way down the road. He had done no dreaming, been in no dark place. From Jeddy's first step into the room until now he had missed no word nor action, sitting there with the outer corners of his eyelids drooping like the first Gus's. Now it had gone far enough, he thought, with Joel getting out the kerosene.

"I'll pick ye a fight, Bill," said Gus, "bein' as you're itchin' so for one."

Thick-set and clumsy, he stepped over the feet of his father and brothers and came tramping down the aisle. His face was unchanged, square and mild in feature, but his eyes had narrowed and hardened, and he moved as he would have moved upon a stubborn stump which, stubborn or not, would come out, roots and all, and leave the ground clean for plowing. As Bill watched him come, his mouth grew morose, and the battling air began to leave his shoulders, hips, and knees. Gus was the only man on the Road it had never occurred to him to tackle; he had as soon put fist into hill or tree as into Gus Bragdon; there are men to dance up to and make a pass at, and men even the drunk know enough to let alone.

"You better go back and set down," Bill muttered. " 'Twa'n't you. Hain't nobody don't know you never had ought to do with ary girl but Sarey Gary."

"Git out from under foot," said Gus.

He lunged past Bill and, dragging the great Bible from the shelf inside the pulpit, dropped it over Joel's little fire. The thud of the book and the crash of the bottle sent flying through the door against the elm resounded, the one and then the other, through the room. "You hadn't ought to let Joe handle matches," Gus told Hamesh. "He ain't fit." He turned back now to Bill, and they stood looking at each other, like ox and wolf, Gus reasonable but grim, the breadth of his shoulders pulling hard at the seams of his neat, stout suit, Bill surly and short-breathed, his lank body showing through his rags.

"'Twa'n't me, no," said Gus, "but seems that don't make no difference to ye. What you're bound to have here is a fight."

Bill lashed himself. He had started this, and he would see it through.

"'Twa'n't no fight," he growled, "and 'tain't goin' to be in here. Git out that door. Or shall I knock ye through?"

"Ye'll knock me if I go," Gus said, "but I ain't goin'."

He made a sudden move toward Bill and their faces came close together, Gus's not quite so high as Bill's, his eyes glinting upwards. He was roused a little from his usual calm, but it was hard to say how his heat showed, for his voice was quiet and his breathing even; perhaps in his hands, that there was force in them though they were empty of tools, and in his eyes, that they were not cold.

"Think I'm goin' out and git mauled by the gang of ye for nothin'?" he asked Bill. "Tackle me yourself. Or be ye afeard to?"

"Afeard—" Bill choked.

"Yeus. Afeard—"

Gus's big fist came out and hit the air. Bill hopping nimbly away from it, turned his own back on the door. His lips tightened and thinned over his teeth. "Afeard?" He skipped up and landed his first blow on Gus's chest; the dropping of the Bible had jarred the meeting-house no less; Gus's body was like a stone wall overgrown with moss. They moved about, eyeing each other, Bill mumbling expletives and threats, Gus silent as he would have been at work in his own field. Bill's right to Gus's neck, Bill's left to Gus's ear; all of Gus's blows missing, for he was slow and, as far as anybody knew, had never raised a hand against another man before, but it was plain that if one found Bill it would lay him out. Gus Bragdon did not play. His fists swung as if he carried an ax.

"Damn ye for a—"

The time came. Gus's hand went plunging up and caught Bill under the jaw. It might have hit his shoulder or his nose or slid between his shoulder and his ear, but the time had come and it caught his jaw. Bill made a deep sound and stumbled, and fell through the doorway onto the steps. Gus stood where he was. The room was as still as if no one were in it.

"Gus!" Sarey whispered. "Gus—you've killed him."

Gus turned a look on her. He said: "I hain't neither. You keep out of this."

Then, clearing his throat, he said to Hamesh, "You better draw up water and throw on him. He's had bigger thumps than that and come around." A smile stirred his eyes. "I shan't never take on no Linscotts, Ham, unless they *be* drunk. You'd be the end of me, amongst ye."

Hamesh and Ezra stood uncertainly. Nothing had gone as had been planned. Bill was knocked cold, Jeddy was drunk, and Joel was a fool. It became their place to take the next step, but the direction was not plain. Hamesh looked at Gus and felt no hate; these two had hunted cattle together in the woods, night after night, had once been lost for two days in an alder swamp, sleeping among the ferns and eating huckleberries. Ham left Gus out of it and made his threat to the others in the room.

"Well, 'tain't the end of it, this hain't," he said. "And some of ye's goin' to pay yit. Ye may figger because she'll be into the ground before ye have another one of your singin' and prayin' bouts, it'll all blow over. But Linscotts don't fergit so easy. They don't fergit so easy, I tell ye! We'll keep in mind for a good while that she's a-layin' up there in the woods somewheres in a hole we dug for her— 's if she was a— 's if she wasn't nothin' but a cutter out of the barn—"

Jeddy, far past noticing fire, fight, or talk, sat rocking his jug and shedding tears on it, holding and stroking it as if it were a baby, a girl-baby in a blanket Aunt Let Ely had twotched up. He sang crooningly.

> "*There come to my wi-inder,*
> *One mornin' in spring,*
> *A swe-eet little ro-obin—*"

Gus stopped Ham from going blindly after his brothers.

"You hold on, Ham," Gus said. "I got suthin' to say here. You hold on." He looked at Asa, seated in the Allen pew. "Mr. Chairman, I make a motion a grave be dug here in the meetin'-house graveyard for Keturah Linscott."

The last words dinned in Jeddy's ears. He bent forward, tears running down his face.

He said, "What is it ye say, thar? The graveyard? Would they let her lay in the graveyard? . . . Ain't no Linscott ever laid . . . all nice . . . like that so . . ."

Ham raised his head. His eyes were dark and desperate, hanging on what would happen next.

The Elder rose ominously.

"The unredeemed, even, must see where your eyes are blind, Brother Bragdon," he said. "No Society can pass such a motion. The churchyard is the Lord's, not ours, and only them as have believed in Him can have the comfort of it. Only them as have kept His commandments and acknowledged Him. You are beside yourself, Brother Bragdon, to speak such words for Him to hear."

Gus stood staring at the wall, waiting for the Elder to be done. It was clear words made no impression on Gus. His mind saw only the one way. Keturah Linscott, the little wild one with black hair stringing, lay dead in childbed; her father had drunk himself weak, and her brothers had drunk themselves ugly. Nobody would put it past the Linscotts to burn down a church or a set of buildings, poison heifers turned out to commons, or let their dogs loose on sheep, if they got started on a rampage. There had to be a way of getting around such ones. And Keturah, sixteen years old, lying still and cold, could do no harm in any place.

"Hain't nothin' in my Bible," Gus said finally, "says who can get buried in a churchyard, and who can't."

The Elder, leaning forward, had more talk over about commandments, and church members, about sin and shame and the wages of sin. Moses Dockham hopped up, squealing and squeaking about God and John and Luke and Judas Iscariot and other people Gus doubted that he knew; Mose was as drunk now with religion as he had ever been with ale; his mouth always went like a mill clapper. Some of the womenfolks took their chance, too, to let their tongues wag. Gus opened his own mouth and closed it three times. When he did speak, it was into a silence.

He said, "Ye don't talk reasonable. Ain't none of ye doin' nothin' but rant and rave. Ain't no reason why Keturah Linscott shouldn't git buried here. I made it into a motion."

"Such a motion, Brother Bragdon," warned the Elder, "will never be passed by this—"

Here Gus interrupted. He had heard enough. His ears rang as if he had worked at stone blasting and cutting all day.

"If ye can't pass it," he said, "ye can leave it lay." He turned and went with Ham to the door. "Ye can bury on my place if ye see fit," he told him. "I got a spot picked out, high and dry, the beat of any ground they've got here for buryin'. I'll have a fence around it, too, before snow flies. Ye can put her there if ye're a mind to."

Bragdons were not hard if touched in the right places. They would hunt longer than anyone else for a man lost in the woods, and stay up nights to see after a creature ailing in the barn, making no hullabaloo, wasting no pats or soft words, but tramping or dosing, dragging ponds or blanketing, hour after hour, and hour after hour. They made bull calves into steers and ram lambs into wethers, for it was necessary, but did not beat their horses nor drive unshod cattle over ice to drink. They sheared their sheep but did not bring the blood; the runt of a Bragdon litter was never left for the sow to lie on, and creatures found lingering in traps in the woods Bragdons either let go or killed. They made no talk of pity; but, as the demands came, Bragdons did these things.

"Brother Bragdon—"

"Ye don't talk reasonable," Gus said, facing in once more. "Ye don't act with no judgment. Church ain't what I thought 'twas. I'm better off to stay to home and tell my Bible to myself. Ain't no use in me lingerin' here. I don't see with ye noway."

"The changes needed in your heart and soul," said the Elder, "ain't been worked yet, Augustus Bragdon. I'll be praying the Lord to make you into a humbler man—"

"I'll jest git my hat," said Gus.

He tramped up to his father's pew, and as he started down again they rose with set faces, one after another, his father and five brothers, and followed him.

"*And the songs that he sang,*" sobbed Jeddy,
They was prettier by far
Than ever was pla-ayed on
A flute or guitar."

The Bragdons reached the spare floor, seven sturdy figures, seven pairs of feet in heavy boots.

"Nor I don't see with ye, neither. If Gus don't see with ye, I don't see with ye! . . . Wait for me, Gus, I'm comin' along."

It was Sarey, little smooth-haired Sarey Gray, her cheeks white as paper and spotted red, sixteen years old and built like a child, but standing up in her woman's dress and pushing past Roxanna into the aisle. Mindwell snatched at the escaping breadths of blue calico but her fingers missed. Nothing now could detain Sarey. As Gus stood up to fight the Linscott gang, and went on standing to defy her father, her mite of courage had grown in her until for tonight she had no doubts, and did not hesitate; her eyes shone, a bright sea-blue, and her step was as light as woodbine tapping.

"Wait for me, Gus!"

The Elder gripped himself in his seat. For once his mouth was dry of words, his mind confused. He thought, "I feel old." It did not seem this could be his daughter, his second daughter. The second one sat quietly and did as she was told. It was the other one, the older one, he had felt concern for; not this one. Sarey was a child yet, always at home. Who was it that had said, "You've never had ought to do with ary girl but Sarey Gray"? No man had ever had ought to do with Sarey. She was a child—

"Go back to your seat, young woman!" burst from him. "When the time comes that you leave the House of the Lord like this, you'll leave mine too. Go back to your mother. This man has besmirched this meeting-house and this Society, and himself worse—"

Sarey had been shouted at before and trembled. Now she scarcely heard. She reached Gus and clung to his arm, her cheek against his sleeve. He looked down at her. She was such a young thing to run after him so in the face of everybody, smooth and white and no weight at all to her. Smart at her work; it had been his way to notice what her hands could do before he began looking at her face and figure; but lately her eyes and the fineness of her skin were in his mind night and day, the way she walked like wind in the grass, the small warmth of her hand as it lay in his pocket. She was a little, young creature to stand up so close to one who had done what he had done tonight, one with shoulders like his, arms and hands and chest and loins, crisp hair and pegged boots like his.

He said: "Well, I don't know. What'll I do with ye? We ain't got our roof up yit, ye know."

Sarey said nothing.

"And who's goin' to marry us?" asked Gus. "Looks like your father won't."

Sarey giggled.

"Elder Johnson would," she said. "I could walk to the beach. Couldn't you?"

"Sarey Gray!" gasped Mindwell. "*Have* ye lost your wits?"

"I don't see what makes ye think so," Hannah Bragdon spoke out. "Other women besides her has got married, Mindwell. And she ain't got to be in a rush. She's welcome to stay to my house if she can't stay to home. Go along, Gus."

Jeddy broke off his humming and looked up with glazed eyes at the group of seven men and a girl in the doorway.

"I—I ain't got nobody along of me," he said. "Rest of ye goes together and I set all alone . . . I lost suthin'. I don't know what it was, but I lost suthin' . . . I don't see what it was. I got my—I got my cider jug here all right. They wanted me—somebody—they kep' a-sayin'; 'Leave it out there; put down your jug out there, and come in.' They wanted—wanted me to let go holt of the—the last thing I got . . . Don't nobody ever take a drink along of me. I hev to set a-drinkin' all alone—"

Moses Dockham started up, squealing and squeaking.

"Drink makes a devil or a dunce of every man that puts his mouth to it."

Gus, full of scorn for these who ranted and raved and saw what was not there, compassionate in his own way for Jeddy Linscott, feeling Sarey young and proud on his arm, and thinking of his good twenty acres, said, "It won't make neither a devil nor a dunce out of me." He took up Jeddy's jug and drank deep from it. "There ye be, Jeddy," he said. "I been a-drinkin' with ye. Now ye better come out where the boys is."

"Augustus Bragdon," Moses Dockham shrieked, "your name is writ on the paper."

"My name has been struck off," said Gus. "It's fixed now so I go it on my own. Sarey and me." He looked down and asked her, "You all ready to set sail?"

She smiled up valiantly, and so it was that in the summer of 1870, James Gray's younger daughter left the Nubble Point church with one of the unpious Bragdons, going through the summer dusk to dance for the first time to the tune of Thoc Blaine's fiddle until her feet could scarcely move another step and Gus must carry her along York Road to his mother's. His arms were gentle to her that night, and his shoulder steady for her head to lie against. When she stirred and offered to get down and walk, he told her: "Ye rest easy. I shouldn't never know I had ye." He meant there was no weight to her; he knew well enough that it was neither stone nor bag of grain nor new calf he carried; all his senses stung with telling him over and over it was Sarey.

"Ye could sleep," he said. "I'll speak to ye when we git there."

NOONTIME

1895

THE Elder retained his pulpit for ten years, preaching every Sunday and leading prayers every Wednesday night, and once each season held baptism in the river behind the meeting-house, standing waist-deep in the water and reaching with strong hands toward the sinners who came down the bank to him. In all this time he never bespoke his daughter Sarey, nor were there any Bragdons in his congregation. Even when a stroke felled him in his eighty-fifth year, he would not let Mindwell send for their second daughter, but lay straight and proud in his bed, calmly waiting for the end. He had five summers of waiting, and five winters of looking across from his small window to a meeting-house with locked doors and cold chimney and unbroken snowy yard. Not even Mindwell knew, except by guessing, what it meant to him to see all he had built up gone to naught so suddenly; for he did not speak of it. The day he died he whispered hoarsely: "Tell my people to rally round. I am at rest in God." But there was no one to whom Mindwell could give the message, for his people had gone back to being farmers, even Mose Dockham was drinking again, and the young men would wander all over the three Derwiches by night in search of a strain of music they might dance to.

There were other changes, too, than in the church. The old died off along York Road. Three years after the Elder, Aaron Bragdon went, and then Shem Joy and Lyman Allen. Crazy Isaac and Aunt Sal Peters finished their long terms, and when Betsy Joy went as wild as her Aunt Sal had ever been, the sheriff came and took her off on the train to a place intended for such people in Augusta; it was no longer the way to keep the insane in barred rooms at home and pound on the walls at them when they grew too noisy. Those who at the time of the reformation of 'Seventy had been girls sitting on the church steps and boys hanging over the graveyard fence, married and moved into little new houses out along Assabenbeduc Lane, beyond Gus Bragdon's place; Hattie Bragdon and Berias Blaine, Lovice Joy and Trumann Selden, Polly Selden and Amos Hamilton, Betsy Dockham and Orrin Cheney, Adeline Cheney and Charles Bragdon, and the rest. The gray cottages of York Road were occupied only by the old or very poor, or were deserted, and travel there grew light. Visitors at the summer hotels along the beaches, determining Mount Assabenbeduc should be more accessible, had been the means of a good carriage road going through from Kittery Turnpike past the foot of the mountain and along the course of the Lane, so that Gus Bragdon had not needed to buy his right of way; and all through traffic used the new road. Ham and Ezra Linscott and their wives, fisher-girls from the mouth of the river, moved out to the other side of the mountain and began making baskets for a living, bushel baskets for farmers, berry baskets for farm women, and sweet grass trinkets for the summer folks. All these couples multiplied, and their children seemed to grow up overnight, many of the boys going away, before they were out of their teens, to the west and the south, whichever direction there were railroad tracks; they thought as much of engines now as ever men had of boats. Many of the best of their fathers' generation had gone these ways too.

Organs came into the homes, and women and girls sang, pumping sturdily, "Stay on the farm, boys"; but still many went, not only to the railroads but to the mills in the cities and to the frontier towns where life was gay. For those who did stay, Fourth of July picnics on the mountain were not good enough any more. Any young man who was anything had a horse and a sleigh and buggy, both vehicles painted shiny black and striped in red, and whatever the season could drive a girl several miles to a dance or to the beach. The mountain was useful now only for lovers' walks on Sunday afternoons. None but the oldest women still stepped back and forth to the whir of a spinning wheel, and they and the middle-aged were all who could knit without a struggle, fingers flying as effortlessly as breath came. The young girls made patchwork and hemmed, painted on cloth, and pasted stamps on dishes, crocheted and embroidered and passepartouted.

Portable sawmills began their invasion on the woods, bringing hard lines to the Seldens and others who owned stationary mills or dams or had mill privileges, the engine being cheaper and more convenient than water. Trees need no longer be drawn to mill for sawing; the mill could go to them. And these mills brought in Canadians, particularly Nova Scotians, men with long brown mustaches, high-pitched voices, and Scotch-English accents; brought in increasing numbers their wives and mothers, rawboned, forceful, energetic women; brought, too, the woodchoppers, French, who lived in tar-paper shanties which they carried about with them from place to place as long as the roofs would stay atop the walls. The community was not so tightly bound together in one unit as it had been. A woman huddled in her shawls as she rode with her husband through the snow no longer asked, when another sled passed, "Who was that, Sim?" but "Was that anybody we know?"

In these times a doctor was called to attend a

birth, and when death came, an undertaker asked to lay out the body. It was necessary now to have certificates of birth and death, and records were published in the Town Report. Women thought something of style when they had new dresses made, watched the magazines, and laid patterns on to cut by; it was no longer enough to have a rig that was whole and warm. Men's suits now came from stores; the few sheep still kept did not produce wool enough to clothe their masters and even the woman who could spin no longer carded.

In 'Eighty the superintendent of the school conceived the idea of having the pupils use all the same reader, and brought in one day a fine stock of Munroes for which he took the odd books in exchange—Kate Bragdon's which had been Gus's, a still neat though much-thumbed volume; Stephen Blaine's which had been Enoch's and was filled with doves and scrolls and verses addressed to girls, and the rest. It was not long after this that the town of Derwich began supplying all books to the children in its schools, and readers, spellers, and geographies began to be lost in the woods or dropped into brooks or left at home when vacation was over; what was not their individual own had less value in their eyes. Nearly every child finished his eight or nine years in the district school, and so many went beyond that it no longer meant quite so much to have it said a boy had been graduated from the academy; it did not mean the boy was separated so far from his fellows as when Thoc Blaine's father had achieved this distinction. "Oh, Cap'n David!" people had once said. "He's got quite a head on him. He's a well educated man. *He* was graduated from the academy down here!"

The little old houses along York Road had three fireplaces, if not more; but stoves came in, and Gus building his house in the 'Seventies left only one hearth open—this in case stoves did not turn out all they were cracked up to be; Berias Blaine, Trumann Selden, and the others who built a few years later out beyond him, had no fireplaces at all, and chimneys grew smaller with the passing decades. The number of horses increased, the supply of oxen dwindled.

Whether much or little, everything changed.

Even Asa Cheney's store, now Asa was gone and his son Abner had the handling of it, became a different place. The same shelves and counters were still here, and the floorboards with their ink stains from the time when old Ephraim Shorey had kept school, but Abner sold flour and cheese, oranges and extracts, oil and grain, tonic and candy and postcards, as well as the tea, crackers, and salt cod of earlier days. The fireplace had been bricked up and an airtight put in. There was a new partition across one corner, and in it a narrow window behind which Abner sorted letters and put them into boxes, now a mail train stopped every day at the Junction.

One night in November of 'Ninety-five Abner stood by his counter, wiping it with a damp rag, dusting off the end of the cheese as it rested on the top of the cracker barrel, and swabbing around the bunghole of the keg of cider.

"Well, I maintain ye can look at 'em yourself," he was saying. "Ain't none of the young fellers what they was once around here. Ain't half a dozen of 'em could start out on a piece of ground of their own and make a go of it."

Berias Blaine and Trumann Selden, chewing together beside the stove, said nothing. They whittled and spat, staining the zinc rug on which the stove rested, and sometimes their quids were tucked into pockets in their cheeks, making a bulge like a squirrel's nut. Willy and Shem Joy, Charlie Hamilton, and Fred Dockham, who had stopped in to toast themselves before starting for Beaverdam for a dance, stood, scarcely more than boys, near the post-office window. They did not expect mail but liked to peek through at the boxes and cut their initials where they could.

Only old Mose Dockham, huddled on a stool beside the counter, gave Abner his full support.

"Yis!" he nodded fervently. "Undoubtedly so, Mr. Shorey."

"If they want anything, it's an education, like

Benny Bragdon," Abner went on, "and can't git nowheres without it. Now there used to be ones, like old Elder Gray, Benny's own grandfather—he knowed his books, but books wa'n't everything he knowed. The Elder, he never had much, but he made a livin' out of that rock heap up there and what little pay he got for his preachin', and must have left something besides it. Anyway, Mindwell, she don't run no bill—"

Trumann spat and said, "Pooh, I guess you'll find what she has comes out of Sarey Bragdon's pocket."

"Well," Berias put in, "there's Roxan too—"

"Pooh," Trumann said, "she's one don't have nothin' for anybody but herself. She's great for fixin' up and ridin' out, but Sarey tells Ad that sometimes they go cold and hungry, both, down there to McIntires'."

Abner did not feel for gossip to-night. He had big thoughts in his head.

"Well, however that is, the Elder got along. He took care of himself and had a family, which is more'n Benny'll do unless I miss my guess. I don't know, the way young fellers is late years, most of 'em, I'm just as well satisfied my young ones is girls."

"Yis! Yis!" declared Moses. "Ye're right, Mr. Shorey. Yis!"

"Young ones, he says," chuckled Fred, nudging

Willy. "How old is Mat, anyway? Twenty-five if she's a day, ain't she?"

"Mat's no spring chicken," Willy answered. "Nor Flora neither, for that matter."

Abner could not hear their words but knew the mockery behind them. His face reddened, and he grew busy drawing a glass of cider which went sliding down the counter to Mose. Moses' fingers closed about it greedily. He would say "yis" all the evening for a glass or two of this, and be back in the morning "yissing" for a cut of cheese off the end of Abner's knife and a few crackers out of the barrel. Times were hard for Moses; his wife was dead and neither his daughters nor his sons' wives would have him in their houses with his habits what they were.

"Yeah, but what you goin' to do with them girls *when they grow up*, Uncle Abner?" Willy asked boldly. "Ain't nobody good enough to marry 'em. What you goin' to do with 'em? String 'em and hang 'em up to dry?"

A neat step fell outside the door, and young Stephen Blaine came in briskly, walking with his weight on his heels and his shoulders well back, a spring in his knees. Closing the door, he saluted the group with two fingers to his hat rim, and took a seat on a stool next to Mose.

"Well, Steve!" Abner exclaimed, glad of the interruption. "You home?"

"Home again," said Stephen. "Give me some cider, will you? Put a drop of something in it to warm me up. And look out you don't get that rag near anything that's going into my mouth."

He sat swinging a trim shod foot, his gloves on his knee and his derby hat knocked back on his head, and drank off the cider. His hair was cut so short and his black coat and gray trousers fitted so snugly that he seemed almost unclothed beside these others in their overalls and baggy jackets. Even his mustache was waxed, and the ends rolled until it was no more concealing than a slate pencil laid across his upper lip.

"Well, you didn't stay so long as you figured on, did you, Steve?"

"No. No, I didn't, True. Got too cold. New York Harbor's the coldest place the Lord ever made." He wiped his mouth and tucked his white handkerchief back into his pocket but left the corner showing. "Why, you never saw anything like it, the way it's been the last few weeks. Out there on that tug with the wind blowing a two-forty clip all the way from England, it's as much as a man can do to keep breath in him."

"New York Harbor!" Berias said. "I had it from your father your job was buildin' on a bridge up to Lawrence."

"Yeah, that's what I heard," Willy said.

Stephen tossed Abner a coin.

"Well, that job didn't pan out. They're putting it off till spring, I found out when I got there. So I jumped a freight for New York and was working on a tug within three days. Quite a sight seeing all the big boats come in. A lot of cargoes of bananas. One fellow told me he ran afoul of three tarantulas while he was unloading one boat, caught one running up his arm under his sleeve, an old riptail roarer. Have to keep their eyes open on that job. I talked to the captain about taking me on for the next trip, but he had his crew. He took my name though, so I might get a call most any time; nice fellow, he was. No letter for me, Abner?"

"No, nothin' here yet, Steve."

"Well, you keep an eye out. I've got two or three irons in the fire. I'll start for a warmer clime, next trip I take."

He began pulling on his gloves.

"You about ready to pull for home, Uncle Berias? I'm going over the Lane."

"Yes, I'll bate you are," Berias said, shaving shreds from his plug of tobacco. "No, I shan't be startin' just yet. I ain't in any such rush as I cal'late you be."

"Aunt Hattie'll lock the door on you!"

"So'll Gus Bragdon on you," snickered Willy. "You'll have to step lively if you get over the

Lane before Gus turns in now. He's savin' up oil lately to buy himself another strip lot."

"Well, I'm glad you mentioned it. I wouldn't keep Gus up for all he'll ever own," returned Stephen, bowing slightly from the waist. "A man that works as hard as he does needs his sleep."

He went out, leaving the boys laughing. Berias and Trumann twisted the corners of their mouths.

"Pooh, he may not find Kate quite so glad to see him back this time," Trumann said. "Sarey hints to Ad that Kate don't have the patience with his comin' and goin' that she once had."

"Oh, Steve'll be oneasy for a spell and then settle down again," Berias grunted. "He's like his father before him. Uncle Thoc tells how once Enoch went out of Porchmuth, cook on a sand boat, and stayed a week or so, and when he got home he complained he couldn't sleep so well on land, and Granther had to stand outdoors all night a-throwin' water ag'inst the side of the house."

"Thoc makes them yarns up out of whole cloth, don't he?" Abner asked. "Stands to reason Old Cap'n wouldn't never have stood outdoors all night—"

"I thinks likely Granther started that one a-rollin' himself," Berias answered. "He was every mite as good at it as Uncle Thoc. No, they never made 'em up, exactly. That is, they always had something to begin with. Now, that time, I s'pose Enoch might have made great talk, like Steve, when he got back, about what a trip he'd had aboard that sand boat. And bein's as Granther had put his own ship around the Horn a many times, it maybe didn't sound like much to him, and he set out to take Ene down a peg or two—"

Stephen stepped along blithely through the dark. The first place he came to was his own, and he hesitated beside it but did not stop. Willy had been right that it was getting late for knocking at Gus Bragdon's door, and he could always get in here; he knew every nail and screw, every window shutter and loose board of the old house. He regarded it, dark against the sky, with the same pride he had felt in it as a child; the first house built on York Road, a fine place two stories and a half high, with four great chimneys, twenty-four panes of glass in every window, a fanlight over the door and hand-carved panels in the hallway, a gate and a brick walk, and on the roof a cupola from which on clear days a man could look off to sea. Very fine ladies had once danced in that parlor, but it was dark tonight, was always dark unless Stephen came home. Thoc and Enoch and Catharine used only the kitchen and the two small bedrooms behind it; Catharine said it was as much as she could heat and more than she could keep clean with always two men and sometimes a dozen underfoot. Catharine would rather have lived in a Frenchman's shanty if only it was new, no cracks in the finish, no plaster falling, and no rats in the cellar walls. She envied Sarey Gray and Hattie Bragdon, Lovice Joy and Polly Selden, Adeline Cheney and Betsy Dockham for marrying men who built them little houses out along the Lane. A Blaine thought having a Blaine was as much as any woman ought to ask of this life or the next, she said.

Stephen walked now under Bragdon pines hedging in oak trees that had taken root as Blaines', trod soft Bragdon needles which buried deep the rocks and soil that had once been Blaines'. But he did not think of his birthright, nor of the etched glass, riding horses and Oriental shawls for which it had been sold. Whistling, walking on his heels with his shoulders high, he was intent on lessening the distance which separated him from Gus's daughter Kate.

The house sat in a clearing beyond the pines, small and undistinguished as compared with his own. No brick had come from England for it; no three men with clever fingers had labored a hundred days to carve the panels of its hall. Gus Bragdon had built it himself, with such as he had or could buy within a radius of five miles. The first and second summers of his marriage, while Sarey carried and bore Benjamin, their first child, at Gus's mother's house, Gus had dug and stoned the well, blasted out the cellar, put up walls and roof and finished off three rooms, a kitchen in the ell and, on the west end of the main part, a sleeping and a sitting room. In the winters he worked on the Navy Yard to earn the cost of it. When Benjamin was six months old, they moved in, and it was a good deal to have, the three rooms and a shed and barn connected so they need not go outside to tend their stock, a sink and a table and two chairs, and a stove Gus had bought for a dollar; a big bed for Gus and Sarey and a trundle for the young one, and plenty of featherbeds, pillows, blankets, and comforters. It was a good deal, and they were proud of it, but they meant to have more. That very fall Gus set to work to make a lounge where Sarey could stop in comfort to nurse the child and Gus could lie to do his figuring before he went to bed.

He never saw the use of sitting up over a slate and pencil, as Sarey did to add how much her hens had brought in that week and to subtract what the feed for them had cost. To Gus nine times twenty-eight made two-fifty-two, seventy-five out left one-seventy-seven, and he was ready now to figure how many one-seventy-sevens would be needed to add to ten-seventy-five to make up the amount of six per cent interest on a five-hundred-dollar note for two years. At the end of that time, he estimated, he would have the principal reduced to two hundred dollars. The note had been written to Asa Shorey in payment for a wood lot Asa had been about to put a sawmill on. There might be a hundred thousand feet of lumber on it now; at a dollar a thousand worth a thousand dollars tonight; Asa had sold too cheap, but he needed money. A man who held this lot for twenty years or so would realize five or six thousand on it; twelve and one-half per cent interest compounded annually on what he had put into it, where the bank would pay two and one-half or three. Gus's mind went over these matters as he lay on his back on the lounge, while Sarey, her feet twisted around the legs of the chair, her thin shoulders hunched over the slate, and her face screwed into an anxious grimace, added how much her hens had brought in that week and subtracted how much they cost.

As long as the Elder lived, the Bragdons had no traffic with the Grays, but when he died, Sarey appeared at the funeral and afterward went often to cry with her mother. Sometimes she took along a spice cake or jars of different kinds of pickle, and one day Mindwell gave her the big cherry bedstead which had been her father's, and a maple chest and a little rocker and his picture in a frame decorated with mother-of-pearl. Roxanna was married to the man who owned the stable in the village, and had no use for such old-fashioned truck, but it was a great help to Sarey. Now Gus must finish off a parlor for it, and while he was about it, must sheathe the end of the attic, too, for Benjamin had grown too big to lie on the floor of the little dish cupboard off the sitting room, and they needed the sitting room itself as a place to put the girls to sleep, Kate and Lovice. Little Jeff would be better in the trundle bed; he was getting so he nuzzled all night long for what his mother's breasts no longer held.

When Aaron Bragdon died, Hannah, refusing to go on living with Leteshy and her husband and big brood of children, came down to stay with Gus. They finished off the other end of the attic for her, and she brought her bed and the cane-seated chairs Aaron had whittled out and painted first red and then black, her spinning wheel and her rugs into which she had hooked the Civil War uniforms of Silas, Paul, Albert, and Edward, her ginger jar full of buttons, and her cookstove. She liked to bake her own bannock and stew her own beans, carrying water up and down the backstairs, and throwing her waste out of the window into the chicken yard. Hannah was well and strong at eighty and kept busy. All day at her spinning her quick, short steps went back and forth, back and forth, and when it grew too dark for her to see, she felt about for her knitting needles. Hannah could knit a mitten or a stocking in one evening and get seventy-five cents a pair for them. She was never without coins in her bureau drawer or peppermints in her pocket. Sarey, in the kitchen below, jerking feathers out of fowl or working butter, often felt resentful that she had neither leisure to earn money in such pleasant ways nor privilege to put it to such self-indulgent uses.

But the small house continued to stretch until when Stephen Blaine approached it that night in the fall of 'Ninety-five it had seven rooms, also a back entry and a sinkroom, and in the long front hall a curving staircase with black walnut newel post and banister. It was sufficiently furnished, chairs, tables, and beds enough for all who lived there or ever came, dishes and rag rugs enough, lamps instead of candles, three pictures and a looking glass and the clock which had been a present from Roxanna. The woodwork was painted and the walls papered, and the outside covered with three coats of white. Green shutters set off the windows to advantage, and a porch ran the whole length of the south side of the ell. Gus had put a chain pump in his well and made a neat pile of what wood was left over after his shed had been filled for the winter. Maple trees, twenty years old now, lined the driveway, and the woodbine Sarey had planted sheltered the porch, her lilac bushes beat about in the wind, and last summer her roses had bloomed all across the east end of the house, gracing the front door. The shed was stocked with tools as well as wood; the cellar held vegetables and apples, cider, vinegar, salt pork, and all kinds of canned stuff. Two hundred fowl had gone to roost in the henhouse. Three hogs and a litter of seven pigs snored and snorted under the barn. Above them stood five cows, a bull, a yoke of steers, a horse, and enough hay to feed the creatures until spring; grain in the chest and sawdust in the corner. Gus's and Sarey's fences closed in forty acres now, Gus owned seven wood lots, and every one of the three notes he had signed had been bought back and burned. It was a good deal they had accomplished already, and they meant to do more.

But Stephen, taking no account of these things, thought only of Kate. Through the window he could see her standing alone in the kitchen.

The stove which Gus had bought for a dollar twenty-five years before was on one side of the room, a low, very black stove, shining from polish but so cracked that the flames showed through. On another side sat the lounge Gus had built and Sarey padded and covered, and the big drop-leaf table where the Bragdons ate their meals. There was the yellow oak clock on the mantelpiece, and a set of hanging shelves full of almanacs, town reports, old letters, slates and pencils. Kate stood beside a small table which held a pile of papers and the lamp. The soft, reddish light seemed to cluster about the outline of her face, slender and dark and intent on the bundle she was tying. Stephen paused to study her with a critical delight a Blaine of many generations back might have lavished on a Raphael.

Kate was tall, her body good in the lean but soundly built style of peasant women; small, high, firm breasts, muscles stirring easily as she worked; broad, capable hands; a slim throat, her long, full head resting lightly on it like a bird's; deep brown hair pinned in her neck but cut in a curly fringe across her forehead; eyes, gray, long and narrow, nearly bare of lashes, calculating and cold to meet but warm and tender to know; nose too large for beauty; teeth large too, she showed them as she bit the string; mouth thin and red, the only color in her face; chin strong and thrust outwards, would have been more becoming in a man. Kate was handsome, rather frightening, grave and sincere; over all she wore an air of feeling herself a stranger, unknown and unknowing, travelling alone through a world whose wonders and terrors she could not describe if she would, and in any case. would not.

Having proudly named her familiar points to himself, Stephen crossed the porch and rapped on the door.

2

"You goin' some'eres, Kate?" Gus asked, seeing her take off her apron and hang it on a nail and put her hands to her hair.

He lay on the lounge, had been asleep but now

slid into waking, his hands clasped over his chest, his body stretched flat and hard and the toes of his boots turned up. His mother sat by the stove with her feet in the oven, clicking her needles faster and faster.

"Mother wanted me to come over to grammum's when I got my work done up," said Kate. "You want anything before I go?"

"Want anything? No, I don't want anything. . . . Ye'll find ye'll need plenty on ye. Close down to zero tonight."

"November's giving us quite a try," said Kate. She shook out her pins and took a steel comb from behind the clock; it sang as she drew it through her hair. She bent low from the waist, combing up from the nape of her neck, then backward from the parting behind her bangs.

"When I was your age I couldn't ha' stooped over that fur to put a comb to my head or my hair would 'a' been a-moppin' up the floor," said Hannah. "I had a master great head of hair."

"Mine's not that long," Kate said, setting pins. "It all runs to thickness."

"Mine's finer 'n yours, too, old as I be," said Hannah.

Kate said: "Yes. Mine's like father's."

"Might be," Hannah admitted grudgingly. "Your mother's nothin' near so fine as mine is, though. Hern is growin' gray, too. Ain't you noticed? It's all them drugs she takes. Here be I, eighty years old, and not a gray spear to my head."

It was true. She sat there by the stove like a withered brown nut, her small body bent almost double, but her hair dark at Kate's own, her neck strong, and her crooked fingers nimble.

"If it wa'n't for these chilblains," she said, "I'd be smart as ever I was."

"You ought to keep your mind on seeing there's hot rocks in your bed these cold nights," said Kate. "You don't take any care of your feet."

"Time they learnt how to take keer of themselves," said Hannah.

She drew them suddenly out of the oven and let them fall to the floor. It was a gesture, and the jar sent a pang through her knees and hips, but her expression did not change; she knit rapidly, four and two, four and two. Hannah Bragdon had been known for many years as the fastest knitter on York Road. She could knit a stocking in an evening! So never a stocking must be started after supper but it was made by bedtime. When she could not keep her own pace, she would be old. Four and two, four and two, four and two.

"By the time you git there, they'll all be to bed," said Gus.

He sat up on the side of the lounge and began unlacing his boots. At forty-five his hair, too, like his mother's, was untouched by age, but a pale color, and crisp. His mutton-chop whiskers lay like small fringed rugs on either side of his thin mouth and rounded, out-thrust chin.

"No. Grammum goes to bed late when she has company. They set up and read out loud to each other."

"Anything to use up wood and kerosene," said Gus.

"Well, when wa'n't that allus like Grays' folks?" Hannah demanded. "That time when Asy Shorey went in thar and took 'em a present of a bag of meal when everybody knowed they hadn't had a mite of bread sence Thanksgivin', and here 'twas Christmas, and wa'n't Mindwell a-settin' and a-playin' over hymns and they'd had a traveller come in and tune up that thar organ for 'em and paid him fifty cents! Asy, he said Mindwell said they thought it was the best Christmas they could have, so they got it. And there they was without a mite of meal in the house! I don't know, some folks."

Hannah wanted to stay; she liked it here with Gus and Kate. Tomorrow Sarey would be back from her visit to her mother's, and bring the other young ones with her, Ben and Lovice and Jeff. When Sarey was at home, Hannah kept to her own part, and many long winter evenings lay ahead of her. But she stuffed her yarn and needles into the pocket in the folds of her skirt and trudged off up the stairs, her small lamp in both hands.

Gus should see his mother knew enough to go to bed at bedtime. She could put on a jacket and finish this stocking in the dark. One that knew how to handle needles like Hannah Bragdon didn't need a light. Burning pains shot through her feet, and she kicked angrily against the stairs as she climbed. She had forgotten her hot rocks again. Plague take her feet. Four and two, four and two, four and two.

"Your mother comin' home tomorrer, is she?" Gus asked.

He had put his shoes under the side of the lounge and sat studying the cracks in the floor boards. A man ought to have hard wood for a woman like Sarey to do her scrubbing on. Pine would always crack and shrink, and the way she dug and tore at it wore the splinters up.

Kate, bringing plants in from the window sills, said: "Yes. We'll all be back in the morning. She just wanted to be with grammum through Thanksgiving. They get lonesome over holidays."

"Never could see what thar is to holidays," said Gus, "different from any other time. Sun comes up, or else it don't, whatever day it is, and after a while it gits dark again."

"Well, they make a lot of them when they all get up there to grammum's. Easter she paints up eggs, all colors, and Christmas we hang stockings, all of Aunt Roxan's and us, everybody, even grammum. And Thanksgiving she sets a plate for each of us in the family, so if we ain't there she feels it. She always lays a place for grandfather, too."

"That must be so they'll have something to take on about," said Gus. "Your mother and her folks always had to git in a good cry, or they didn't have no kind of a time at all."

Something in the nature of a twinkle passed between them, but they did not smile. Gus went to the stove and took off the cover to scratch among the coals, closed the draughts and opened the oven door to let out what heat there was into the room. Kate brought a roll of striped outing flannel, her nightgown, from the stairway and spread out newspaper to wrap it in; a crumpled paper, used before for wrapping and would be again; they did not often have one.

"Granny'll get you mush and milk for breakfast. That do you all right?"

"Ain't nothin' better," Gus said. "You blow out your light when you start."

She heard him open the sitting-room door and close it behind him, heard his stocking feet padding across the corner to his bedroom. He and Sarey still slept in the little downstairs chamber. He rarely saw the upstairs of his house. A room to eat in and one to sleep in were all he had a use for. Whatever else he did was done outside. The bedroom door closed. The buckles of his suspenders clinked against the footboard of his bedstead, and the cornhusks of the mattress rustled as he climbed in and lay among them. Here he would sleep, and wake to hear the clock striking two and three; a time to figure and scheme, his eyes blinking thoughtfully in the dark. If he dropped off again, his roosters would wake him, and he would be out in his yard by six o'clock. Earlier than that it was too dark, this time of year, for a man to accomplish anything. Only in summer he had light long enough to get in a good day's work; in July and August he could always be at something by three. In winter a man who farmed it had to make up his mind to lay by.

Alone, in this minute or two, Kate thought of many things, her thoughts explaining what she was, how young and how old, how much Bragdon and how much Gray, where she was hard to the touch and where yielding, what she loved and hoped for and believed in; but none of this showed in her face. There was to be seen from the outside only what Stephen saw, her features and figure, what she was doing and how she did it, neatly, capably. No wonder he did not know Kate Bragdon. She raised her head at his knock, paused for an instant to listen, and moved to the door as if she had a premonition who it would be.

"Stephen Blaine!"

His hat came off and he laid it against his chest,

making her one of his stiff, slight bows. No other man along York Road or the Lane could have done it so. It was Stephen back again, with the moonrise brightening behind his head and his eyes laughing at her. This time she had counted on his staying; they had talked it over together and he had promised,—this time he would stay until the job was finished and prove how quick and sure he was with his hands, how he always knew where a bolt was needed and could match two pieces of wood until no one could tell they had not grown so. Stephen would work hard and faithfully in Lawrence, while Kate here at home kept to her quilting and her hemming, Sarey pinched closer than ever on her eggs and butter to have the more to sell, and Hannah upstairs wove cloth for sheeting as she had once woven her own. And in the spring—

"You're right. That's the name."

He took her and kissed her swiftly, her throat and mouth and hair.

"Oh—Stephen—"

Tonight it was a silver sky and bare branches behind his head. Other times it had been blue sky, or warm twilight, or birches bowed to the ground with ice. He had been hers since they had begun to grow up, though she was two years older, and anywhere that she could go alone, about her father's place or between York Road and the mountain, she had been with him in one season or another. All her senses quickened at the touch of him. Now she smelled only cold air and woodsmoke from the chimney; but once there had been the fragrance of sun on new wood as they stood among the stacks of shingles bought to roof the shed, once that of a spruce tree in the corner of the schoolroom as they decorated it for a Christmas concert, many times the smell of mayflowers and the must of a deserted Frenchman's shanty as they sat in its doorway to tie up their nosegays with vines. Tonight it was still; but he had kissed her with the sound of water trickling past, or frogs singing, or nuts dropping, or other Bragdons, the Seldens, Joys, and Hamiltons calling down that they had reached the top of the hill and where were Kate and Stevie? Kate-and-Stevie, people said, running their names together.

"Stephen, I—"

He did not listen to her until he chose, and she had no spirit to force him. It was Stephen back again, his thin, hard face, his eyelashes, his breath, his hands upon her.

At last he said, "You might ask me in."

"Yes. Come in."

He stood by the stove and spread his hands above it. Not much heat came up. Kate stayed just inside the door, her eyes on him. His still laughed. He seemed to dare her to find fault with him.

"You've grown taller, Katie. And your hair's curlier."

"No, I haven't. And it isn't. It can't be."

"Why not? Are you the Great Rock that you can't change?"

"No, but it takes me time. You haven't been gone long enough for me to change any, Steve."

He slapped his thigh with one hand and reached for her with the other.

"Good. I'm tickled to death. I want you to stay just the same. Your hair was always curly enough, and if you put on another inch, you'll catch up with me. That wouldn't do, would it?"

She did not go to him, but stood looking at him. He came to her, and she moved away, taking up her bundle from the table. He laughed.

"All right, Katie. Let's get it over. What's the matter? We'll sit down here and have a nice fight. You told me to stay away until spring, and I—"

"I don't want to fight with you, Steve," Kate said. She almost laughed herself, her mouth softening. The yielding to him filled her eyes with sudden tears. Gus would have stared to see her. "I don't know *what* to do with you. You're so—you're so—"

"Yes, I am so, ain't I?"

"Stephen, don't! I can't. I'm in a hurry. I've got to go up to grammum's tonight. Mother's there, and Lovey and them, and they're expecting me. *Really*, Stephen—"

"All right, Katie. You're the boss. I'll walk along with you."

"Not all the way."

"Well, to the pasture fence. How old will you have to be before your grandmother'll think you're grown-up enough to have a beau right out in public?"

"I don't know. She don't seem to think girls ought to—"

"Funny how a woman like that ever got grandchildren!"

"Yes, *'tis*—why, Stephen Blaine!"

"Guilty."

"Will I need a jacket underneath my cape?"

"Yes, and your earlappers pulled away down and buttoned."

"Is it really so cold?"

"Colder 'n the old Harry."

"Just think. And not December yet."

Kate blew out the light and pulled her cape around her. Stephen let them through the entry and turned the key in the lock. Gus, come morning, would have to go in and out by way of the shedroom. Now he slept soundly on his stretched ropes and cornhusk pad, covered with comforters Sarey had made the winter they had stayed at his mother's, before Benjamin was born. Upstairs

Hannah had finished her stocking and laid it away in the dark. Her back ached, and her feet were stiff with cold; her fingers fumbled as she put her great, ruffled white nightgown over her head and struggled in its depths to let out her buttons and slip her underclothing to the floor. Emerging, she peered once out of the window to make a guess at tomorrow's weather, and saw two figures turning into the short cut through the woods to Mindwell Gray's place. The moon was high enough to make the fields quite light now, and she saw them clearly, a sturdy young woman in a heavy cape and hood and a young man beside her in a trim topcoat with a derby hat on his head.

"So he's back again," she grumbled. "Another gre't start and a morsel of an endin'. Well, when wa'n't that allus the way with them Blaines? Lingisters, all of 'em, a-winin' and a-dinin', and now see where they've got to by it. Kate must think a lot of herself to cotton up to him."

She looked again.

"Kind of a little runt, too. Aaron was a head taller'n him before he got bowed over. Seems like they don't grow so big now as they used to. Suthin' stunts 'em. Aaron now, he was six foot three."

She crawled in between the blankets, chewing her tongue to keep from groaning with the cold, and thinking of Aaron and his brothers, how tall they were and how stout, which one could throw another quickest when they used to come around her father's house in the evening and wrestle on the grass. Aaron was slower than some, but when it came to building, he could handle the biggest logs. Isaac was a good chopper, but he couldn't beat Aaron; Aaron didn't hit so often, but every blow brought a chip. Yes, they had come tall in Hannah's time, tall and stout and willing to go at life with an ax and a gun. An ax and a gun and a woman, and some way they made out not to starve and kept from freezing and raised up young ones tough as little polecats. Yes, six-foot-three it was Aaron had stood when he and Hannah were married.

3

Mindwell Gray's place was on a hill, not more than fifteen acres, pasture and all, and most of it ledgey, with a brook cutting its way down through from the mountain to the river. The house, one of the little old ones, stood only a story high, a kitchen to right of the chimney, a parlor to left, and three small bedrooms along the back, their windows darkened by evergreen trees and grapevine. A lane straggled up to it from the main road, picking its way among the rocks and keeping close to the brook, but the approach most travelled of late years was a path across Mindwell's pasture and Gus Bragdon's, a very narrow path, made mostly by Mindwell's and Sarey's distorted, plodding feet.

Tonight Mindwell and all her descendants except Kate were under the Elder's roof, and all the youngest sound asleep, but the older ones still clustered around the stove. Mindwell herself, a stout woman now and well on in years, but with the same fresh, cool, somehow sanctified face of her youth, appeared as if enthroned in the cushioned, straight-backed chair the Elder had built for her before he died; it had a wider seat than ordinary, and shorter legs, and she occupied it solidly, her feet set square on the floor, one hand with its broad, chaste wedding band dangling from the end of the chair arm and the other holding a book on her narrow shelf of lap. She did not speak often, but watched and listened with a mildly judicial air.

Roxanna in black merino skirt, crimson velvet waist, and big gilded buckle, sat near her mother, her ruffles sweeping the floor and her fingers flying at their tatting. As she talked, she kept glancing up to laugh, a handsome woman with sound, white teeth and good color in her cheeks. The pinched ageless little figure in the rocker was Sarey, huddled over her patchwork, her face gone flabby and old and chalk-white, her eyes still blue but now sharp and certain, darting almost viciously in first one direction and then another.

She said little. Her second daughter, Lovice, on the rug by Roxanna, seemed lost in watching the pretty mystery of the shuttle; she was another Sarey, as Sarey had once been, timid and dreamy, but in better health and more aware of her own charms; it was plain she copied Roxanna in the way she sat and held her head and placed her hands. But she did not talk. Benjamin, her older brother, lying on the couch with his long, thin arms under his head and his eyes staring at the ceiling, was most likely to be the one to answer Roxanna, when she needed answering.

"You ought to come down and pay me a visit, Lovey," she said. "It's as much as two or three years since you was there. You'd be a young lady now and get asked out. I could get Cyril Bannister to take you over to the Town Hall a Saturday night. How'd that suit you?"

Lovice could only catch her breath and flush. Cyril Bannister was the clerk in Drury's dry-goods store, and she remembered the way he had looked at her when she went in to buy black cotton gloves for Sarey, the day before a baby sister's funeral many years before. As a little girl wrapped in a Paisley shawl and set down off the top of the cart in which Gus had driven to the village through the early spring slush, she had made her way to the door between the two Drury signs and opened it into a dim, still room with counters running the length of each side and the walls covered with shelves of white boxes. Cyril Bannister had come toward her softly, facing her inquiringly, but saying nothing. The place smelled of new cloth and strange dyes. "I wanted to git a pair of black cotton gloves, size 5½," whispered Lovice. He turned and looked through several boxes, his hands very white, and his nails clean and rounded off short. At last he laid a pair before her. She knew she should finger them but did not dare. "If they ain't all right, can I have the money back?" she whispered. She could not lift her glance as far as his face. His voice came down to her coldly. "Why shouldn't they be all right? They're black cotton gloves, size 5½. Just what you asked for." His voice terrified her. She was feeling giddy from the smell of so much that was new. She could think of no reason why the gloves should not be all right, but she had been instructed what to say. She shrank into the folds of her shawl, staring at the floor, and said thickly: "I guess they'll be all right. But if they ain't all right, can I get the money back?" She heard him putting the boxes away, and feared he had lost patience and the gloves were gone from her forever. Her mother must have gloves, for the funeral tomorrow. The baby was dead. "Oh, let me have 'em!" Lovice implored him. Her glance flew upward, and, seeing the gloves still on the counter, she snatched them to her and promised, trembling: "I won't find no fault, if you'll let me have 'em. Here's your money." Trembling, she pushed a twenty-dollar bill across to him, and wondered why he looked at it and then at her so oddly. "Ain't it enough?" she asked him, frightened. It was the first bill she had ever handled, and she had no idea of the cost of gloves. He laughed and said: "Plenty. A little lady like you shouldn't be buying cotton gloves. I've got some fine silk ones, and some beautiful kid—" But Lovice had gone running out of the store with her change in one hand and the gloves in the other, and hid in the cart until her father came and turned the horse toward home.

"He works in at Drury's, don't he?" Benjamin asked.

"Yes. He's a fine hand at waitin' on folks. Everybody likes him. Smart as a trap too. Nobody sees why he don't get married. He must be—why, he must be thirty-five years old anyway. He looked as old as he does now when he came there, and I know that was before Minnie was born because I was into the store once when Josie Merrifield come in and bought some baby's stockings of him, and I know I didn't have any young ones of my own at the time because I thought, 'I bet she wisht she could spend that money on something for herself.' I didn't realize then how a mother feels about doin' for 'em, after she gets 'em. . . . But I know Cyril was clerkin' there at that time."

"He must have saved up a very good sum of money by now," Benjamin said. He added quickly, "Though there are other good uses for money besides saving it."

"That's what I always say," Roxanna agreed. "It's a slow way to get ahead, to be always saving your money. Now, I suppose if *you* had a good job, Benny, you'd buy yourself an education with it. Then in time you'd be the minister in a big church with a big salary, and plenty of chance then to do your savin'."

"Servants of the Lord don't work for pay, Roxanna," Mindwell interposed in her heavy, deliberate voice. "Benjamin won't never find a place that needs him any more than this does, nor wouldn't however fur he wandered. Where else in the civilized world is there a church that ain't been open for fifteen years, nighabout?"

"Grammum is determined not to see my way, Aunt Roxanna," Benjamin said bitterly. "I'm past expecting her to. Religion means too much to me for me to *ever* go forth to preach it until I have learned the words to use. Who am I to preach? A man who never sat in Sunday school in his childhood, nor heard anyone speak with an inspired mouth all through his youth! I'd never have seen the inside of a church except that I unlocked the door with her key and crept in to pray alone in the cold. I have never been trained as a minister, nor even as a parishioner. I have never heard a sermon; how could I deliver one?"

"If you've read your Bible," Mindwell said, "you've done all you could, and that's enough. That's all the education your grandfather had, and he brought a many souls to his Master before he took to his bed. You've got a build like his and a voice like his, and I'll believe to my dyin' day you was meant and appointed to take up his work where he laid it down. But you ain't done it."

Benjamin sprang to his feet, towering among the seated women.

"And why haven't I done it? *Why* haven't I done it? Because I'm tied hand and foot. I love the Lord Jesus Christ. I am consecrated to His service. But He has told me I must not represent Him until I am ready. I must read, and study, and travel up and down the highways, and *I must not undertake to lead a church until I have been ordained.* He has told me. It is His will. I have known it from the summer when I was fourteen. One night I slept out in the woods beside the pond, and He came and told me. Do you think I would disregard His command? His personal command to me?"

Benjamin's eyes seared his grandmother.

"Yes. He said to prepare myself. But how am

I to prepare? Nothing to enroll in a school with, nothing to get there with, nothing to live on while I'm there. And why is there nothing? Because my father is a poor man with a starving family? No; because my father is one that digs and saves and *hoards*, and would rather have deeds and bank books and silver pieces in the chest under his bed than a son in the service of his Maker. I am not free even to read my Bible and the few books I have collected without being sought out and growled at and given more to do than my shoulders can hold up under. There's never one day I can call my own, nor one night when my lamp can burn and I don't hear about it, one way or another."

He turned to the window and stood looking out.

"How in the world did it happen Kate went down to the academy?" asked Roxanna, not so impressed as she might have been. She could not keep her mind so long on one problem. "I never was clear about that."

"How did she happen to go?" repeated Benjamin. He turned again into the room, his face long and dark, his eyes hot. "How did she happen to go, the two years she did go? Well, I'll tell you, Aunt Roxanna. She went because my mother put her shoulder to the wheel and sent her there. Between them they raked and scraped for every penny she had, and mother did the work for the two of them. And she could do it because Kate was a girl. She couldn't do it for me. I never could be spared, and I never have been spared. But I want you to know if it had been in the power of my mother I should have gone, and I have faith God will hold it to her credit."

He came and stood beside Sarey, who looked up at him in a small flurry of pleasure and embarrassment.

"She's not well," he said gently. "You can see to look at her what she's been through since she left her mother's house. Nobody will ever know better than I do what she's had to bear. Driving year in and year out, a good deal of the time without fit food for her to eat, always being ridiculed and criticized and made to look small. She's like a bird that somebody has fastened a turtle shell over, and they keep hitting the turtle shell so she has to stay in it to live at all. But unless something happens so she is let out to fly and sing, she —I don't know as we'll any of us have her very long."

He glanced sharply from one to another of their startled faces, bent to kiss his mother, and left the room. As he went up the stairs Jeff spoke to him from the bed they shared in the loft, but Benjamin did not answer.

"Mother!" Lovice cried. She left Roxanna, running to crouch before Sarey and bury her face on

Sarey's small, bony knees. "Whatever does Ben mean? He sounds so *awful*—"

"There, I don't know," said Sarey, as bewildered as the others but not so frightened, for she had heard a good deal of Benjamin's strange-sounding talk and never seen it come to much. "It's suthin' more out of his books, I s'pose. He's an awful deep-thinkin' boy, and nobody can make out what he's gettin' at sometimes. He takes right after father that way, sartain."

"What he don't have," said Mindwell, "he don't have his grandfather's git-up-'n'-git. If only Benjamin could do as well as he can talk, the way your father could!"

"Well, Sarey, you do look poorly," Roxanna said. "Your eyes look as if they was goin' to pop right out of your head. I don't doubt you're draggin' yourself to death and gittin' no thanks for your pains. You never ought to have been in any such place. It wa'n't as if I didn't warn you how wrapped up Gus Bragdon was in himself and wouldn't have eyes for how you fared. Yes, I do declare, marm, I never see Sed look so poorly."

"I know it," Mindwell answered. She sighed. "She's thin as a rail. She ought to have suthin' to build her up, but I don't know what 'twould be, I'm sure. Seems as if she's took everything anybody ever heard was good."

Mindwell's and Roxanna's eyes rested anxiously on Sarey. Lovice had not left her mother and now raised her head, bursting into tears.

"Well, she needs a rest," she sobbed, "and she won't take it. She could if she would. She don't need to work the way she does, with two great girls around the house. Kate and I've both tried to git her to give up, and she *won't*. She's—she's gittin' all wore out—"

"There," said Sarey, "don't take on so, Lovice. You'll be sick out of it. I'll live till my time comes like everybody else." She chuckled suddenly. "Why, I feel as if I'd got that house built right onto me, and if I was to crawl out from under it, it would tumble down into the cellar square on top of Gus and the young ones and Granny Bragdon and all of 'em. That's just the way I feel, and there ain't no way around it."

So much attention had put new life into her. She glanced across at Roxanna's shuttle and tangled rosy thread.

"That looks like awful pretty work to do, Roxan," she said. "Who learnt it to ye?"

"Why, everybody's at it down to the village," Roxanna answered. "We all do it at club meetin's. It's no trick at all, once you get onto it."

"Lovice, you'd better try to pick it up," Sarey suggested. "It would make an awful handsome aidgin' for some petticoats. You'd ought to be gettin' ye a few pretties together, you and Kate, both of ye, ag'inst your gittin' married. It'll be all I can do to stodge and twotch up comforters enough to keep ye warm into bed. I never was no hand at fancy stitches, but, land, what chance did I ever have to study 'em out?"

"Married!" Lovice sniffed. "Who'd I marry? Harvey Linscott?"

"You know that's a comical thing," chuckled Sarey, "the way Harvey Linscott has took to tendin' out on Lovice. That's Jed's grandson; you mind, Roxan—Ketury's boy."

Roxanna dropped her work and looked up quickly.

"Sarey Gray! You ain't tellin' me you'd let Lovey have anything to do with—"

"No!" Lovice exclaimed heatedly. "I wouldn't *anyway!*"

"No," Sarey agreed, "she don't go nowheres with him, but there ain't no reason she can't treat him polite when he stops in. He don't 'pear to want nothin' better than jist to look at her, and I'm sure that don't hurt her none. Gus says he's an awful worker in the woods. He follers the sawmills, you know. He's very neat and clean, too. He don't hang around with the rest of the tribe much. He wa'n't so dretful smart in school, Kate said, but that's the most I ever heard ag'inst him; he's several cuts above the rest of 'em. I don't think of any young feller around that's any steadier."

Roxanna broke in indignantly. "That's all right, Sarey. That's the way you look at it. But you never could see further 'n the end of your nose in such things. Look what you done for yourself. Now you're fixin' to let your girls git right into the same ditch. What I say, I say no young one is any better than them that went before him, and if Ene Blaine was the one Ketury had, as folks all thought, bein' as Catharine was always so straight-laced with him that whole year they was goin' together—if Linscott and washed-out Blaine is all there is to this Harvey—"

"There now, Roxan, that'll do," said Mindwell, for the first time stirring in her chair. "I've heard enough 'n' more 'n enough from ye, the both of ye. This ain't fit talk to have over before Lovice, and you know it. Everything ye've said shows ye're thinkin' of Lovice as a woman when she ain't nothin' but a little girl. I hope she can manage, in spite of ye, to keep sech ideas out of her head for ten years yet; that's what I hope. I hope her mother's poor example will mean more to her than anybody's light talk; that's what I hope for ye, Lovey."

Lovice hung her head, twisting her handkerchief in the agonized embarrassment of any sensitive child who hears other children scolded. The other children, Roxanna and Sarey, bent guiltily to their work. The room grew quiet.

At last Sarey spoke again in a low, firm voice.

"One thing I will say, whether anybody wants to hear it or not. I will say I ain't done so bad for myself as you always try to make out. I've been drove, but I've drove myself; ain't nobody had to drive me; I ain't the kind to hang back. Gus is hard, but he ain't bad; an' you ain't never heard me say I knowed of anybody else I'd ruther had. I guess life ain't easy anywheres you live it; I never heard of anybody's that was. I ain't gone cold nor hungry neither, and whatever ain't been spent on finifyin' has gone where Gus thinks it'll do the most good in the end. It ain't been squandered."

"You're hittin' out at me," Roxanna said bitterly, "about how Ed spends on horses. Just because Gus had to pay that one note for him—"

"No, I ain't," Sarey answered. "I ain't hittin' out at nobody. I'm just sayin' I don't want so much hittin' out at Gus. There's good things ye could say about him, or ye could say nothin'. Ye both claim to think so much of Lovice, ye might think whether it's good for her to hear her father run down. I guess all of us Grays will do well to guard our out-speakin' a little mite. That's all I've got to say, and I'm done."

"Let's—couldn't we sing?" asked Lovice anxiously.

"It would be a good thing," said Mindwell. She hitched forward and raised herself by the strength of her hands on the ends of the chair arms. "We'll have no arguin' and quarellin' under your grandfather's roof. I still think what I think, but I'll hold my tongue. What d'you want to sing, Lovice?"

Lovice thought she liked "He's the Lily of the Valley" the best of all.

" 'Tis a good one," Mindwell said.

The organ stood in the corner between the dish cupboard and the cellar door, as accessible to her as her bed or her provisions, and used more often than either. She let herself down on the fringed stool before it with a puff of relief.

"Number Seventy-eight, girls. Come."

"I'll be right there," Sarey answered cheerfully. "Didn't Benny say that's what I need—singin'? I guess likely I do. Sometimes after I've let my voice out I feel ten years younger."

As they crossed the room to where Mindwell sat and Lovice stood holding the lamp, Roxanna murmured: "You don't need to worry about that fifty dollars, Sarey, you nor Gus neither. I shouldn't never have asked ye for it if we'd had any other way to turn the day we got that letter. Ed'll pay you back the first free money he gets hold of. It's six weeks now since the last funeral, and hacks is all that's been out of the shed. It keeps us awful close."

"Say no more about it, Rox," Sarey answered cordially. "You take care of it when it comes handy, and not a minute sooner. I had quite a time a-gittin' of it, but Gus hain't said a word about it since, so don't you spare yourself short."

" 'He's the Lily of the Valley,' " Mindwell sang in her strong alto, not so deep and rich as it had once been, but still true. Sarey's and Lovice's soprano and Roxanna's contralto joined her. " 'The bright and shining star. He's the fairest of ten thousand . . .' "

As they swung into the second verse, Kate came in quietly and sang from where she took off her hood and cape, rubbers and leggings at the end of the stove and hung them on hooks above the wood-box. Her voice was alto, too, deep and rich as Mindwell's had ever been; and she sang as they all did, as if singing were no effort, but the joyous outgushing of a living spring which had been stopped for a while by a stone across its mouth.

"One hundred eleven," Kate said as they finished. She went to turn the pages for her grandmother; none of them needed words or notes, but turning the pages to the right number was part of the ceremony. She did not take time or thought to greet the others, nor they her. They were the

Grays singing together, and in every pause thirsted for that rush of music in their throats. Kate's voice led the others, martial and gallant. "'Shall we gather at the river, where bright angel feet have trod . . .'"

"Mine's sixteen," said Sarey. "Sixteen!"

Once or twice Mindwell said, her face shining, her eyes bright and glad, as Kate turned the pages to a new number: "Oh, how your father did love to sing that tune! How he would run right up on them last notes and *bust* into the chorus! I never could keep up with him on the organ." Once Lovice said softly: "First time I ever heard that was the day we buried Little Ruth. That was before we started comin' over here to grammum's, and I hadn't ever heard hymns much." Now Sarey's tears came. Roxanna put her arm around her sister, and Sarey said: "You done it, Roxy. You done it awful sweet for her." And the Grays sang through their crying, "'Tell me the old, old story of Jesus and His love.'" Then Kate turned to "Will There Be Any Stars?" And after that Roxanna wanted "Hear Dem Bells," which was not in the book. Mindwell played from memory. None of them had ever seen or heard a Negro, and none had lived the freedom of any but the most restricted and reserved of New England lives; but they sang this song with their heads thrown back, their eyes half closed, their mouths open wide, and their shoulders swaying, for they were the Grays, shut away among their own, and the music had taken them into itself.

"Hear dem bells! Don't ye hear dem bells?
Dey's a-ringin' out de glory ob de Lamb!"

4

The Blaines were not in bed when Stephen reached home. Catharine had gone, but Thoc and Enoch still sat here in the kitchen, with Berias and Trumann Selden who had stopped in on their way home from the store. This room was not like the other kitchens along the Road and Lane, despite all Catharine could do. Large and high-posted, it had—besides its stove and table, couch and straight-backed chairs—Enoch's great walnut desk, broken and scarred by its long journey over rough waters to this country and hard usage for many generations since; the mahogany framework of a Duncan Phyfe sofa with the upholstery gone and the springs torn out and boards nailed across and a comforter tacked on it; two little French chairs with worn blue leather seats and the remnants of urns and roses painted on the backs; an open-front cupboard filled with odds and ends of transparent china, a dozen or more pink Lowestoft plates, a nearly complete set of willow ware, and the few bright new tins Catharine had contrived to buy for herself. Her good dishes, which she had bought and was still buying with grocery coupons, she kept in the parlor cupboard where they would be safe. The top of a Governor Winthrop desk was stuffed with books collecting dust, the pigeonholes jammed with papers, all yellowed and most of them illegible, and the drawers full of bits of jade from China, stone images from India, mummies' hands from Egypt, coal from Pennsylvania, little gold nuggets, arrowheads, compasses, jumping beans, old coins, stamps, motheaten sponges, whale oil and goose grease and buffalo horns, ships in bottles and carved ivory and catnip mice and pearls from oyster shells.

Thoc came out of his chair now with the agility of a boy, though he was close to seventy and too bulky for his small feet.

"Well, by the Lord Harry! If it ain't Steve!"

"There, I knew he was comin'," Berias said. "I had it in mind to tell Catharine when I come in; but you was tellin' that yarn about Billy Joy, and it went clean out of my head. He was in at the store."

"Well, I say, faith be king!" exclaimed Thoc in delight. "Here's the boy back again, Ene; what do you know about that? Lay off your coat, and sit right down here, Steve. Take the arkettyvine. Go ahead; go ahead; take it. Catharine! *Catharine!*

Steve's home again, and I'll swear he knows he's got a stomach in him!"

"If I've got that, it's all I've got," grinned Stephen. He dropped his coat and hat on the table and came toward the stove, fixing his thumbs on his hip bones and pressing inward with his fingers. "I can count all my vertebræ from the front."

"I don't s'pose Bragdons had a crust or a bone or anything to throw to ye?"

Stephen aimed a kick at Berias as he passed, and shook hands heartily with Thoc and his father, all their faces lighting; Thoc a rotund man, head bald and pink except for a fringe of white hair across the back, eyes small and bright and creased around with laughter, the slack of his soft cheeks brushing the wings of his collar, and an ebony scull charm swinging from the heavy watch chain hung on his immaculate white waistcoat; Enoch taller and very thin, thoughtful, even morose, not so quick to speak and smile as before he married Catharine Shorey, but still a Blaine with the Blaine gift for giving back a quick answer.

"Well, sir!" said Enoch; and Thoc, "Well, well, sir!"

"Didn't mean to turn you out of the arketty-vine, sir," said Stephen.

He stood for a minute with his hand on the back of the chair Thoc had vacated. It was a big wing chair mounted somewhat awkwardly on rock-ers, one that grown Blaines had sat in for several generations, and their children had always liked to cuddle in. Cap'n David, seeing how little Thoc, Sam, Gilly, Ann, Rachel, and the others were restless until settled there, and thereafter were content, named it the Ark of Divine Safety. Children's tongues had made it the "arkettyvine," which now it was.

"But I won't let her go begging," Stephen said, throwing his long young body into it.

"*Catharine!*" roared Enoch.

"I'm a-comin'," Catharine's voice answered. "Do you think I'm stone-deef? What's the matter with Steve that he's back here so quick? I s'pose he's—"

"Well, sir, now it's good to have the boy back, ain't it, Ene?" Thoc insisted, beaming around on the whole group. "I've got some idea, too, how hungry he is. I was younger'n he is now by a long sight the first time I walked down to Porchmuth and back again. Brother Gilbert, he was with me. I was eight or ten, and he might have been a dozen, and we struck off one morning across lots through the woods. Wet? My soul, we was as wet to the knees before we'd gone a mile as if we'd walked into a river to push off a boat."

"He ne'er forgets to gie the grass, ilk blade its drap of dew," murmured Enoch.

"What's that?" asked Thoc, turning.

"His Burns again," said Stephen, grinning at his father. "Don't mind him, Uncle Thoc. Get right along with your story."

"Oh, Burns, is it? Well, all right. I don't know what Burns knows about it, but I know there's an old Scotch saying father used to get off a good many times, 'You have to get up airly if you want to walk with God,' and I thought of it that morning as I walked over Oak Hill with Gilly. Oak Hill, you mind, was where the Cochranites, the Children of Nature, used to have their meetings years ago. Father recalled them. He used to tell how they'd build up a great bonfire over there and dance around and around it without a stitch on, singing and making a great to-do, and anybody that was converted to 'em had to go dressed and dance with 'em, a-pulling off one garment at a time and throwing it on the fire until they'd sacrificed 'em all and was purified. I recall thinking that over that morning we was walking to Porchmuth and wondering what them fine red oak trees thought of such foolish goings-on."

"Well, whatever they thought," said Berias, "they had to think quick, because even then Gus Bragdon was a-beggin' to be born so he could hustle over there with a pick and shovel and dig 'em up while they was still worth somethin'. You mind they *was* the trees Gus dug up, one of the first things he done after he built over there in the

Lane. He'd dig out the roots and pull over a tree with a fall, cut off the biggest root and hew the trunk down to that size and haul it to Porchmuth Navy Yard for a dollar an inch. If the root was eight inches through, you see, he'd get all of eight dollars for it, after he'd hauled it down there! They used 'em for boat ribs on the Yard at that time, but it wa'n't more than a year or so before they started usin' steel ribs, so if Gus hadn't put up a fuss and got born just as he did he'd have been out a year's work and as much as sixty or seventy dollars."

There had been much laughter and slapping of thighs all through this, except from Berias, in whom, as story-teller, amusement was not becoming; and the room shone with merriment and good-fellowship when Catharine came into it—a tall, gaunt woman in a hastily buttoned blue flannel wrapper and her hair in a braid, her eyes sunk deep and black under her bushy eyebrows, and all the bones of her thin, square face protruding powerfully. She took a quick look about her, and scuffed the heels of her shoes threateningly across the wide floor boards as she came toward Stephen; but he did not notice her until she put a hand on his shoulder and gave him a small shake. She could not work up a real fury against him as she could have done against another. If her life had gone for anything at all, it was this boy.

"Stephen, what you here for? Be you sick, or anything?"

"Hullo, there, ma! Sick? No. Starved to death, that's all. Could you get me just a bite? . . . Gosh, Uncle Berias, that's a good one. I never heard that one before. Did you ever see another man in your life went hell-bent for work the way Gus Bragdon does? Say, if he heard anybody was paying a cent a carload for old shoestrings, he'd start saving his up and tie his boots with marsh hay . . . Well, go on, Uncle Thoc. What was doing along the river the morning you and Uncle Gilly struck out for Porchmuth?"

With grimly resigned face Catharine set about preparing a meal in the midst of story-telling. It was not a new experience for her, and she had no qualms about her interruptions. Her pans and dishes rattled, doors banged, and he who did not keep his feet under his chair would get them stepped on and knew it well enough.

"Oh, the river was full of craft that morning," Thoc resumed. "Full of craft. Some anchored, and some moored to the several wharves. Gilly and I recognized 'em all right off quick. Father learnt us boats if nothing else. We see sloops that day—tall, raking masts—pink-stern schooners, a fore-and-after, brigs, both square-rigged and hermaphrodite, and I recollect Captain Staples's full-rigger was just into Rand's wharf from China with a cargo of tea. Gilly observed right away she'd got a new foremast. Gilly was a great one for—"

"Move over, Thoc!' snapped Catharine. "I've got to get into that woodbox."

"Have ye, Catharine?" asked Thoc, mildly. "Ye *have!* Well, now, I don't see how you're going to do it. That box ain't an inch over three feet long—"

"Oh, stop your nonsense," she told him. "Clear out of my way. The fire's down till I don't know whether it'll fry anything or not. I wisht I had somebody could keep me stocked with dry wood. I'm sick to death of burnin' this green stuff, and the chimney's well-nigh plugged up with sut. *Move*, can't you!"

"Calm yourself," Thoc admonished her. "Come, calm yourself. I'm a-moving, but you ain't in ary rush for that wood. Fires don't go out in a minute. No, Catharine, you ain't in near so much rush for that wood as you think you are."

"I've heard that before," said she, diving into the wood box and out again to rattle stove lids and pots and pans, and fill the fire box. "Everything you and Ene say I've heard so often before that I couldn't stomach to laugh at it even if it was funny, which it generally ain't."

"Catharine," said Thoc kindly, "was born with a very small ticklish spot in her, and ain't nobody found out where it is yet; but when they do, she'll go right off into laughing fit to give her a pain in her side. . . . Well, all else I want to say about that Porchmuth trip is where Gilly and I had our dinner. We had it at John Rand's victualling cellar in the basement of a brick building just a few doors southwest from the old Spring Market. John Rand's was where the masters of the vessels was most likely to eat, and any folks from out of town on business. When you stepped down into it a man in a white apron and shirt sleeves with his frilled cuffs turned back would ask you—very polite, he always was—'What is it today, my little gentlemen, meat or fish?' I recall Gilly and I that day had fried haddock, bannock bread and butter, and a cup of tea for ninepence each. They baked the bannock on plates leaning against the bread block before the fire, and they fried the haddock by putting it on a long-handled frying pan with the pan on the coals and the handle resting on the slats of a high-back chair turned back to the fire. They made their coals out of oak chips from Raynes's shipyard—"

"I s'pose they was *dry* chips, wa'n't they?" Catharine demanded. "There, I guess, Stephen, there's a mouthful of suthin' ready for ye, and maybe ye can eat it if ye ain't too partic'lar. Of course this ain't John Rand's nor any restaurant up to Massachusetts, and it may not suit—"

"Suits me fine," Stephen assured her. He went

to the table and dipped in hungrily—cabbage hash rich with salt-pork gravy, hot brown bread and cheese, and steamed cranberry pudding.

"I say, faith be king!" Thoc exclaimed. "Here I've been a-telling over about old times, and what we want is to hear from you, Steve." He moved across to the arkettyvine, now it was again empty, and sank into it with satisfaction. "How did things look, where you've been?"

So between bites Stephen told of his few days' work on the bridge in Lawrence, and of the month on the tug in New York Harbor, of bananas and tarantulas and Navy Day, of fog and cold and wind and the swarthy appearance of foreigners landing at Ellis Island. He had the Blaine sense of how to tell a story, not held back by consideration of truth but keeping near enough to it in the main, ready with emphasis and exaggeration, expressive words coming easily to his tongue. He told, too, of the manufacturing that was quickening everywhere and bringing in new life and strange ways wherever it went, how he had heard that the old families of Derwich Village were fighting the shoe shop which threatened to build a long double row, a whole street, of ugly little houses all alike, fighting the trolley-car line which might send a great yellow cart rumbling and whistling over steel tracks past their very doors and their gardens full of lilacs and larkspur, Canterbury bells and London pride, cinnamon roses and lady's-delight and strayaway ambrosia.

"But they'll come, both of 'em," Stephen said, draining his mug of cider while Enoch poured more for the rest. "They'll come. You mark my words. This old world won't stand still, not even in Derwich."

5

Nearly every morning through the winter Gus went into the woods after a load of limbs. Every morning while Sarey still slept he stepped out of bed into the bitter cold and drew on red flannel underwear she had made for him, stockings of his mother's knitting, flannel shirt and corduroy pants and overalls, felt boots and rubbers. Armored so, he went to build the kitchen fire and set the kettle on, then felt for cap and coat on pegs behind the stove and, with two milk pails in one hand, made his way through the dark shed to the barn. He was not sleepy; he did his sleeping by night. Now it was growing daylight and he could get at his work, so broad he turned his shoulders sideways to go through a door, a hard, stooped, ruddy-brown man with pale eyes and thick-skinned hands that did not shrink from an iron latch on a January morning.

The chores done, he went back to the kitchen and sat down at the table, whether it was set or not, and Sarey hastened to put food before him. He ate quietly, rapidly, hugely of whatever he saw; Gus was not one to think of leaving something for those who would come after. He ate what he wanted of what was there, but asked for nothing else; offered neither praise nor criticism of the meal; cleaned his plate until it would be difficult to prove it had not been washed, crossed his knife and fork upon it, and pushed back his chair. Sarey brought him a parcel of biscuits with barberry sauce between them, hard-boiled eggs and dried apple pie, and two whisky bottles filled with sweetened tea and wrapped in newspaper, and he put these into the pockets of his greatcoat and went out into the snow.

"Now you be careful," Sarey called after him sometimes. "You mind that time Charlie pitched off his sleds up in there and broke his leg and well-nigh froze before they found him—"

Gus never answered. A man went where he had to, and managed as well as he could.

The kitchen had been hot and stifling to him in his heavy clothes. Now cold air came stealing in. He mounted his homemade blue sleds, sitting so low his head was on a level with Bell's flanks, and drove into the Lane, passing Berias Blaine's and Trumann Selden's places, where no one was yet up, and turning into a woods road which led along the course of the river and across a pond, farther and farther away from any other flesh and blood than that of an occasional deer, a rabbit or two, and a few birds. Foolish ones, Gus called the birds, these left behind when all the rest had flown off to some place where picking was easier than here. Tough little fellows; they dipped and soared as if it were summer, or bit and tore at the bushes in a frenzy of industry, or sat dully on an icy branch with foot tucked in among their feathers, depending on the kind of spirit they had. Foolish ones, perhaps, to hang on here, the few of them alone, just because this was the place where they had pricked the shell; but they seemed to be making out. Gus's attention slid away from them.

Always when Gus went into the woods his mind was on the trees. The boundaries of every lot were familiar to him, and its corners, whether a pile of rocks, an iron stake, a jutting ledge, or a lone evergreen. He knew the landmarks—the Spreading Beech, the hopyard, the rye yard, the Spruce Swamp, the Great Rock, the Horse Hills—and had visited them all in every season from his boyhood on. This had been his playground, his courting place, and his field of business. He knew every different kind of tree from afar and could tell its habits, how long it had lived and might still live; the feel of its bark, whether the shelly maple, the pebbly ash, or the smooth and sticky pine which oozed out a good, clean, live-tasting gum in May;

how long it took a birch to stretch and cover marks left upon its skin by a wandering lover with a knife. He had been here many times when all was as now, cold and still, with purple shadows lying across the sunlit snow, and at other times when it was bare ground and running water except beneath the evergreens where drifts still lingered, and when berries hung red and blue and black on the stripped lots, and when foliage was falling, leaving the hardwood trunks and branches proud and free against the racing clouds.

Not only the matter of the value of the trees was his concern. His neighbors would have said so, but they did not know. It was true his thoughts ran mostly to how tall they were and how thick through, how straight, whether his and if not, whether it would be wise to buy them, whose land they grew on and what bounded it, how far they were from wheel road and from railroad; but there was more to it than his thinking. Trees were what he fully understood of all that lived. They never confused him. They were born and had a period of growth, some longer and some shorter, and then died. They drove their roots deep, and every day pushed a little higher toward the sky; but nobody saw their growth. Even the pine now. A pine grew from twelve to eighteen inches in a year. Every spring each tree was finished off at the top with a small bunch of buds, and by another spring each bud had become a branch spreading wide and the main stem had put out another bunch of buds higher up; but nobody saw it grow, and most people had forgotten, when it came to sawing, how very small a tree it had once been. Not Gus; he remembered; he had watched it all the way and never grown impatient as he waited. This was a way of doing which seemed to him natural and right.

His contacts with human beings were less close. He found them whiffle-minded, jerked this way and that by every clod and turn in the road. They talked too much and had too many feelings. They were like young ones playing on the beach, running and squealing as the waves came in, making a great tumult if a crab nipped them or they trod on a jellyfish; but the trees stood as firm as rocks while tides came in and went out and the moon changed. Among people there was too much wishing and wondering, recalling and anticipating, too much poking fun and feeling bad; this one must always be showing the rest what he knew; that one must indicate he would not be stepped on; the rest fell over one another getting their pucker stubbed, speaking their minds, having their sensitivities hurt, complaining of their symptoms; there was no end to it. Gus went eagerly into the woods and came reluctantly out. Trees were what he knew.

Still there was no doubt it meant something to

him to see Kate or Jeff coming up Hamilton's Hill as he rode over the brow of it at sunset. If Jeff was there with his sled or wagon, it meant he had filled the pails and tank and teakettle with water, the wood boxes with wood, both large and small, and the pail with chips and edgings; otherwise Sarey would not have let him leave the dooryard. It was a conduct prize she held out to him all day, this going to meet his father, though no one knew, least of all Gus, why it meant so much. Gus only drew up on the reins while Jeff climbed to the top of the load; then Bell plodded on again, steaming. Jeff, broad and sturdy, a noisy boy in the schoolyard, red-faced and blue-eyed under his stocking-leg cap, was entirely content to sit quiet beside his father while Bell drew them through the snow or mud, and the little sled or wagon bounced along through the ruts behind.

If Kate came, it meant that she was anxious, though Gus never knew this. Sometimes Sarey worried all day long, her face more tightly screwed than ever. As she plunged her hands deep into pale yellow butter, working it, or dressed a hen for the market, she kept looking out at the thicket into which Gus had gone, and saying, "It's dretful slipp'ry today. If your father was to miss his footin'!" or "I wisht your father would stop in to Dr. Foster and have him listen to his heart. I've got a notion it acts up sometimes lately. Of course he wouldn't say nothin'. I keep a-thinkin', what if he should have a spell up in them woods all out of sight 'n' hearin' of everybody?" All day Kate, working with her, would answer cheerfully. But if it came close to dark, Ben had brought the milk in, and supper was ready on the back of the stove, and still Gus had not come, she threw a shawl over her head and walked up Hamilton's Hill. If she reached the top, she waited there until she heard the sound of his wheels or of the bell the horse wore on her collar, and then ran home again, her breath coming free once more. If Bell and the load and Gus on top of it surprised her, coming suddenly down out of the dusk, she smiled and shouted: "Your supper's all ready. I'll be right back. I'm getting me a breath of air." He only thought she liked to be outdoors better than the rest of them, that peace and quiet suited her as well as it did him. Only Grays wore themselves out a-worrying; Kate was a Bragdon.

It was one Sunday late in the spring that he walked into the woods up by the Elbridge Allen lot, wearing a straw hat and clean overalls and carrying one arm across his back, and found Kate there before him,—Kate and Stephen Blaine.

They had come a piece through the growth, and now Kate sat on a stump at the edge of the adjoining stripped lot. Her flowered organdy skirt billowed over the moss and roots and small bushes, and lace clustered so high about her throat that her chin brushed it as she turned her head. It seemed a strange place to wear such a costume, but it was somewhere, and this was Sunday; she had been careful about holding it up and they had come by way of the clearest spots. She had few such dresses, but even those few grew limp from hanging in her closet and rarely were worn out. Her hat, something of straw and roses with a long black velvet ribbon, lay on a branch; and her head was tilted back, her eyes on the pines, her face strong and grave above her finery. Stephen lay on the moss beside her, leaning on his elbows and whittling. He looked more than his two years younger by daylight; younger than he was; the mustache became a toy in the sun, and his mouth under it showed full and sweet.

He looked up quickly at the sound of a step in the underbrush.

"It must be father," Kate said. "Yes, it's father. . . . Hullo. Who'd expect to see you out here in the woods?"

"I be quite a stranger," Gus agreed.

He was always more approachable on Sunday. Sarey waited for Sundays to speak to him of something Mindwell or Roxanna ought to have. If they must have it, she waited for a Sunday when he went into the woods and she felt able to follow along after him. He would be at his easiest there, though never very easy. He paused now beside these two and rested one foot on a neighboring stump.

"What's goin' on? Mayflowerin'? Late, ain't it, for Mayflowers?"

"Yes," Kate nodded. "They're about gone by. No, nothing's goin' on. Steve and I are out here on business."

"Business, is it?"

"Yes. What do you say this lot is worth?"

"This one? This Elbridge Allen lot? . . . Why, Almond Tuttle owns it and he's got a price on it. I guess anybody could git it for less, though. You thinkin' of buyin', be ye?"

"Yes. That is—Steve is."

Kate looked at Stephen, smiling, and he rolled over and sat up, hugging his knees. Gus regarded them both soberly.

"Yes," said Stephen on a deep, outgoing breath. "Kate says I've got to settle down. She's been saying it for years now, but she said it today in such a way she's got me scared. I'm licked, and I know it. I've got to start scratching for property the way a hen scratches after worms."

He got to his feet, suddenly serious. He had a very likable face, warm and bright, a friendly, generous face.

"And she's right about it, too, Gus. I know that as well as anybody. I—well, I don't mean to speak against my folks, but being so much with father and Uncle Thoc wouldn't do any young fellow any good. I've never heard anything but books and yarns, and you know as well as I do nobody ever earned honest bread and butter by them."

Gus knew it very well. He quite agreed.

"I've had my ambitions," Stephen said, "but I've never heard them anything but laughed at, at home. Father and Uncle Thoc are all for laughing at—at anybody that tries to get ahead. But I'm through listening to them. I tell you, and I tell Kate, I'm through. I'm going to get me a piece of land plowed and get to work on it, and see if I can bring back the home place there from all running to seed. I've got a good start; I've got a horse and some cows and tools and riggings, such as they are, and I'll make a showing by a year from this fall, now you mark my words. I'm going to light in there, and I shan't let anything trig my wheels."

"He can do it, too, father," Kate said quietly. "He can do it if he will."

"Sure," Gus answered. "Sure he can. See what Harvey Linscott has done to that old field over by the Elder Gray place. That feller's a worker; he'll make his way."

Stephen had no admiration to spend on Harvey Linscott.

"I'll tell you what I've made up my mind," he

was going on. "I've made up my mind I'm going to put in two years over there and show Kate what I can do. The land wants using, and the buildings want fixing; and I'll tend to both. In a couple of years I'll have 'em in such order as she won't be ashamed to come into. Now you may not think I mean it after all my darting hither and yon, but I'll show you, Gus, and I'll show her. I'm not all Blaine; there's some Shorey to me, and you'll find it out so. I've played around long enough. Now I'm going to buckle down."

Kate sat watching him, and listening, and Gus with her. Their eyes were grave, and he felt they still awaited something else, looked for something in him which they were not sure they found.

"That's the way he feels about it, father," Kate said at last. After another silence she remarked in a new, fresher voice, "That's why we're interested in wood lots. I tell Steve you think it's as good a way as any to take care of anything anybody gets ahead. We thought he might be in a couple of years where he could give his note for part of the price of this Elbridge Allen lot. It's one that looks as if it was growing well."

"Yes," Gus answered. He took his foot off the stump and replaced it by the other, his elbow resting on his knee and his hat pushed back so that he could see the tops of the Elbridge Allen trees. "Yes, it's doin' well. Almond wants a thousand for it, but I'll lay he'll take—well, seven hundred 'n' fifty. In twenty, well, say thirty years, it ought to bring—why, it ought to bring right around ten thousand dollars."

"Ten thousand, Steve!" Kate repeated proudly.

The sum had caught Stephen off his guard. He stood looking at Gus incredulously. It was some generations now since Blaines had thought in figures of that size.

"Yes, this is one of the lots that's comin' right along," said Gus. He looked steadily back at Stephen. "I've had it in mind I might git it of Almond myself if it come right, but I ain't got the price ready yit; and as I see it I'm too old a man now to saddle myself with notes. Maybe you'll git in a position to speak with him before I do, if you keep at it."

"I'll keep at it, Gus," Stephen vowed roundly. In his heart he swore he would beat the old penny-squeezer at his own game this once if it was all he ever did. "I'll keep at it all right. Make no mistake about that. Three years from now this lot will be mine and paid for."

Kate regarded her father.

"I should think there'd be other lots than this one you could buy," she said, "now Steve's set his heart on it."

"So there be," Gus told her. "I shan't be ready to buy nothin' in under three years. So if Stephen is, he'll git it, that's all, as fur as I'm concerned, and I'll have to do with suthin' else."

She understood him now, and took the challenge for them both. Gus did not know when he had ever seen her look so gay. She pulled her flowered and velvet-ribboned hat off the branch and stood up.

"That's what you'll have to put up with, father," she said. "Something else. This lot is going to be Stephen's. He's going to work hard; and it may be no fair, but I'm going to help him. I'm going to see Uncle Ed tomorrow about getting me the school to teach next fall. I'll pay you for my board and save besides it. . . . Come on, Steve. We'll trace out the boundaries of this lot of ours."

She flung her ruffles over her arm, and the two went away up the edge of the stripped lot together. When they had gone, Gus sat for a while on the stump where Kate had been, poking thoughtfully among the moss with his stick. Then he walked for an hour or more through the woods, coming home early by the back way, and tramped about in the shed chamber before going to change his clothes and do the chores. Sarey, lying in the bedroom with a wet cloth on her head, wondered irritably what he could be hunting for up there, and called to him, but he did not seem to hear.

In the evening he brought small pieces of heavy

dark wood into the kitchen and spread them out on the table, opening his knife.

"What's that?" Kate asked.

"Well," Gus answered, sliding the pieces through his thick fingers, "it's black walnut. Some I had left from that stair rail in the front entry there. I had an idea if you was a-goin' to keep school you'd need a good stout ferrule and a handle for your bell. Ain't nothin' better than black walnut when you want suthin' stout, to last."

6

The summer passed. Kate studied for her examinations and wrote out the answers to the questions at a bench in her Uncle Edward's shoemake shop, while he sat by at his pegging; and when he had sent the papers in to the supervisor in the village, word came back that if the Committeeman for District Number Nine was satisfied, she might have the school. Uncle Ed was satisfied; he peered through his spectacles at her number work and said she wrote the clearest hand of anyone he knew, bar none; why, it read like printing.

Stephen worked as hard as she, if not so faithfully, or with such good results. He planted more than he could keep hoed, mowed a bigger piece than he could handle, and tore off more old shingles than he could replace with new before a rain came to soak down the English scenic papers in the upstairs bedrooms. His judgment was not all it might have been, Gus saw, but his will was good, and his courage high. Nothing daunted him. "I'm going to have the gosh-darnedest mess of cabbages, Kate," he said, when his neighbors were already eating peas and his, not yet in bloom, lay pale and choked with weeds. "If you folks need any extra cabbage, you just call on me. I'm the boy, if it's cabbages you want!" When his cabbage began to rot from being in too low ground on a wet year, his talk turned to muskmelons. "I'll tell you, Kate," he said. "The way to make money these times is to start in something new. Now this climate is just right for muskmelons, and I don't know anybody that's raising 'em. Do you?" Kate didn't. "Well, that's it," he rejoined in triumph. "Now this is my idea. I've got some books and catalogues together right now that tells what a good many men—what your father, for instance—would like gosh-darned well to know about muskmelons. But don't you say anything. I'm going to keep it dark. But next spring I'm going to plant my land *all to muskmelons.* Then I'm going to the beaches and drum me up a trade. If I can get in with the hotels, they'll take every one I can raise at a good price, and by next fall you and I'll be in the money. We shan't have to wait as long as two years, if you ask me. It all hangs on whether I can get in with the hotel men, and I guess I can. I've always found, wherever I went, I didn't have much trouble making friends."

The next spring came, and he bought himself from his potato money a spruce red gig and a small black driving horse and for a while rode to the beaches nearly every day. On Saturday or Sunday Kate sometimes went with him, dressed in the same pink-flowered organdy she had worn walking in the woods or in a yellow challie of a summer or two before. On these occasions he drove his covered buggy, and they rode on cushions and springs over the Flat Rocks and through York Woods, past Mount Assabenbeduc and out by the main road to the cluster of hotels at Short Sands or the one big boarding house and several cottages at Wells. He had made friends. Everyone seemed to know him and people clustered around wherever he stopped his horse. Kate, sitting tall and quiet, envied him the ease with which he smiled and the grace with which he removed his narrow-rimmed brown hat, and bowed with it lightly brushing the front of his tan-and-brown checked coat; envied and feared it and was very proud of it. They always had dinner at one of the hotels, though Kate would have been glad to bring a lunch, and at these times the manager often came to their table and said he had it in mind to make muskmelons a permanent item on his menus. He always laughed, and Stephen did, and Kate was never sure how much was meant by what was said, but it was clear Stephen had made friends. She thought to herself, "And done it without cheapening himself." For she had a notion of the means by which many men won popularity, but Stephen had never once been late home in the evening, or stayed away all night, and everywhere she went she saw him treated with great consideration and respect, as if a little distance separated others from him and all his cordiality had not made them see fit to cross it. At the table among so many others or as they strolled along the board walk on the beach, even she grew humble before him, felt tall and awkward, as if her hands were too broad since his were slender, and wondered if his friends made comment that Stephen should choose a girl from upcountry. But she said nothing of it, and as they rode back through the woods in the twilight he became hers again, the boy who was two years younger, a Blaine with all the Blaine weaknesses to overcome before he could entirely please her, and she spoke to him quietly of what he would do about his planting or his hoeing in the coming week.

"Oh, I've got my hands full next week," he told her. "Monday morning I start in on that piece down back of the barn—"

But the end of June came, and he had not

dropped many muskmelon seeds about his place, and a late frost had struck most of the few plants which were thriving. He was more interested now in celery. You had to dig a trench for celery, he said.

This same June marked the end of Kate's first year of teaching, and Supervisor McLean was writing out a paragraph which would appear about her in the Derwich Town Report for the years 1896–97.

"The school in District Number Nine has been presided over the last three terms by Miss Catharine R. Bragdon, and I have found the discipline good and all the scholars making reasonable progress in their several studies. Miss Bragdon has had no previous experience, and signs of this are at times apparent, but she is possessed of keen mind, great patience, and remarkable dignity of mien, and bids fair to be, a few years from now, as successful a teacher as the town affords."

This was the summer that Roxanna's Minnie was graduated from the Academy. No one from Sarey's went down to see her stand up before the others and hear her sing her solo, for the graduation came during a hot spell, and Sarey was in bed with dizziness, leaving everything about the house to the girls; Hannah's knees were so stiff now she could not get downstairs. But Roxanna wrote Sarey all about it in a fat letter so very like Roxan no one else in the world could have written it.

Sarey read it, lying in the near-cool of the parlor on the cherry bedstead which had been the Elder's.

Dearest Sister

I am going to set Down to write you a few Words of comfort if I can but I don't know Whether I Can See to write so you can Read it or not. My Eyes is awful bad of late sometimes They pain me so all I can do is Set Here and cry. How are You Feeling now. I don't see why you had be took down Sick just at this time. Minnie was so disapointed not to have a Single one of her own folks there to Hear her. She done awful good her voice is just as clear as a bell and She can hit the High notes as sweet as ever you could which is going some to Say because i always said your Voice held up as good as a Chord when you run it up. i wish marm could of heared her she would have been proud enough. I should think one of your Girls might have brought her down here for the day but there i dont spose they could or they would have and there, i dont know how marm would have stood it anyway it was so close and hot in there I got a Headache onto me that i cant seem to shake. I dont know what is the matter with me of late but i know i ain't right some way. I'm inclined to think it is Internal. I'd have the dr. in but there it's no use. i cant pay him. it cost awfully for Minnie's close and she didnt Have a mite better than the Rest neither, but We aint had a Funeral since Jacob Harrisons' three weeks ago and old Mrs Harrison aint paid for that yet.

Poor Old Soul there was one that suffered if anybody ever did I guess. He had a pipe Cancer and They say it eat right down his throat and out through his Neck and he suffered and took on something Awful at the last of it. Of course they dont give out its Cancer but i guess that's what it was all right. They never opened up the casket at the Funeral and of course if it hadn't been for Something like that they would of opened up the casket. There i dont know it seems as if human beings has an Awful lot to bear but i spose its Meant for Some Good i hope so I'm sure. Ed has got a boil on his leg.

We had a Supper down to our Church last night and we did have a good Frolic. There was a real jolly crowd there and everybody Entered right in. I dont know when i ever had such a rinktum. i kept thinking how You and Marm would of enjoyed it, and it would bring Tears right into my Eyes. Poor Old Marm setting up there in that old house all alone day after day i can't get her out of my Head. It worries me so for fear something will Happen to her up in there and Nobody won't know anything about it till Afterwards. She'd ought to have somebody with her. I dont know Who could go. I'm sure i couldn't as things are. I dont know why it is anybody's Hands has to be tied so. Time will come when i wont have any Mother and then i dont know what I *shall* Do.

I'm sending you a Sample of Minnie's dress and some of the Lace I made to put On It. I got Almy

Winters to Make it Up because I ain't no Hand at Cutting and fitting and it looked awful nice. It cost something though. i dont know how i'll Manage to Do the same by Mabel when her Turn comes. Poor little Young One, she's Awful listless. I know she dont have what shed ought to have to eat, now thats just the it of it. Right at this time in her Life shed ought to have a Mouthful of fruit once in a While and eggnoggs and custards and them things. She's awful picked. She complanes an awful lot of her Back.

I'm going to tell you this because my Heart is so Full I cant keep it Back. the Teacher sent Mabel to the doctor one day she had the Nosebled in school and he wrote me a note saying he found she'd got Weak Lungs and I'd have to Coddle her this summer or he wouldn't be Responsbel. Well Sarey i cant coddle her. i cant do it if its a matter of life and death i cant do it. there aint a thing but potatos and cheese in the House to eat and aint Ben for a Week. And i cant even keep her in Bed because i'm too near Down Sick myself. I dont digest my food and my head and Eyes is awful bad. it dont make much difference about Me but when I think of my Poor Little Young Ones. Well, there it don't do to think. I suppose the Lord is watching and it Must be All for the best. I hope so I'm sure.

I hope it ain't so Hot where you are as tis here. its ben awful hot for ten Days now. You take Care of yourself if you can.

With love and Kisses to my Darling Sister,

ROXAN

You will have to overlook this awful Hen-scratching. I Belive i'm going to be like marm the way she has the Rumatism so. The Joints in my fingers swell up by nights so their awful tender to touch i dont no how much Longer i'll be able to Hold a Pen.

Wednesday. This is a nice morning. I've got a whole potful of portulacas in bloom out here by the back Door. My Roses has been hansome but their most Gone by now. When the Roses is gone then anybody begins to think of winter. The dear Lord only knows how I Dread it this year with Mabel the way She is and Nothing to do with.

You try to take care of yourself. I've worried so about you i'm Just about Sick, i wish i had something Nice to send you but there what use is it for Ones like me to Wish.

This was not a Sunday, but a hard Friday in the hayfield for Gus, with only slim Ben and little Jeff to help him, and Sarey was far from able to follow her husband on a walk into the woods if he had been free to go there. But she could not rest until she pled Roxanna's and Mabel's cause to him. Her mind was full of it. She lay and tossed among her pillows while the sun went down the sky, peering in blinding streaks of light and gusts of heat around the drawn shades, and until she heard scraping of chairs and clatter of dishes and knew the family was at supper. Then she crawled out of bed, put her feet into shoes, drew on a wrapper over her nightgown, and made her way weakly out the front door and around the side of the house to her rocker on the porch. As she sat there she took combs and pins from her pocket and put her hair in order, and the neatness and the evening air made her feel more like herself than she had felt in weeks. She even rested her hands on the chair arms and rocked a little, the boards creaking comfortably under her slight weight. It was early July, and peas hung ready for picking on Gus's vines, potatoes were in bloom the whole length of the planted piece, and small green apples were setting on in the orchard. There was the smell of syringa and fresh-cut hay, and a strong, deep one of pine which an afternoon shower had stirred up. The cows had been tied and milked and replaced in the pasture by the horse and oxen who must have their nibble of green grass before nightfall. When Gus came out of his door with his supper in him, he calculated to find his day's work done and well done and himself free to turn his mind on tomorrow.

"Well! You so's to be out, be ye?"

Sarey looked up at him with a faint smile. He was such a stout one, through with his work, full of supper and power and peace. Whatever he wanted, he took. Whatever she wanted, she must ask for, scheme and connive and bow down for. This was only one of the differences between them.

His face was burnt dark, hers was white from lack of blood and being always under cover. His hands and arms were strong and steady, while hers were always tired and trembled sometimes as if she had the palsy. Her body was forever complaining; it was weak, or ached, or felt sore or cramped or prickly; she had to keep moving it, first one part and then another. He never thought of his; he put it in a chair and left it there until it was needed in another place. He did not even have to smoke a pipe or take a chew as any other man would have. He was free, while she was bound. He stood to one side to weave the pattern of his life while she became entangled in every thread she touched.

"There," she answered. "Yes, I've got this fur."

He made no comment. His face was mild and placid as he sat across from her, his shirt open at the neck and pulse beating rhythmically in the hollow beneath his Adam's apple; the dark blue, figured material of his shirt was stained black with sweat across his back. His eyes studied the field and orchard, narrowed to the computation of how much each would produce, and how soon, and what it would bring in the market. The land did not mean to him what trees did; he did not love it, only worked it, and from the pull on his own muscles, from pride in the security of what he owned here, from the silver pieces in the chest under his bed took his reward.

"Your peas is a sight earlier 'n last year, ain't they?" Sarey asked.

Gus nodded. "Yes. Yes, them peas has come on good." He added: "My pole beans is kind of pindlin'. They need more wet."

"How soon'll we have cucumbers?"

"Middle of the week, I thinks likely."

"It seems as if I could eat a little cucumber."

Silence fell, and Sarey sat in it imagining that she had already got Roxanna off her mind to Gus and he had said he would see what he could do. The frogs were singing wildly in the marsh, and she almost relaxed in the cheerful clamor but then roused herself. She would open her mouth and begin and the worst would be over.

"Gus! . . . Gus, you got to bring home grain tomorrer?"

"I thinks likely I'll have to git a bag or two of oats and one of cracked corn. Why? You want to git down to the village?"

"Oh, land, no!" She was worn out already. "Anybody'd think you could see I ain't fit to go anywheres."

"Well, I didn't know," he returned mildly. "Ye spoke of grain. I took it ye had it in mind about the room."

Kate and Lovice came out, carrying tin pails,

and Sarey knew they would pick the peas for market tomorrow. No green stuff would come her way until the customers in the village were sated. Kate brought a shawl for her mother's shoulders, and Lovice said it seemed good to see her up but she must be careful. They climbed through the barnyard fence and went down the pasture lane to the hill piece, for going by way of the field would have left a path through uncut grass. It was nearly dark. She did not know how they would see to pick, but young eyes must be better than old; and of course in the morning there would be the dew to contend with. Gus made a movement as if to go to round up his horse and oxen, and Sarey knew she must speak now.

"Yes, I was thinkin' of room," she said. "I want ye to bring along Roxanna and one of her young ones as you come back. Ye can take the democrat wagon."

Gus, standing now, glanced at her and then turned again toward the yard.

"No, I can't neither. I got to git grain, as I said, and the horse can't haul that and three besides it. There's the whole livery stable to take her if she's on the travel again."

"Well, now, you wait!" Sarey cried. "There ain't neither. The last time she druv a horse up here, there was a party of picnickers hired every cutter Ed had to home and would have took that one if he'd had it, so they lost a number of dollars by it right there. Besides, she ain't fit to try to handle one of them stable horses. She's all run down, and she gits the rheumatiz in her hands awful bad and her eyes ain't right; and Ed can't bring her because he's sick. He's got a dretful bad boil on his leg. You know what a time he always has when them boils gits onto him. I don't know, I'm sure, Gus, why you can't plan so's to bring her and Mabel back with you. Mabel's the second young one, and the doctor says her lungs is weak and she'd ought to be looked after. I want to git her and her mother up here for a spell where I can—"

"You want 'em up here so ye can wait and tend on 'em," said Gus calmly, "and do a lot of cryin' and takin' on. I've seen it gone through with time and again, times enough. Now she ain't goin' to git up here, not by me, and I don't never want her in this house over another night. That's my say, and you'll see I stand on it."

He went out through the yard toward the pasture, and by the time he reached the pump was beyond Sarey's sight. She sat alone, upright in her rocker, her eyes glazed with anger. So that was his say. Well, he would see. For once in her life *she* would show *him*.

The next morning when Gus brought in the milk, Sarey stood in the sinkroom wrapping squares of butter and counting eggs. She did not look up from her work, and it was Kate who put his breakfast before him. The sun had not yet risen and the air coming in at the window beside him was fresh and cool, but it would be very hot later; Gus could tell by the sky. He ate rapidly, thinking to get to market and back again by midday and be ready to haul in the hay Ben and Jeff would have spread and turned. When he came out from the bedroom, dressed in his gray suit and sewn shoes, he looked for his buckets and boxes of produce by the door and did not find them.

"The stuff is into the wagon," Sarey said shortly, her back turned on him. "I loaded it for ye and Ben hitched up. Now maybe you can git it to the village."

She spoke as if Gus's share in the work here was very small.

He went out to his team, paused to run a hand over the buckles of Bell's harness, and made a change or two in the arrangement of the buckets. It did not do to put breakables over the axle. Once before when Sarey had loaded for him, he had found two eggs broken. Eggs rode better well toward the front. He pushed them forward to where they would rest between his feet, and left the shade of the seat for butter boxes. Coming around to climb in, he was surprised to see Lovice sitting there, in a white dress and bonnet and holding a plaid duster over her knees.

"You goin' to the village?"

"Yes," said Lovice. She glanced at him and then dropped her eyes to her hands, fingering the fringe of the duster. Her voice was almost a whisper. "I thought I would. If you don't care."

He took his place behind the whip socket and clucked to the horse. Bell moved off amiably, out of the yard and over the Lane to York Road, past the Blaine place and Shorey's store and the meeting-house and out into the main road. Lovice, never raising her head, saw only the sand dripping off the rims of the wheels, Bell's tail switching at a fly, the dry ditches, the tufts of sweet fern, blades of grass, and leaves of clover along the roadside; but all these she saw with great distinctness as if they had been enlarged, caught, and held before her. Gus did not notice them, nor her. He was looking straight ahead, anticipating every turn and every upgrade which would slow Bell's progress, thinking of how much he had to sell, who would buy it, and what he would get for it, and how soon he could be home again.

"I'm goin' to stop at Aunt Roxan's," said Lovice at last, with a great effort. "Mother wanted I should."

Gus looked at her sharply. He had forgotten that she rode beside him.

"If—if you don't care," said Lovice.

"Well, you'll have to be on the lookout for me

when I git back there. I ain't got no time to waste. You be all ready and out to the road when I git along."

"I'm—I'm fixed to stay down," quavered Lovice. "Mother wanted I should pay a little visit down here . . . If you—if you don't care . . . So you —won't need to bother any, only to let me out."

He might have wondered why she made such a piece of work, for he had never given any of his children real reason to be afraid of him. But she was Lovice, breathless and always all of a twitter like her mother before her, and it was likely leaving home even for a visit had taken something out of her; he could see now she had been crying. He doubted she would be able to do the work Roxan Gray would pile on the back of anyone who would bend to it, but her mother ought to know; this was women's business, Sarey had ever favored Lovice, and they were Grays together. He thought again of the butter, whether it would be getting too soft for the doctor's family's liking, and of the peas which filled a bushel basket and would be among the first to reach the market. He could get a good price for peas today. Lovice had to touch his arm in reminder when they reached Ed McIntire's, the big green house with wooden lace edging all the roofs, the gray stables with scarlet horses' heads painted on their doors, and the yard where no grass grew but a shiny spring wagon and a four-seated buckboard stood ready for gayety and a rusty hearse just starting out suggested a different mood.

"Here's Aunt Roxan's—"

"So 'tis." Gus cramped the wheel and handed Lovice the limp leather bag with crocheted draw-strings. It could scarcely have held more than her nightgown and comb, and perhaps an apron or two. "Well. Take care of yourself. When you git ready to come home, you be out here any market day about ten o'clock."

"Yes, father—"

She stood looking at him, her color soft through her blue-white skin, her hair smooth and shining, her eyes ready with tears. Gus may have thought of Sarey as she had been, but it is certain he thought of his melting butter and of the hay which waited for him in the fields, and that in his middle age he had lost what little patience he might once have had with drooping womankind. He moved into the middle of the seat, glad to change the position of his legs, and jerked a little on the reins.

"Well," he repeated. "Take care of yourself. Come, Bell, come."

Lovice stood watching him riding away down the street, his broad back in the greenish gray coat, his brown, creased neck and rough, home-cut fringe of hair under the straw hat. Hard as he looked, impersonal as he had been to her, he was her father, the last link she had with home, with the little room she shared with Kate and to which in the dead of night Ben and Jeff came sometimes to talk, all four of them sitting on the bed with their feet tucked under them; with the kitchen stove and table, the yellow oak clock and its twanging bell, the worn places her feet knew in the stairs, setting-sunlight on the cellar door, the feel of the chip dirt, the smell of the barn, the cherry trees and the cordwood piles, her mother's sleeves wearing through while the rest of the dress was still good, the sound of her father's step and the small bustle of preparation it set up ahead of it, roosters in the morning and whippoorwills at night and wild flowers blooming over both banks of the Lane. No runaway ever stepped off a train in a great city with a keener sensation of having lost himself than Lovice Bragdon felt as she watched Gus go out of sight down the main street of Derwich and thought over and over, stabbing herself and turning the little weapon in her wound, as a Gray would: "He is going farther and farther. Now I can't see the lines of his neck, only his hat and shoulders, as if they met . . . Now I could call to him. I could shout, 'Father,' and he would hear and stop. . . . But now he couldn't hear me, however loud I shouted. . . . Now I can't hear even Bell's hoofbeats. . . . Now they're almost gone, and I *must* stop watching. Because they say if you watch a person out of sight—" Lovice was nineteen years old, but she had never been away from home without her mother before, and never to stay overnight. She did not know what life would be, even a few weeks of it, down here by herself, and she had not wanted to come; but Sarey had sent her. She went tearfully into the house, and was still tearful when, two hours later, she hid behind Roxan's lace draperies and watched her father going past again on his way home. Nervously she studied his face, the way he sat, to see if she could guess what his feelings were.

"What *must* he think?" she wondered. "What *will* he say? Oh, dear, I don't see what *made* mother—"

But Gus did not look toward Ed McIntire's house, and he sat as he always had, holding a firm but not a harsh rein on Bell. There was nothing to show, on the outside, how he might be within.

It was near noon when he drove into his own yard, under the welcome shade of the maples. Sarey's flowers lined the driveway. Dish towels hung white in the sun against the background of the dark green woodbine. The parlor blinds were closed, as usual, and smoke puffed from the chimney in the ell. The barn door stood open. Gus rode in, and stabled Bell, and made his way through the shed and up the stairs into the shed room, his arms full of buckets and boxes and a few paper parcels. Kate glanced up from a pie she was setting in the window to cool. Her face was flushed from her work, above her black calico dress with its yellow vine leaves, her sleeves rolled up and her collar turned in.

"Well. You back," she said.

Gus piled his load on the end of a table and stood looking at it.

"There's that corned beef your mother had writ down on the paper," he said. "Better git it into the cellar as quick as you can."

"Yes," said Kate. She brought a platter. "Hot weather for meat."

"Ain't fit for anybody's stomach this time of year," he said. "But she had it writ down." He fumbled for the paper in his vest pocket. "I guess I got it all. . . . Sugar. There's the sugar. Saleratus 'n' cream tartar. How much was the last saleratus?"

"I think it was twenty cents," said Kate.

"That's what I had in mind. Twenty-three today. . . . And crackers. I guess that's crackers."

"I guess you got it all," said Kate. She began turning the saleratus into a cracked pink sugar bowl kept for the purpose on the shelf above the cooking board.

Gus passed her and went through the deserted kitchen to change his clothes. He was gone ten or fifteen minutes. Returning, he wore his blue shirt and overalls and peg boots. His clean-shaven face looked strangely fresh, as always on market day, and his mustache and few whiskers almost golden from their weekly combing and brushing. But there was no market-day good humor about him, nor had there been since he first came in. Kate sensed this.

"Set right down," she said. "It's all on but the biscuit."

"Where's your mother?"

"She's not here," Kate answered. "Will you drink some coffee, or is it too hot? I could stir up some lemonade."

"Where is she?"

"She's gone over to grammum's."

"What's she over there for?"

"She's on a visit. Set down, father. Everything'll be spoilt."

"You know what she done? She took some money out of my chist."

"I know it. She said she had a right to it, father. She said she earnt it as well as you. She said she never laid hand to anything before but what you give it to her, but this time—"

"What did she want of money?"

Kate set on a plate of biscuit and leaned against the wall, facing him squarely, her face grave and calm while drums beat in her head, and her voice quietly drowning out the confusion beneath it. She wondered what it would be to live seeing only one side of any question, only one person's point of view. It was her gift and her cross to look from all angles and find as much reason in one as in another. Sometimes it seemed to her she was nobody, being everybody; and then again being everybody carried her to strange heights and gave her a power she wielded with as much joy as terror, as a surgeon should his knife.

"There's plenty of need for money at grammum's, father," she said. "Mother couldn't go over there to stay and not take something with her."

"Take something! I guess she took something. It's likely she took four or five dozen eggs and around five pounds of butter and two dressed hens and two pecks of peas. I got to market this mornin' with jest barely enough for my customers. Every box, bucket, and basket was stuffed in the bottom with old newspaper. There wa'n't nothin' left over for the stores, not even enough to trade in for groceries."

"She hadn't ought to have done that," said Kate.

"It was takin' advantage."

"Yes," said Kate. "I told her so. It wasn't right. But seemed like she was possessed."

"A man has gone to jail for short measure."

"She was kind of out of her head, like," Kate said. "She took everything she had cooked up here, too. I been baking all morning to get caught up again. She took potatoes and canned stuff and vinegar and a lot of salt pork. She made three trips over there and back with Jeff's express wagon. I didn't know but she'd drop in her tracks. I don't see how she stood it, hot as it was."

Then something passed silently between these two, as it sometimes did, a kind of common amusement, and a faint compassion for the bantams of the flock, the little people who tried to stand up to the rest, fighting so fiercely and so vainly against such impossible odds. Yesterday Sarey had been sick in bed, but today in her wrath and righteousness she had gone about snatching whatever she could get her hands on and smuggling it away, like a child preparing to besiege himself against his elders. They seemed to see her, scuttling and panting back and forth across the pasture. Now she would be feeling triumphant, yet she had only, from all the Bragdon store, a few silver pieces, a fowl or two, some meat and eggs and butter and vegetables. They had all the rest, and were at home—the home she must by and by retreat to in disorder.

Gus pulled out his chair and sat down, filling his plate with bread and potato and pork gravy. "She must think she and Mindwell will work up some awful appetites," he said once, "to take so much."

"Aunt Roxan and Mabel will be there too," said

Kate. "Mother sent down word by Lovice for them to come right up."

"Was they comin' by hearse?" inquired Gus. "I see it startin' out from McIntire's as I come by. Or ain't they dead yet?"

"Father!"

"Well, Roxan's been dyin' for nigh onto fifteen or twenty years, ever since before her first young one was born. Anybody but her would have got to it by now. . . . But I thinks likely your mother and Mindwell will pull her through again. They're good hands at it. . . . What's Lovice doin' down to the village, with them all up there?"

"Lovice is helpin' Minnie with the house and young ones."

"That so."

Later Gus asked: "Where's the boys? They down poulticin' Ed's boil?"

Kate saw no reason why she might not laugh at this. Ed McIntire was certainly no relative of hers.

"No, they're still in the field. Things was so stirred up here this morning they didn't get to turning the hay as early as they'd ought to. But in this heat I guess it will dry out fast enough." She added as she cut the warm blueberry pie: "I see they're coming now. You needn't be took back by anything Ben might say or do. He's in one of his states."

Ben and Jeff splashed at the sink, Jeff drenching his curls and slicking them flat, and took their places at the table. Kate pushed the food toward them. Gus was cleaning his plate, tipping it with his left hand, running a thin-bladed knife around and around and across it, scooping up the last trace of potato, the last globule of pork fat, a drop of berry juice. He was intent, and did not lift his head.

"Stir it up from the bottom, Jeff," said Kate, of the gravy. "Leave a little of the good for Ben."

"He can have it," Ben said. "I'm not over-anxious. Give me a cup of tea. That's all I want."

Ben's wrists were lean and white, his hands big and thin as he held the cup to drink. His eyes, above the gilt rim, were bent on his father's weaving head. There was hate in the stiffness of his slight body, in his neck and hollow cheeks, even in his dripping hair. He set the cup down with a sudden crash, before it was empty.

"There, father," he said. "That's the last time a dish of yours will ever touch my mouth!"

Gus crossed his knife and fork, deliberately, and turned his attention to pouring water from the earthen pitcher which set always beside his plate.

"I guess you'll be put to it to eat soup," he said.

Ben threw himself back in his chair, his fists driven into his pockets, his forehead thrust out, and his chin drawn in.

"I shan't eat your soup," he said. "Soup nor anything else at your table. I've had about enough of you. I've slaved for you all my life. Before I was ten years old you had me on one end of a crosscut saw. I've tore my in'ards out for you. I've raced and drove, and bore with your houting, and you've never raised your hand to do a thing for me but let me eat here. Well, I want you to know I'm through with that, too. I'm clearin' out. I've stood all I can. You began before I was born bringing shame to your family, making a name for yourself by leaving the Lord's House and breaking your pledges, and you've been dragging us down with you ever since. Now it's come to where my mother can't have her own folks in her own house. You've drove her out, and you've drove me out; and I praise the Lord that He is just and will see you pay for it."

"Looks like thunderheads," said Gus, studying the sky. "Be a wonder if that hay don't git wet before it's dry."

"It may be it will," said Ben, standing. "It may be the Lord will see your hay gets wet and your potatoes rot and lightning sweeps down on everything you own. It may be. These things come sometimes when they are least expected. You would do well to look to your soul, Gus Bragdon. I am going to look to mine. I been denying it long enough. I'm going to throw myself into fighting everything you stand for—greed and cruelty and ignoring of the Lord. I lack much for so great a work, but the Lord is on my side, and with Him as my Captain I shall win. Within a week, if you pass that way, you will see the church doors open once more, and of a Sunday you will hear my voice from the pulpit. The day that you come in, and bow yourself before your Maker, I shall be, for the first time, your son."

"One o'clock," said Gus. "Well—"

Ben opened the back stairway door, took up a carpetbag from the bottom step, and left the room without a glance, his head held stiffly on his long neck, his overalls hanging loosely on him. Kate sprang up and followed to the porch.

"You're crazy to talk so, Ben," she said. "That ain't religion. That's meanness, and shows your soul *does* need lookin' to. Father never brought shame on you nor any living person. There's not a better man in this place, nor one that knows his Bible better; and if he left the church, the church wasn't what it ought to be; I've lived here longer'n you have, and it's the other ones have done the houting, not him. Like now. You stand there and run him down just like mother would, and he don't say a word back. He never does. But *I* will. I'll tell you now you're a liar and you're black jealous because he's stronger than you are. That's what the matter with you. Now if you want to go, you go along; but don't you open your mouth again on this place unless you can say something decent . . . When you're as good a man as your father is, you'll be fit to stand in a pulpit—or fitter'n you are now."

She wheeled and went into the house. Gus, watching Ben climbing the fence between the pastures, said: "He'd ought to have taken some of that corn beef down cellar. And some beans. Your mother's crew's gettin' so big I don't know as she's prepared to ration 'em."

He went to the well, and drank, and to the barn for his fork. An hour later Kate drove the hay cart into the field, Jeff sitting in behind. She made seven loads that afternoon, taking each forkful from her father and laying it where it rode best. Her arms were as strong and far more willing than Ben's had ever been. Jeff did the raking after. The sun blazed down hot, and all the field was golden-brown, Gus and Jeff a large and a small black spot against it, Kate a blue stripe beneath her wide hat. Between loads they drank deep at the well, and wet their faces. The sun dropped lower and lower, and the outlines of haystacks turned the color of orange peel. The cooling air shimmered above the hot ground.

"You'll have to be at your supper," Gus said.

"No," Kate answered. "Granny will see to it."

"Your grandmother—"

"Jeff and I brought her downstairs. She was pleased enough to come. We made a chair of our hands. It wasn't anything. She is so little."

That was the summer the Nubble Point Meeting-house opened for the first time in nearly twenty years, and there was a reformation, and a baptism in the river. Roxan McIntire was badly off with her nerves, and one of her young ones, too, and they came up to her mother's; Sarey Bragdon stayed over there three months to help see after them, and she and Roxan went berrying every week day up on Long Hill; Sundays they would all walk down from the Gray place to sit in the front pew and sing loud and fine. Lovice Bragdon had to be at the village with Roxan's family, and Gus made out as well as he could with Kate and Jeff and Hannah. Ben never went home now. There had been words passed, people said, when he made up his mind to be a preacher. This was natural enough. Gus would never see what there was in a kind of work which paid nothing except what a few worshipers could give—a half-dozen hens, a side of fresh meat, a peck of apples, or a pail of honey fresh and dark from the hive. But Ben was satisfied. He preached every Sunday with an inspired tongue, and on Wednesday evenings he led the praying. If the congregation was not so large, nor quite so fervent, as in his grandfather's time, it was because things had changed; there were not so many living here nowadays; four or five houses along York Road had their windows boarded over, and one in the Lane, and people were not so quick to throw themselves upon their marrows as their grandparents had been. Ben's voice was as clear and his words as resounding as any ever spoken by the Elder himself.

7

It was the death of Hannah that brought Sarey home. One morning in September Hannah hung out a wash and then went in to lay herself on Gus's bed, but slid down beside it. When Kate came in from the potato digging, she found her there and lifted her up, but there was no life in her; and Jeff went running for his father, and afterward his mother. Sarey hurried in without a word and pushed by Gus to put her hand on Hannah's head.

"There, yes," she said. "She's gone, poor old cutter." She sighed. "Well, you might as well git started for the village, Gus, and send somebody up here to help me with her. You might as well git Perkins. He's jest as good if he don't cost so much. He's got a nice way with him."

So the undertaker came, and the coffin, and the flowers; Ben came to make a prayer, and Mindwell and Roxan to sing; camp chairs came, and neighbors, and bearers; and when they had all gone,

Sarey was still here, making out butter as no one else could, cleaning the cellarway, and sweeping her carpet with wet corn meal and shredded paper, and no one spoke of her having been away. Not that it was the same now as before she went. She seemed in rather better health, and held herself straighter. Her son was a preacher. Every Sunday she dressed up in the best she had, a blue linsey-woolsey with black velvet belt and collar, and went over the Lane to church, and if the mood took her, stayed overnight or even longer with her mother and Ben. Roxan, renewed, was back in the village now, but Lovice had not come home, nor did she write so often as at first; Lovice was being weaned away. Kate and Jeff remained the only ones Gus could be sure of finding when he came in at night, and even they were off all day at school, and many of Kate's evenings were for Stephen.

Gus did not mind this. He had no sense of need for anyone. By day he worked, and by night he lay on the lounge of the kitchen, figuring, or sat in the bedroom with a lamp on the commode, looking over the papers and the money in his chest, which he kept locked now. The outline of his key always showed plain on the vest pocket of his overalls. But it was true the sound of a man's voice was more welcome to him than it had once been; and he did not resent it that Harvey Linscott dropped in so often in the evenings, and sometimes stopped as he was passing the field where Gus was at work, and took a hand himself.

Harvey was long and lean, with Linscott body and Blaine legs, a friendly fellow but frightened, like a stray dog long unclaimed. He had a small head, with the dark hair of his mother, heavy and straight, and thin, honest face, watchful and eager. His clothes were always very clean. He washed them at the brook, and whenever he stayed at his grandfathers' house, slept in the barn on the hay.

"I can't abide bugs," he told Gus. "Spiders may git in a nip or two, but they're neat, like. I can't abide bugs, no way."

Most of his life since his tenth year had been spent around the sawmills. He had followed them down east and up into New Hampshire. He was quite a traveler, though he had seen nothing but the woods. He liked to tell Gus how tall the trees had stood down in a town they called Sabattus, how many feet of lumber had been stripped from how many acres, the joke they had played on the sawyer by dressing up a peavey in his clothes, and how he had marked the pine boards, the oak boards, the maple boards with his blue chalk. But still he was not too much of a talker. He could sit for fifteen or twenty minutes and say nothing and not fidget; and whatever he did have to say struck

Gus's ears as sensible. Lumber, now, was a thing to speak of that a man could listen to.

One night in October as they sat mending on a harness, Kate came into the kitchen suddenly. They had not heard her step on the porch, and there was no sound of Stephen's whistle in the yard, though the two had gone out together less than an hour before.

"You send your beau home awful early, don't you?" asked Harvey, grinning sidewise at her. "Nice a night as this is, too. I thought you was ridin' somewheres behind that spankin' black mare."

"Yes," said Kate. "I was."

She folded her shawl and laid it in the stairway, and sat down in the rocker by the window. Her face looked thinner than Harvey had ever noticed it, and very calm and cold; her eyelids lowered when she faced the room, as if she found discomfort in looking at anything so close by, and she turned again toward the dark outside. To Harvey Linscott she was everything a woman could be, and more than any other woman ever was; so far above him he wondered they could speak together and find a meaning in it. In all the days that he had sat in the schoolroom with her, he had never known her fail to answer any question as the teacher wanted it, never seen her fight in the schoolyard, nor heard her cry. Whatever anyone else did, she could do better. And now she was grown into a woman. Lovice he wanted, but did not dare to ask for; Kate he did not even dare to want.

"It's an awful handsome piece of horseflesh, that," he said now, working his big needle through a strip of leather. "That Peter of Steve's. . . . Thing I'd like to own sometime, a neat-steppin' horse."

Kate said, looking at the dark, "Why don't you buy him?"

"Buy? Buy *Peter!*" Harvey stared at her, the harness sliding off his knee. "Why, Steve wouldn't no more sell that horse!"

After a minute Kate said: "I guess he would. He ought to be glad to. There won't be anybody over to Blaines' to handle him. Stephen's going to the Klondike."

"The Klondike! He is!" The harness was on the floor now, and Harvey bending forward with his hands on his knees. Only Gus kept on working, pushing the needle through holes he made with his awl, and pulling it out underneath. "Why, that's where they've found the gold the papers tell for!"

"Yes," said Kate.

"Why, they've found millions of dollars up there. I heard tell down east this spring of seventy-five feet of ground where they dug out $120,000 worth of gold. Just two claims, it was. All they had to do was dig."

"Yes," said Kate. "I've heard so."

"They sluice up in the spring, they say. Some men workin' on a percentage has cleared from five to ten thousand dollars apiece within sixty days. Why, Steve'll come back a rich man. Will he work that way—on a percentage?"

"I don't know," Kate answered. "I don't believe he knows. He's just going."

"Goin' right off?"

"Going in the morning."

"He is? He is! Well, I guess—I believe I'll jest step over there." Harvey's face was alight as he stood up. "I s'pose he'll have his stuff to be gittin' together."

He hurried out. It was the first time he had ever left the house without asking what they had heard from Lovice. Gus took his hat from a nail behind the stove and followed him as far as the porch.

"Harvey," he said. "Here. I don't s'pose—you don't think of lightin' out along with him?"

"Me?" Harvey answered from the shadowy yard, only his hands and the side of his face showing. "*Me?* No, Gus. . . . Lord! . . . Lord, I ain't one for anything like that. I don't see how I—they say prices is awful high up there. Potaters was a dollar a pound, they say, last winter. Awful for potaters, wa'n't it? Eggs as much as two dollars for a dozen. I guess it would be hard lines on a feller like me that wouldn't likely find no gold anyway. . . . Lord, no, Gus. Not me. With Blaines now, some way, of course it ain't the same—"

"Well," Gus said. "I jist thought I'd speak. . . . Nice night, ain't it?"

Harvey, hurrying out into the Lane, did not hear. It was Kate who answered.

"Lovely," she said.

She had crossed from the back window to the front, and stood looking out with her arms folded on the sash, her chin on her wrist. She could not see her father, but knew where he stood, and he could see her plainly, in outline against the lamplight.

"I done my best, father," she said slowly.

"I thinks likely."

"He's been talking it now for a month. He couldn't put his mind to anything else. I said everything I could think of. I argued and I plead. But it wasn't any kind of use. No kind of use at all. Over there to Blaines he never heard anything but Klondike, Klondike, Klondike. Ene was reading books about it, and Thoc was telling what he would do if he was young. I don't see as Steve could have stuck it out if he had wanted to. And he didn't want to."

"No," said Gus. "Well."

"But it's the end of him. That's plain. If he can't stay by now, he never can. It's taking every cent he can rake and scrape to get there, and he'll come back poorer than he went. Where one gets something out of it, ninety-nine gets nothing. Even Harvey Linscott can see that."

"Harvey's no fool."

"Steve's no fool!"

"No," Gus agreed from the dark. "No, no. Steve's no fool, sure. He knows well enough what his chances is. He don't expect to find a fortin. The Klondike's only a word to git him started off again. . . . No, Steve's no fool. He's just—a Blaine."

After a minute Kate left the window and came out to stand on the steps beside her father. She was exactly his height, and her shoulders were broad, too, like his. Under his coat, which she had caught up in the entry, the swell of her breasts did not show, nor the slimness of her waist, nor the long, fine lines from hip to knee. Only her neck revealed the woman of her, and her face and warm, sweet mass of hair.

They stood looking at the yard. It was very still. The pale leaves of the maples hung quiet; the woodbine did not stir; the plants in the garden patch beside the cowyard were covered with old grain bags and blanket and newspaper, against the frost. The low land was their field, and the first and second hills, and beyond that their pasture. Beyond the pasture the trees of one of Gus's wood lots stood firm and dark. It all lay so still it seemed that, if they could reach, they might stroke it, like a sleeping cat.

"That lot down by the pasture," Kate said. "The Shep Selden lot. That was the first one you bought, wasn't it?"

"The Shep Selden? No. No, I never bought that. That was one I had from father."

"What was the first one you bought yourself?"

"First one I bought was the Asy Cheney, the one he had from Sime Butler. They called it the Peables lot then, but I guess more knows it now as the Asy Cheney."

"You signed a note to get the money for it, didn't you?"

"Yes. Yes, I signed a note down to the bank."

"You've bought a good many since then."

"A number."

"But that was the first one. . . . I suppose you must have felt different about that than any of the rest, being it was the first one."

This was woman's talk.

"It was a good lot," said Gus. "I see what it would git to, give it time."

"It about grown now?"

"Yes. Full-growed. It's had twenty-five year sence I bought it. I'll sell when I git my price and not before. I can wait as well as the next one. I'll have $5,000 for that lot when I let it go."

"Five thousand dollars! . . . I suppose when you first bought it you used to walk through it a good deal. I suppose you used to think: 'This here is mine. The lumber and the limbs and the bushes and the ground, they're all mine. Even the growing,—that's mine.' "

Gus did not answer. He had no words.

"I want to buy a lot," said Kate. "I want to buy that Elbridge Allen lot."

"Well, now, that's a good lot," Gus said, as if it had never before been mentioned between them. "It's doin' well. I guess anybody could git it for seven hundred now. Almond is needin' money pretty bad."

"I've got three hundred saved," said Kate. "Will you take my note for four and let me have the money?"

"I guess you could git it from him for three hunderd down."

"I'd rather be owing you."

"Owin' is owin'."

"You needn't doubt I'll pay it, father."

"No."

"It's only I'd rather be owing you than him."

"Yes. . . . Well . . . I can let you have it . . . Six per cent . . . Want it right off?"

"Yes. Any time. I want the lot. I want to get the deed. And have it."

"Well. I'll go in and make out your note."

He went inside and closed the door behind him. Kate heard him scratch a match to light his hand lamp and cross the kitchen floor toward the bedroom. She sat down against the post, and laid her head on her knees. She was a long time like this, and all the lights in the house had gone out. There was not a sound or a movement anywhere. Then she lifted her face, letting the frosty air sting it, watching the trees against the sky.

8

It began to seem Lovice would be the first of Sarey's children to marry. She came home for a visit in the winter, and Kate and Sarey and Mindwell found her greatly changed; even Gus could see a difference. Roxan had not overworked her, that was clear. A great intimacy had sprung up between these two; they went about to parties and meetings, and sewed and read together, and Lovice had learned to toss her head and give as quick and brittle a laugh as Roxan's own. Kate suspected it was Minnie, short, fat Minnie, no longer a child and never an ornament, upon whose shoulders fell the tasks and responsibilities Lovice had gone to the village to assume. Lovice had many new frocks, all in shades of blue and violet, which she and Roxan had fashioned, slippers with high heels and pointed toes, embroidered stockings, and a white fur muff and cap and tippet; not even Lovice knew where such finery had come from; somehow Aunt Roxan had managed it. She did her hair in a new style, in a great pompadour, turning her head into a heavy, white-and-gold blossom on the slender blue stem of her body. Her hands were soft and her nails neat and shiny, and she knew little tricks of holding muff or handkerchief, of resting her chin on her fingers, of letting the point of one toe show daintily beneath her ruffles as she sat small in a big chair.

"I guess ye've had quite a time at Tiddi-aye-do," Gus said, watching her as she sat by the stove warming herself after their cold ride up from the village. "I guess ye've seen all the sights and done all the doin's."

"I haven't missed anything I had a shot at, father," she answered gayly. She had no fear of him now, whatever she may have felt when she lived here. He was a man like any other, and she lavished her pretty ways on him. "It's my chance, and I'm takin' it. It seems to me if a girl don't see something and learn something before she gets married, she never will."

"Married?" asked Gus.

"Well," Lovice pouted, and smiled, "Most people do get married, don't they?"

But Gus did not hear much of her chatter. She saved it, and Kate and Sarey saved their questions, and Abner Cheney's girls and Adeline Selden and her daughter Pearl saved their calls until a time of day when men folk are in the woods after limbs or at the barn about their chores. From one o'clock until four of a winter day a likely man did not intrude upon his kitchen, and womenfolk could sit and piece on quilts, pull up their chairs to the table for a cup of tea and slice of cake, and exchange a few words in comfort with their own kind. It was a treat indeed to have Lovice Bragdon come home in midwinter with news of Roxan McIntire and her family, indeed of the whole village. Even her Aunt Hattie, wife of Berias, tramped over the Lane to take a look at her, and Hattie Blaine was no gadabout and rarely put foot outside after the first snow flew.

"My sakes alive, Lovey, how you have growed up!"

"Have I?"

"Well, I should say you have. Ain't she, Sarey? I guess Roxan has made a woman of her for ye. Well, now, you sweet-pretty thing, you!"

"Lovey, did you really take music lessons?"

"Oh, yes! I've took them ever since Aunt Roxan come home from up here. She arranged it with Cyril Bannister he could have a room there and pay for it by teachin' Minnie and I piano. It made it real nice for all of us."

"Cyril Bannister? That's the one works in Drury's—"

"Last time I called into Roxan's she didn't have no piano—"

"Uncle Ed got it from a man that his wife died and he didn't have any other way to pay for the hearse and hacks."

"Oh, I should dearly love to hear you play!"

"You'll have to strike up on grammum's organ."

"But organs ain't the same, Kate! You ought to *know!*"

"I guess the keys are about alike. How's Minnie doing?"

"Not so very good. She didn't practice at it hard enough. Cyril got kind of out of patience with her (you *couldn't* blame him!), and she give it up. Mabel's tryin' now, but she don't seem to have the knack—"

"Well, Lovice, you must know Mr. Bannister awful well. What's he like? Is he nice?"

Lovice, flushing: "Pretty nice."

"Lovey—did he ever ask to see you home from anywheres?"

"Plenty of times, you goose. What do you think?"

"Oh, did he *really?*"

"He takes me to a dance every Saturday night, regular as the clock."

"*Lovice!* Do you *dance?* . . . Sarey Bragdon, did you know what she was up to?"

"Sartain I did. Roxan learnt her, and I'm glad of it. You needn't repeat this to Ben and marm because they look at it different. But I can't see no harm in keepin' step to music, nor never could."

"*Round* dances?"

"Yes, round or square. I don't care which; they're all of 'em set to music. Roxan says Lovey whirls as pretty in them waltzes as anybody she ever see on the floor."

The Cheney girls and Pearl seemed to see her whirling on her pointed toes, enveloped in a mist. Pearl's face grew long with envy, but Mat and Flora were past hoping for themselves, and hung on the adventures of Lovice as if she were a creature from one of their novels come to life.

"I'll bet you'll marry Mr. Bannister!"

"Not for a long time anyway. After you're married you settle down. Aunt Roxan says there was fifteen years she was tied to her young ones, and now's she's just beginnin' to live her own life again."

"But I'll bet you *could*, any time you wanted to!"

"Maybe!"

"Roxan? Does Roxan go to dances?"

"And Ed?"

"No. Uncle Ed don't dance—"

"Ed's awful good that way, though," Sarey interposed. "He'll go and set by and take 'em home when they git ready. 'Tain't many women has such—"

" 'Tain't many men have wives like Aunt Roxan," cried Lovice. "Handsome and young-lookin' as she is! Ever so many takes us for sisters. I wisht you could see her in a wine-colored satin dress she's got, and a sealskin cape—"

"Satin and sealskin!"

"They're things she's had and dyed and turned and kept so you'd never know they wasn't just from Boston. She hasn't had a thing new but two taffeta shirt waists and a velvet hat with a plume since I went down there. But she keeps makin' over."

"Her health must be a sight better 'n 'twas."

"Well, she has her ups and downs. Yes, I think she's some better 'n she was last summer."

"Lovice, how does it seem to have the electrics goin' through the village?"

"Oh, it's fine. Some of the great ones still put up a fuss because the cars make a little noise and they don't like the looks of 'em. But I think they're handsome. I love to hear 'em, the way they come whirrin' over the tracks, and I don't know why 'tis, but when I hear an electric car whistle I always feel as if something nice was goin' to happen."

"I'll bet you've had some great times on them

electric cars. I'll bet you've been to Porchmuth on 'em."

"Yes, I have. And once last summer to Old Orchard Beach, and rode on the merry-go-round."

"Did you, honest? Did Mr. Bannister take you?"

"Wouldn't you like to know!"

"No, Lovice; did he?"

"Well—yes, he did!"

"Oh, just think of it! He's such a pretty man. He must have a lot of money, too."

"See the way she sits there, lookin' modest, the little minx! How does it feel, Kate, to have a sister that's the belle of the ball?"

"Feels fine. Only thing that don't seem right is for her to be my sister. Lucky for you, Lovey, I don't walk in on one of your parties with my skirt pinned up the way I wear it when I go into the woods. What would your fine friends say to that?"

"Well, you wouldn't, Kate. I wish you *would* come down."

"There!" exclaimed Sarey. "One at a time, if you please. I ain't quite up to handlin' this place alone, to say nothin' of your father in the field."

"Oh, Kate'll have her turn when Stevie gets back. Wait till you see Kate and Stevie ridin' around town in a buggy with gold rims to the wheels. What do ye hear from Steve, Kate?"

"Nothing. Only he's got him a claim and he's digging. It's awful cold up there."

"Ain't found a nugget yet?"

"No."

"Ain't come to any sign of gold yet?"

"No."

There was more of interest to be had from Lovice, who, while she denied she would marry soon, wore a turquoise in a circlet of chip diamonds on her forefinger, and took dainty stitches on a white linen pillow sham.

Gus heard none of this, but one night as Sarey came into the room where he had lain in bed for some hours already, he said suddenly, "To my way of thinkin', ye'll do well not to let Lovice go back down there to McIntires'."

"Not let her go back!"

"Seems to me it's high time she took a hand here to home."

"Well, I guess if I don't complain, you needn't. She wa'n't never no kind of use outdoors."

Sarey was in bed when Gus added:

"What I mean, I mean, as I see it, she's been down there with Roxan long enough."

"I know what your feelin's is toward Roxan," Sarey answered, "and I've learnt it ain't no use for me to try to change 'em. But Lovice is past eighteen and free to do her own choosin'! Happens she chooses to see my folks the same as I do, and 'll have a chance to profit by 'em. . . . You ought to be proud as Lucifer of that girl, Gus, and if you ain't ye're blind. I can't make ye out, and I've give up tryin'. . . . But you needn't worry about Lovey. She's fixed now to look after herself and don't need nothin' of either one of us."

All the rest of the winter and spring Sarey gave every spare minute to piecing and tacking comforters, to seaming and hemming sheets. She cross-stitched "B" on each of a dozen cotton towels, and sent away and bought a lamp with a great white china base and shade and roses painted on them. All these things she laid away in the closet in what had been Hannah's room, and the letters she and Lovice exchanged were never read or discussed with anyone. An air of happy secrecy marked all Sarey's doings, and she continually sang at her work.

It was fall before Lovice came again, and then she was unexpected. She had caught a ride on one of the teams from the sawmill, as far as the end of the Lane, and came hurrying along a frozen rut to the house, huddled inside the white furs, now worn a little thin; rabbit skin does not stand up like other pelts. Sarey ran to the door to let her in.

"Why, Lovey Bragdon!"

"Hello, ma!"

They kissed and clung together.

"You all right, dear? There ain't nothin' the matter?"

"No. Of course not. I just took it into my head—"

"Well, there, I'm glad you did. Some way I've been kind of lookin' for you lately. I kind of had an idea you'd be poppin' in one of these days. I don't know. I have these feelin's, and they're most gen'ally right."

But Kate, looking up blankly from her supper-getting, exclaimed: "Well, Lovice! Good Lord! Whoever heard tell of you? I should as quick think to see Mrs. McKinley walk in here tonight."

"You would!" Lovice exclaimed. "Well, I don't see why. This ain't her home, is it? And most likely she hasn't heard yet that this is the night they're goin' to serenade Charlie Hamilton and Cora Dockham."

"That's right. Folks are going over there tonight, ain't they?" Kate said. She reached through the doorway into the cold sitting room to lay Lovice's cape and furs on the top of the sewing machine which had been her last year's Christmas present to her mother. "I'm surprised you heard of it, so far off."

"Oh, I heard of it," Lovice said. "I come up to go. And you're goin' with me."

"Me to a serenade?"

"Yes, you, Stick-in-the-mud!"

"Land," Sarey cried, "you couldn't! Just you two girls alone!"

"There, ma, only up the road to Amos Hamilton's. Don't be foolish. Come on, Kate, will you? Because if you won't, I'll go by myself. I vow I will. I've done all they do down to the village until I'm sick to death of it. I'd *love* to go to a serenade!"

"Nothing but a great racket," Kate said.

"There, you see! You know! You've been with Steve! And I've never been with anybody. Well, now, you can take me or I'll go all sole alone, just as you say."

"Oh, I s'pose you might as well," Sarey agreed doubtfully. "Ben won't like it if word of it gits to his ear, nor marm neither, but after all, as you say, 'tis only up to Amos's. And there, ye won't neither of ye be young but once."

So when the ringleaders of the serenade, a crowd of young men and boys, went past Bragdon's on their way over the Lane under cover of the dark, Kate and Lovice, already dressed even to their outside wraps, were in the parlor peering out through the blinds at them. They made a strange company, going so hurriedly and so quietly by in twos and threes, some carrying shotguns, others bells, others tin pails or copper wash boilers. Their shadows were like those of trees bare of leaves but hung with grotesque toys and decorations, all bent in one direction by a strong wind.

"Can you tell who they are, Kate?" Lovice asked. "It's been so long since I've seen any of them—"

"Why, I guess a lot of 'em are from the mill crew that's sawing on the Shem Joy lot," said Kate. "They're strange gaits to me. That one coming now walks like a Linscott. Yes, and the next three or four, they're all Linscotts; you can tell that Linscott roll—"

"Harvey?" Lovice asked.

"Harvey? Well, no, they wouldn't any of them be Harvey. He's different. His is a—well, it's not a Linscott walk. There, there comes Willy Joy and Shem, and Fred Dockham. They three are always together same as before any of 'em got married. They're cases, all of 'em, and always will be, I guess. Don't seem as if they grow up a mite. . . . Well, there, now, that might be Harvey. I can't be sure—"

"Has he got him a girl?"

"Not yet, and I don't see any signs. No, he still inquires for you, Lovey. I declare I wish he wouldn't. It's getting so it's kind of pathetic just to hear him. He's here with father a good deal, off and on. . . . Well, I guess that's the last of 'em."

A few minutes later a different group began to fill the Lane before the Bragdon house: many married couples, some of them with children, several single elderly men, among them Thoc and Ene

Blaine, and a few boys and girls of school age or somewhat older, pairing off. They moved along at a leisurely pace and chatted among themselves in low voices. They would take no part in the hullabaloo but went for the social occasion, for the games and singing which would go on once the merry-makers had pounded and howled their way under the roof of the bride and groom, for a share in the candy and lemonade, the cider and cigars Charlie Hamilton would have on hand if he was wise. Kate and Lovice ran out and joined the parade, going along with Gilbert Selden and Sadie, his wife, and Abner Cheney, who never missed a chance for a good time, and Mat and Flo, his daughters. The Cheney girls took Lovice between them, their arms about her waist, and Kate fell back to walk with Abner, which filled him with pride; he did not venture to say much: she was the school teacher. The many footsteps rumbled like those of a small army over the frozen ground.

They had reached the top of the hill above the Hamiltons' when the clamor burst out. Until then it had been very dark and quiet ahead, but suddenly a dozen blinking lanterns danced from behind Amos' barn down in the hollow and encircled the house. One gun was fired, as for a signal, and a volley answered it. The thunder of stovewood sticks hammering copper and the din of many cowbells crashed into the air. It went on for minutes, while the little company on the hill waited in their tracks with expectant faces.

Into an abrupt hush Fred Dockham's voice yelled: "Open up! Let us in there! Charlie Hamilton, open that door! . . . It's only some old cronies of yours, Charlie, come to give you jest a little good advice! Don't be skeered, Charlie! We won't do more 'n kill ye! Open up!"

"Are ye asleep?" shouted one of the Joy boys. "Are ye asleep, Cora? Come, rout Charlie out! We want Charlie Hamilton, and we're goin' to git him! He'll come out or he'll be drug out!"

"Come, Cora! You'll handle him gentler 'n we will. Pitch him out here!"

"Char-lie Ham-il-ton! Come out here! . . . *Begorry*, ye'll come out here!"

Another blast of drums and gunshots followed, of bell ringing and fish-horn tooting; more shouted commands, more noise, and sound of feet running across a roof, of blinds shaken and a window broken.

"You'd better come out, Charlie darlin'! The boys is a-losin' patience! Better send him out, pretty Cora—or by God, you'll wish you had!"

Up on the hill Abner Cheney said: "We might start along down. He'll give in to 'em now very soon." They all ran, stumbling over the ruts and one another, into the valley, and passed under the Hamilton elms and into the yard just as the first light flashed inside the house. The Hamiltons' was the finest house along the Lane, a two-story-and-a-half with four chimneys, one on each corner; and when the door opened, a hanging lamp with glittering red bangles shone in the hall behind Charlie's head, lighting up the winding, carpeted staircase which, it was to be supposed, he had just come down.

Charlie was small, a wiry young fellow, with tow head and blue, mocking eyes. He stood in the doorway in his white shirt sleeves, with his hands thrust into his pockets, and gave the crowd which filled the yard little reason to suppose that he was frightened. He lounged against the doorframe and rubbed his chin on one hunched shoulder, his legs crossed and the raised foot resting lightly on the toe of the other.

"Well, I say! Gol! What're you little boys doin' up so late? Do your mamas know you're out?"

Goaded, the ringleaders swarmed toward him, and he was caught up on the shoulders of a pair of Linscotts, the Joy boys, and Fred Dockham, and carried, struggling, through the barnyard and down the pasture lane. With blast of guns, drums, bells, and horns, the other serenaders followed after, and only the women, children, and elders were left in the yard. It was the duty of Charlie's father and mother, Amos and Lucy, to attend to them. Amos took Charlie's place in the doorway, a thin, genial little man such as Charlie, too, would be in thirty years.

"Good evenin', folks, good evenin'. Come right in. Come right in and set. Glad to see ye. Cold snap, we've got, ain't it?"

"Well, hello, everybody!" Lucy cried, bustling, full-breasted and wide-hipped, about the sitting room as the neighbors began to stream in. "My sakes! What a surprise! There now, ain't this nice, I'm sure! Wherever have they took Charlie to? I hope to my soul ain't none of 'em been drinkin'."

"Don't you worry about that feller, mother," Amos assured her largely. "He'll look after himself."

Lucy might say it was a surprise, but that could be taken with a grain of salt. What fellow who had been married a week did not expect to be serenaded, come Saturday night? And Lucy was not known to be such a good housekeeper that her rooms would look as neat as this if she had been caught unprepared for company. Even the kitchen, through the open door, was revealed spick and span, and a woman bending over the stove could have seen her face in it.

Cora Dockham, that had been, came downstairs presently, wearing the cream-colored cashmere and blue ribbons in which she had stood up for her wedding. She was a chubby little girl, only seventeen, with a round freckled face and wisp of deep brick-red hair, but this was her night, and she looked very pretty; and not a woman there but wondered, wistfully or compassionately, how Charlie treated her when they were alone together in the room from which she had come down. He seemed a boy still, and boys had such hard hands and destructive ways and cruel thoughts sometimes. It was not long ago he had caught flies to watch them die, and broken his mother's parlor mirror, and dropped his sister's breastpin into the well. But Cora's face was warm with pride, and when at last the confusion in the yard gave warning he was back, she ran out into the cold to meet him and came in beaming, with her hand in his.

"Come along in, fellers—"

"So ye beat 'em off, Charlie!"

"Beat 'em off! I laid every one of 'em flat and had to throw water on 'em to bring 'em to," said Charlie, ducking under Shem Joy's fist with a broad grin. "Well, I'm sorry I had to do it, but don't anybody hold no grudges. Here, Fred, I hit you hardest—you have the first cigar!"

There was much smoking, eating, and drinking at Hamiltons' that night, and hilarity enough to last over many evenings when nine o'clock would find every light out along both York Road and the Lane. Amos went often up and down the cellar stairs with a pitcher in each hand, and Lucy and Cora kept the plates piled high with cake and doughnuts and peppermint sticks and chocolate candy. The descendants of those who had once danced the soles of their boots through on the flat rocks of Mount Assabenbeduc were here, as many of them as still lived in Derwich, with never a whit less jingle in their knees. Thoc Blaine, hot and happy, sweat flooding down his face and drenching the handkerchief he had tucked in around his neck to catch it, sat on the wood box in the kitchen and played "Round the Green Carpet" furiously, while a ring of young people danced around and around through kitchen, sitting room, parlor and back bedroom: the Joy boys and Fred Bragdon and Charlie Hamilton, with their young wives; eight or ten red-faced Nova Scotiamen and a few French choppers from the woods; Mat and Flo Cheney, their plain faces merry; Lovice in a crimson velvet shirt waist and her wavy pompadour; Pearl Seldon and Charles Bragdon's daughter; Harvey Linscott in a new brown suit and plaid scarf tie; the Elys and the Shoreys and the Allens.

"Round the green carpet here we stand.
Take your true love by the hand;
Take the one that you profess
To be the one you love the best!"

The elders looked on with indulgent eyes and tapping feet at the spinning circle. The dancers grew breathless. Enoch Blaine deftly handed boys into the kitchen, girls into the sitting room, and Thoc's fiddle struck up a new tune. Enoch sang the words, the solemn expression on his face never changing.

"There stands up those Dunnybrook rowdies!
Who they are I do not know,
But I advise you, if you marry,
Choose you a young and a handsome beau!"

The girls fought one another in the doorway, each in a small frenzy to be the first to reach the man she had in mind. Willy's wife of a year wanted him, but Shem's wife of three years did also. It was Shem's wife who claimed him. Cora wanted Charlie, but so did Mat and Flo; it was their kindly feeling for her as a bride that held them back to let her win, and left them only saw-mill men to choose. There was no competition for the partnership of Harvey Linscott, yet he did not go untaken. Lovice Bragdon paused before him, flushed and smiling in her crimson waist, made him a little curtsy, and tucked her hand in his arm.

"Ow-w!" groaned Fred Dockham, who by now had a little too much cider aboard. "A curtsy, is it? Now ain't that puttin' on the agony?"

" 'Puttin' on the agony,' " sang someone. " 'Puttin' on the style—' "

Enoch's big voice, coming from where he sat in

a corner and stared moodily at the wall, drowned him out. The room quieted. Ene was going to sing one of his old stand-bys; and worth listening to, it was, every time.

"*Come, all ye good people, wherever you be!*
A comical ditty you shortly shall hear!
The boys about here think they to advance
By courting the girls and learning to dance.
To my fal lo little o' day!

"*If a penny they get, they will quick let you know!*
Away to some tavern to spend it they'll go;
And when they get there, they'll scrape and go in.
They'll rattle their pockets and call for a sling!
To my fal lo little o' day!

"*I think it now time for the boys to leave out,*
And turn to the girls, for they are as bad.
They'll powder and twist and do up their hair
In nubbins and bows, on the streets to appear.
To my fal lo little o' day!

"*They'll out with their snuffbox and hit it a tap;*
They'll pass it to one, to one and to two,
Saying, 'Madame, you'll have a pinch?
Misses, will you?'
To my fal lo little o' day!

"You can tell a good woman wherever she be.
No flattering things about her you'll see—
No ribbons, no laces, nor no such a thing,
But a plain strapped cap tied under her chin.
To my fal lo little o' day!

"I think it now time for my ditty to end,
For fear there's some here whom I may should offend.
If there be any such here to take an offense
They can go to the devil and seek recompense!
To my fal lo little o' day!"

As the clapping and cheering died down, Pearl Seldon cried, "He was singin' that for Lovice's benefit, in her red shirt waist!"

Lovice, coloring, clung to Harvey's arm.

"Singing to that shirt waist?" Ene inquired, turning his head slowly toward it. "I wish I could. I wish I knew a song that was worthy of it. Bobbie Burns ought to be here. He'd write out some lines—"

"*Now* will you shut up, Pearl?" howled her brother. "Button down your hatches, woman!"

"Dance!" boomed Thoc into the tumult, raising his fiddle to his chin. "I say, faith be king, *dance, damn ye!*" And strains of "The Irish Washerwoman" twinkled through the house.

It was much later, as Kate sat a little apart from

the older women whose company she had kept all the evening, that Enoch came up and stood leaning against the wall beside her. There was no resemblance between his tall, thin, morose gentility and Thoc's round, jolly figure, except that it was plain if one of them must be relative to any man in the room, it could be only to the other. Something of the free manner of men who tread the decks of their own vessels, the grace of those who ride good horses and serve old wine in thin glass, of the touch of silk and linen and the aroma of perfumes from the East had come down along the line with them. They had nothing, and were nobody; but their name was Blaine, and wherever they went, as long as they lived, people would listen to what they said and stand aside to let them pass.

"You're not being very gay, Miss Kate."

"What? Well, no. But I'm enjoying myself very much."

"I *have* seen you play games with the rest of 'em, haven't I?"

"Oh, yes."

"But not tonight."

"No, not tonight. . . . I guess—must be I'm outgrowing it, Enoch."

"Too young for that."

"May be . . . I guess the truth is, Enoch, I never was much for it, myself. I'm the quiet kind. You put me off alone and I can walk a good stride, or

I can sing. But in with a crowd of people I—well, it's natural for me to just set and kind of wonder at 'em for making such a touse. Whenever I've done any different, it was—for the sake of somebody else."

"What do you hear from him?" Enoch asked.

Kate leaned forward with her arms folded on her knees, studying the knots in the floor boards.

"He's still digging."

"Thinks he's getting hold of a little something lately, don't he?"

"Yes. Yes, he does. He says by another spring he'll have enough to last him through a lifetime."

"Pretty good, for a young fellow his age."

"Yes."

"That's the way it comes sometimes, without slaving fifty years for it."

"Yes; sometimes."

"Then by summer he'll be home, and I suppose they'll be bringing their tin pans and fish horns over 'round our house again, eh, Miss Kate? Been quite a while since they've done any serenading there."

Kate's head swung slowly above her folded arms. Enoch could not see her face.

"Not for me, Enoch."

"No!"

"No. I shan't be serenaded. There wasn't ever a man made for me. I tried to think Stephen was, but he wasn't. No, I'm one to stick it out alone. I know it now. I'm a strange one."

"Oh, come! Maybe you'll see different—"

"No."

Lovice came running up, her hair loose and flying, her eyes very bright. She had Harvey's hand in one of hers and shook Kate's shoulder with the other.

"Kate! Kate, Harvey wants to see me home. Do you care? I'm tired anyway. I want to go. You can come along with the rest of 'em all right, can't you, Kate?"

Kate took a quick look at Lovice and a long, almost tender one at Harvey, all gratitude and blinking unbelief behind his plaid scarf tie. Kate's face was grave and kind, a little drawn, with something in it of the new mother who has not won her secure position without struggle.

"Yes. All right. You two run along. I can come with the rest." She added, raising her voice as they left her, "You be a good girl now, Lovey."

Outside, it was colder than earlier in the evening; but the wind had gone down, and so it did not seem so. The rising moon hung full over Mount Assabenbeduc. Harvey in his new suit, too short and too broad for him, and Lovice in her blue cape and white furs moved along the road from the shadow of one tree to the shadow of another, passing the silent houses one by one. Lovice said little, but kept looking up at Harvey, showing him her eyes and her smile and her pointed chin. Her hand was through the loop of his arm and the small white muff hung from it softly. This was more in one night than Harvey had expected of all his days and nights.

"You've never said whether you've missed me any," Lovice murmured.

"Missed you! Lord, Lovice! You might know without my say-so—"

"Maybe you'll be glad, then, to know I'm goin' to stay to home!"

"You're goin' to stay?"

"Yes, I am. They can have their old village if they want to. I'm good and sick of it. I've had more fun tonight than I've had in a long time."

"Gosh! It's awful nice you're goin' to stay. Course it'll be pretty quiet after this for quite a spell. We don't have a many serenades—"

"Can't you take me 'round a little bit, Harvey? So I won't get blue?"

"Oh, Lord, Lovice! If you—if ye'd be willin'. I—I ain't got no horse and buggy, but I guess I could git one."

"Oh, Harvey, do! We'll have great sport!" After a minute Lovice added, "These ruts are so bad, let's go through the field."

Gus had built a high board fence along the end of his farm, and Harvey clambered over first and offered his hand to Lovice. She sat on the top, with her heels caught on the second board, rocking a little, laughing, holding her muff against her chin.

"I'm goin' to fall, Harvey! I'm goin' to fall! I'm goin' to—"

He reached up to take her, and lifted her down, and she stood quiet between his hands, looking at him. All the mockery was gone from her now, all the airs and pretences. Her face was childish and frightened.

"Harvey! Tell me something. Are you good? You are good, ain't you? I don't mean to make great talk about it, like Ben does, and other ones. I mean—do you feel good—inside—to yourself?"

"Why—I don' know—"

"I mean, what I mean, Harvey—see, this is what I think about you. Don't you care what I say now. This is honest and true what I think. I think you're kind of slow, and not very bright, but you're awful kind and sweet, and you believe in treatin' other folks well and fair, and bein' clean and polite and workin' hard. You could marry a woman and live with her, and she wouldn't find out anything about you she hadn't known before, anything much. You ain't one thing to home and another one away, one man upstairs and another one down. You don't know any tricks. You really are the way you act. You *don't* know tricks. Do you, Harvey?"

"No, I don't know no tricks, Lovice."

He may have thought she was speaking of eggs turned out of a hat, and aces brought out of decks of cards. He was anxious only to soothe her.

"I don't know no tricks. I'm jest the same as I always was. You've seen me around—"

"Because if you don't—Harvey, if you don't—if you won't fool me—if you won't ever, ever scare me—if you'll swear—then I want to marry you! If you—if you want me—"

"Lovey! Want ye! . . . *Want* ye!"

He held her while she clung to him and cried, small and trembling; and he looked over her little white fur cap at the stars and the full moon. Was this Harvey Linscott, standing in Gus Bragdon's meadow, not far from the rise of ground where his mother lay because the churchyard would not have her? His throat was swollen full, and he would have liked to kneel and pray, but as like as not, if he had, his praise would have been given to the Bragdons, the first one who cleared this land he stood on, and all the others who had come after him.

"Oh, Harvey, I've been so scared. I *am* so—so mixed-up and scared. I don't know how to tell you. I couldn't. I couldn't tell nobody . . . Only things has happened—"

"Little Lovey!"

"Things down to—down to that—that place

where I was. It's been awful. At first it wasn't; it was fine. I thought it was all play. But it wasn't. I was the only one that was playin'. Cyril Bannister wasn't playin' . . . It wasn't just to dance and laugh and learn piano, and maybe get married sometime and live near the electrics and the stores. It was Something Else. I can't say it, Harvey—"

"There, there, Lovey."

"I ain't been bad. You needn't think I been bad."

"No, no, little Lovey."

"But I might 'a' been. You don't know, Harvey. I hope you don't know—how tangled up you get; and it's all close and queer, and everybody keeps on laughin', and nobody comes right out—and you never knew anything like it all before, and you just hold your breath and wait, not to seem foolish . . . Oh, I don't know what I'm sayin'. It's so good to speak to somebody. I been mixed up and scared so long, and nothin' to get hold of or to go by—"

"Yes, Lovey. Poor little dear!"

"Oh . . . Harvey . . . This is so good . . . Harvey, I've got to say just one thing more. I can't ever go down to that house again. Never as long as I live. Don't you ever let mother send me, not even if they all get sick and die. Because it's —I guess you ought to know this, if you're goin' to be my husband—it was my aunt was the worst one of 'em all! I can't hardly bear to say it, but I've got to and remember it. Dearly as I've loved her, handsome as she is, and nice-appearin', and one of our own folks—I know now she's a bad woman, Harvey; just as bad as a woman can be . . . Oh, Harvey, what made her—what *makes* her do so!"

"There, there, Lovey. Don't take on. Little Lovey. My little dear."

The word of hers which stayed with him was "husband." It lay snugly between her wet cheek and his heart.

9

The winter, spring, and early summer were long for Gus and Kate, but fled, filled as they were with dramatic opportunity, for those who were all Gray. The idea of Lovice married to Harvey Linscott, yokel son of an unwed mother, was one Roxanna would not for a minute tolerate, and she spent more time than she could well spare from her family, as she said, in her mother's kitchen, pacing up and down with fluttering skirts and crying out against it. Everything she said Ben agreed with and emphasized by his oratory. For Mindwell the thought of the child Lovice promised to any man took on an awful, even shameful form, and her elaborate avoidance of the subject, while it milled about her day after day, cast a gloom upon the little house. This and the fear of encountering Roxanna, with whom she had not exchanged a word since she had run away from her, kept Lovice at home. She scarcely ever stepped outdoors, except with Harvey, and once or twice with Kate to visit school. Even when Sarey went for her occasional few days' visits with her mother, she could not persuade Lovice to go with her; no, Lovice would stay at home and sew and keep the house.

Sarey's feelings ran up and down like the thermometer. Some days it was the greatest cross she had ever been called upon to bear, that she must stand by helpless while this second daughter, the gentle, lovely one, threw away her chance to marry into the village and sit in a dainty home with folded hands, and chose to give herself to a hulking laborer, a no-account, a bastard Linscott. She could not endure it; it was too much; she wished she were dead; she wished she knew a way to end it all, would Jesus Christ forgive her. She had put up with a good deal in her life, but she had never guessed it would come to this. She remembered the day Lovice was born, how she had sent Ben and Kate up to their grandmother's, to tell her to come down, but they were only young ones and stopped to paddle in the brook; and Gus set out with the horse and cart after the doctor, but a freight train on the new track stood across the road and held him up an hour. He could have crawled through or walked around, but it was three miles beyond there to the doctor's and he would have saved no time by leaving his horse behind; so he was gone from home almost four hours and Sarey lay in the back bedroom alone and bore this young one. Nobody would ever know what she went through, how she had tried to get up to scream from the window, and fallen on the floor and lain there senseless for only God knew how long, and nothing but such pain as then came upon her could have roused her. God alone knew why He had saved her or the baby either, only to come to this.

But other days her point of view was very different. She saw quite clearly how it had been with Roxan; all Roxan's life she had been one to take whatever she could get her hands on, if she wanted it, and she had been tracking down Sarey's children ever since they were born, just because they looked well and knew how to behave (more than could be said of Roxan's own) and because they were Sarey's. Right now she was at work on Ben, and she might get him; but she didn't get Kate, back when Kate was going to the Academy and sometimes stayed there overnight in a storm, and she didn't get Lovice for all her trying. Roxan could put that in her pipe and smoke it; she had not been able to get either of Sarey's girls away from Sarey. There was a good deal Sarey had not done for her children which she would have liked to, but it seemed a girl's mother meant something to her, after all, that nobody else could. This did not seem like the same place with Lovice away; Sarey felt alone in her own house; if Roxan had made out to marry Lovice off to Cyril Bannister, when would she and Sarey ever have been together? Maybe once or twice a year; no more. That, likely, was what Roxan was aiming for: to get Lovice underneath her wing so far the girl would not care if she never came home. But it had not worked, and maybe this would teach Roxan a lesson, and make her keep her fingers in her own porridge dish. Lovice was not going to marry a stranger; she knew better than that; when she was ready to settle down, she would take a home boy, one they all knew, one who lent a hand when he had a chance and worked along with her father, and could draw up and eat heartily of whatever victuals the Bragdons might put on the table. Harvey would never set the temz afire; but he was a driver and nobody dependent on him would ever starve, that Sarey was bound. If Lovice married him, they could stay at home; there was room enough; and later on, when they were ready, they could build on Gus's place or next to it, and Sarey would have Lovice running in and out, to speak to and do up a stretch of work with, like spring cleaning. It would mean a good deal to Sarey, as long as she lived, which probably would not be long; nobody knew how she had felt to think that in the few years left to her she could not be with her second daughter more than of a Sunday now and then, and they must always be company, hardly more than callers, in each other's houses; many was the night she had cried herself to sleep, turning it over and over in her mind.

Some days Sarey could not imagine why Lovice avoided Roxanna, and rated her soundly for it. She caught Roxanna's pique, and felt Roxanna's slight, said it was the strangest of anything she ever heard, what had come over Lovice, and declared the young should show respect for their elders, especially for them who had been kind beyond all reason. The other days she forbore to question Lovice as to why she had sneaked away and come up home, and gave Lovice to understand she shared the secret. "I guess it's just as well you didn't stay down there any longer," she said once. "I didn't know how 'twould be, but I had my suspicions. Sometimes I was all but out of my head a-thinkin' of ye, but one thing I always know: I always know I can trust my young ones, wherever they be. I don't see where Roxan got some strains that she seems to have in her. Ye'd never say she was marm's daughter, and I'm sure nobody ever thought she took after father. Some way her bringin'-up couldn't have been all it ought to have been. She's got a lot of good in her, but she's got a lot that ain't. There, I don't know what to do about it. I wish to my soul I did."

But whichever day it was, Sarey's feelings were something to talk about in her high, sharp voice, and the excitement of the time kept up her health so that she rarely had to retreat to her bedroom in daylight. Gus never went through the yard without hearing the clatter of her words, and when Kate and Jeff came into the kitchen late in the afternoon the two, Sarey and Lovice, were nearly always bent over Lovice's sewing, her tucked petticoats or her crocheted yokes or her dish towels with their fringed ends; and always the hum of their conversation and the heat of their emotion filled the house. Lately no one relaxed, or dropped off to sleep on the couch, however tired; it was impossible to forget that Lovice had renounced the village for Harvey Linscott, and would by and by stand up before a minister to be married to a man no other girl in the neighborhood would have had, though few men were so deserving. When Harvey came, the strain increased, for no one knew how Sarey would receive him, whether with a curt nod, or with a smile and pat, as if he were already one of her own. Lovice said little, dropping her eyes lower than ever over her needle, and Kate and Sarey helped her with the white net of her dress, the rickrack braid on her aprons, or the quilted padding for her pot holders, their needles glittering as they flew in and out, the thread snapping with a sudden sound, while Gus and Harvey exchanged a friendly remark now and then and otherwise were silent.

Sometimes when Jeff had been sleeping for an hour, and Gus and Sarey had gone into the bedroom, Kate tried to break the spell, but not with great success. It seemed a long time to her since she had done much laughing. It was a thing to think of, what a change the presence of Stephen would have made in this room.

"I had a letter from Stephen today, Harvey."

"You did? Where's he at, now?"

"Well, he'd just took passage on a steamer from St. Michael, up there somewheres, when he wrote, bound for San Francisco. He's been way up to Fort Yukon, you know. He had his claims, five of 'em, between there and Dawson City, but he's sold 'em now. I guess it was an awful place to get to and get away from."

"How was it he got up in there, anyway?"

"Why, he went by train to Vancouver, and then by boat to a place they call Dyea and across a lake—Lake Bennett, I believe it was; and then up the Yukon River to Dawson City. Now coming back, he's come down the river as far as this St. Michael and took ship. It's a wonder he ever got out of there alive."

Lovice sang:

"In far-away Alaska where the Yukon River flows
And the mighty boulders stand 'mid strength and might,
'Mid treasures there untold, in a land that's decked with gold,
He is sleeping in the Klondike vale tonight."

"Well, Steve didn't find it was so decked with gold, did he?" Harvey chuckled.

"No," Kate answered. "No, I guess it wasn't hanging from the trees. But I guess, too, it's there in spots."

"Will Steve bring home much, d'you s'pose?" Lovice asked.

"I don't have any way of knowing," Kate answered with reserve. "He's going to take a fine trip anyway. He must have got together something."

"A trip!" Harvey exclaimed. "That so! Wouldn't you think he'd had trip enough! Where's he goin' to?"

"Why, he says in three weeks he'll be aboard a boat bound for Japan and China. That's what he's always hankered for, to see them Eastern countries that he's heard tell so much about there to home. Ene's grandfather, you know, Old Cap'n

Josiah, he was there many times, and Thoc and Ene remember all his stories. Stephen says he's always meant to go, and now he's going. He thinks now to get all the way around the world before he comes back here. He's all high."

"I'll bet he is," Harvey said, his admiration kindled. "Think of any one man seein' what he's saw and will see. Steve always was a great one for gittin' around the country."

"Maybe he won't ever come back," Lovice said, turning her soft eyes on Harvey. "I shouldn't want a man that meant anything to me to go into such heathen places. You can't tell what might happen in China and Russia and like that. Gives me the creeps just to think of it."

Kate folded her work, and took off her white apron to lay it in the drawer. She lit a lamp and took it away with her, saying good night, up the back stairs to her room. She had the room to herself now, Lovice having taken over what had been Hannah's. A few minutes later she stood in her nightgown by the window, looking out. It was the last of June, and warm. The frogs were singing lustily in the marshes. The light from Lovice and Harvey's lamp ran out over the white roses by the door and reached the trunks of the maples which were the age of Kate. She and they had been here twenty-five years now, and it was not likely anything could move them. It would be their place to stand by together and watch while other people kissed and married, parted and reunited, touched one another and laughed and brought forth children. Kate did not think she envied Lovice anything except the son she might one day have; that she wanted with a great longing, not only the son but the weight of him and the pain of bearing him and the deep, stinging joy of the first time she saw him; she wanted all these, and would never have them. She had nothing but trees.

And somewhere Stephen Blaine rode the Pacific, throwing back his young head to laugh at the stories of other men, telling his own yarns with just enough truth but not too much, and his voice running fresh and free.

10

One day in mid-July as Gus drove along the the Lane toward York Road on his way to market, he met Bill and Ezra Linscott and a pack of their boys setting out in the direction of the mountain with fishing poles over their shoulders, rude, homemade rods wound around with cord. Linscotts were always going into the woods, with fishing poles or guns or traps, or with baskets for berries and nuts and wild apples, or equipped to rob beehives; but it was strange enough to see them up so early that Gus drew rein on his horse.

"Fishin'?" he asked, motioning with his whip toward the poles.

The Linscotts grinned companionably.

"Yeah. We be about starved out. The last of the salt hog is gone, and we ain't seen meat-kind for such a spell the womenfolks is on the anxious seat. I lay we'll have to git our hooks into suthin' or we won't dast come back."

"Won't ketch no fish sech a day as this."

"Too bright, ain't it? That's what we told 'em all; but they're up on their ears, so we got out. Poles ain't much to carry, anyways."

"No. Well. S' I to myself when I see ye comin', this ain't no day to ketch fish." Gus flicked Bell lightly, remarking as his wheels began to move again: "We've had good hay weather. Been a long, hot, dry spell."

"Yeah. Been a great stretch of it, ain't it? I s'pose you've got yourn done."

"Yes," Gus called back, without turning his head. "Mine's under cover."

He rode on thinking with some amusement of the Linscotts, how they lived, three families of them, in their two-room shack, men and boys sleeping in the barn, women and children in the parlor, and Jeddy and his wife in the kitchen. Generally they went hungry, but sometimes had great feasts on wild meat and borrowed beans and melons of which the remnant of Stephen Blaine's garden was the loser. At these times other Linscotts gathered with them, filling the shack and spilling over into the yard, and the sound of their jew's-harps and singing ran up and down the Road and across the fields into the woods. They were like dogs, or like children, living for the day, not knowing what it was to look ahead. While Gus peddled his butter, eggs, and chickens, scheming and counting in the heat with drooping eyelids, Bill and Ezra and their boys would lie on brown pine spills beside a brook, dangle their hooks in the water for a while, eat blackberries and take a drink of the rum or cider they would be sure to have along, and fall asleep, a sprawling group, half undressed, in the shade. When it was dark or the mosquitoes grew too thick, they would come stumbling home again. It was a strange way for human beings to live out their lives, and it left their faces, even those of the very old ones, smooth and bright; only the legs of the Linscotts gave out as they aged; their faces changed with the years no more than those of animals do.

On his way back, at this same place in the road, Gus thought of them again. It being twelve o'clock they were likely enough asleep already. He pondered briefly on where they might be, whether by Gray's brook or Dockham's, and his eye ran along the course of first one and then the other, where he knew water flowed among the pines and cut down through the ledges. It was his own minute of relaxation after a busy morning, but did not last long. His glance sharpened. He pushed back his hat and looked again. Yes, he was right; that was smoke, no mistake. Up between two of the Horse Hills, where Dockham's brook wound through a stripped lot that had been one Aaron Bragdon had given to his third son, Charles, a wisp of gray smoke hung like a taper. The fools, they had caught a fish or two, and now were cooking them without a thought for the underbrush which had lain baking for six weeks until it was as dry as tinder and could almost burst into flames of its own accord, nor for the half-dozen dead pines which marked one corner of that lot and stood, tall and brittle, as if beckoning to a spark which they could catch and taste and fling into the Shem Joy lot adjoining. For one of the few times in her life Bell felt a sharp cut of the lash.

"I guess that must be father comin' now," said Lovice. She stood up from the sewing machine and came into the kitchen to help put on the dinner.

Sarey listened.

"No, can't be him. Whoever it is has gone right by."

"Well, for heaven's sake!" Kate exclaimed to Jeff in the field where they were driving poles for the beans to climb on. "There's father, and he's not turning in. Why, see him larrup that horse! What on earth can be the matter?"

She stood looking after the team, with her smudged hand shading her eyes, and was amazed to see Jeff's figure cross her vision at a dead run. Jeff was fifteen now, a broad, stout-built boy, almost fat in what remained of his childishness; he would soon stretch up tall, spinning out the thread of his body into that of a strong man, but at this stage was clumsy, like a young elephant, and for the most part disinclined to hurry. Kate had not seen him move so fast in years as he was moving now, barefoot and in overalls, and when his big hat fell off as he leaped the wall, he did not stop to pick it up but vanished over the hill.

"Father! Father! . . . Where—you—goin'?"

"Git along home!"

"Where—you—goin'?"

"Look out fer her hoofs, I tell ye!"

"Le' me up in. Le' me—here, I'll climb up—back . . . Where you goin'?"

Gus swung his whip toward the Horse Hills. He did not look at the boy beside him. Both sat on the edge of the seat, and Gus's face was grim to the job of keeping up Bell's pace. Sweat stood out on his forehead and wet through his hatband; Bell's flanks were already ridged in a white lather.

"Fire!" Jeff cried above the creaking of the

wagon and the rattle of the wheels over Rocky Hill. "Must be folks blackberryin' up in there dropped a match!"

"Blackberryin'!" Gus growled. "Fishin', 'twas. Linscotts is up in there. Looked first like it was just a fire they'd lit to cook a trout. But I do' know. If 'twas, it must've got away from 'em, way smoke's boilin' up there now."

It came in puffs, white as from an engine pulling out of a depot, and hung in low clouds above the trees. No small picnic fire would stir up such a smoke. They turned off the Lane into a woods road, Bell at a gallop and the wagon rocking in the ruts.

"I thought I see a flame then," Jeff shouted. "Must have got into the top of them alders in the swamp."

"If it only spreads that way, it'll be a good thing. Here, take this horse. Don't set in the wagon. No tellin' what'll happen if she smells that smoke this close. Git out and hold her by the head."

Gus disappeared through the trees, going at a dogtrot. It was cool and still here, not a breath of wind stirring, but out ahead there was a sinister small hiss and crackle, and the smell of swamp and berries and pine pitch was changed by the haze of smoke. He lost no time, but crossed the swamp, jumping from tussock to tussock, and came the nearest way to the old Merriman lot, stripped three years ago by Gus's brother, Charles. Still Jeff was there almost as soon as he. They stood together, their faces livid and the blood thick in the veins of their necks. The blackened territory was still small, no bigger than the spread of a woman's apron, but in the breathless stillness was creeping rapidly out in all directions, small, merry tongues eating vines and bushes hungrily and licking at what lay beyond. If no wind came up, the brook would stop it on one side, and the swamp would discourage it on another; but nothing would hold it back from the Shem Joy, the Lyman Allen, and the Asa Cheney lots but the struggle of men or a drenching rain, and the sky was a clear, pale blue above the smoke. Except for Gus and Jeff there was no sign of life the whole length and breadth of the woods; no fishermen were here; even the rabbits and the squirrels had already scuttled out of reach.

"Here's the egg buckets, father," Jeff panted. "I thought—maybe we could—"

"Drop 'em," Gus said. "Take this coat, and git back to the team. Drive back the way we come as fast as ye can, and rout out the men every house ye come to. Tell 'em there ain't no time for nothin' only to take some tools and git here. Shovels, pails, and sprinklers. Git word to Joseef Allen; he's the Warden. Drive fast, but mind ye look where ye're goin'."

"Yup. I'll do it. And I'll be back here quick as I—"

"No, ye won't. Don't ye come anear here. Ye hear what I tell ye, now, Jeff. I ain't got no time to argue. Ye do what I tell ye, and git home and stay there. If I lay eyes on ye again till I git home, I'll beat ye with anything I can put my hand to. Now clear out!"

By night not a man was left in any of the houses along York Road or the Lane. Even the very old stood in the long line between the brook and the far side of the fire, passing pails of water along the human chain, and the stoutest bent to their shovels, digging trenches and throwing up barricades of dirt. Always many belabored the writhing flame with wet pine branches. And still, in spite of them all, the fire travelled on like a snake which has so far managed to protect its head. All night the fight continued, and with sunrise a wind sprang up, a southeast wind, light but constant, and nothing was left for it but backfiring. Warden Allen came out of the woods, worn and grimy, and sent his daughters to the village to ask for help. That afternoon a crew of twenty men rode over the Lane, and women watched them thankfully; children cheered from the dooryards as if it had been a parade. But twenty more men were nothing to such a fire as this had grown to be. Having eaten the stripped lot and gorged the young pines of the

Shem Joy, by nightfall it was roaring up the sides of the Horse Hills. No one of those at home had any heart to eat. From Kate's window, where she and Sarey and Lovice sat together, silently watching, the hills were like the lips of a great iron cauldron filled with fire, a steaming, bubbling red-gold stew from which a spurt of flame leaped up from time to time and clung to the tallest trees above, bursting up through them with a tail of sparks as if exploding, and one tree flung it on to the next. As the fire travelled into the oldest growth, trees remained standing when the flames had gone on, skeletons against the sky. Though three miles from Gus's house, the roar was plain to hear, and the crash as each great pine was struck. These were not only trees which were burning, but the shade where berry pickers had sat to eat their dinners, the moss where children had walked softly as if on velvet, the old orchards of farms long deserted, the safe in which Nubble Point had placed what little money had been dug out of the ground. And though the wind carried the fire now toward the mountain, there was no telling when it might shift, and fire which came the few miles to the edge of the woods would find all the farmhouses cowering there. The air was heavy, the sky had been lowering all day, but hour after hour passed, and no rain came.

Over in the woods Hamesh Linscott stumbled

out of the dark to one group of the men. Gus was there, and Amos Hamilton and his boys, and Harvey and Fred Dockham and the Joys. All were digging stubbornly, turning up the sterile dirt, all naked to their waists and their skins as black as stokers. They did not look up at Ham's step. The woods were full of men running back and forth.

"It's bearin' down on my place," Ham muttered. "You hear me? I say, the fire's bearin' right down on my place up at t'other end. The wind has shifted a little. I've had to git the womenfolks and young ones out. I guess I'm goin' to lose all I've got."

Nobody answered. Many of them, too, would lose most of what they had, unless rain came; some had lost it already. Ham's place was nothing better than a shack where he hung his baskets for the summer folks to see; a tar-paper shanty a chopper had left behind. Their bodies gleamed with sweat in the fiery light.

"I tell ye it'll git it," Ham sobbed. "They ain't enough fightin' on that corner to do no kind of good. There's all my hay there, and my planted stuff, and my cutters in the barn, and everything I've got."

"You think 'twill get it, do you?" Willy Joy snarled, still digging. "Well, too bad you folks hadn't thought before that fire is bad stuff. Next time you go fishin' in a dry spell, maybe you'll eat your fish raw. The rest of us will be obliged to you, I'm sure."

"I ain't been fishin'!" yelled Ham in despair. "I ain't been fishin'. And we been tellin' ye all day 'n' night 'twan't none of us set no fire. The boys was along o' me all the mornin', and I set in my shed a-makin' baskets. I ain't been fishin' sence last—'

"Well, get out of the way," Willy broke in. "Nobody cares when you been fishin'. Why don't you get to work? You won't save your buildin's standin' here."

"No, nor nohow," Hamesh sobbed, "if nobody won't help me. We ain't hands enough. I dunno anybody else that neighbors wouldn't turn to and help in sech a time—"

"In sech a time everybody has got their hands full where they be," said Willy.

Old Jeddy pulled himself to his feet from where he had lain napping by a stump. His face had not changed much since 1870; only his legs, which seemed shorter than ever and more bowed. He staggered on them.

"Nobody has got time for us, Ham," he said gently. "Ain't you learnt that yet? We's Linscotts. We ain't got no rights, nor no privileges. We ain't no better than field rats to mind we git burnt out, or what all. We ain't got nothin' only ourselves, nor never had. Come along, Ham. G'ove us, ye come along with yer daddy. We'll save yer little 'ouse yet. Ye come along with yer old daddy."

They went away together, and the men kept on digging, backing away and digging again. Gradually they were driven across the Lyman Allen lot, and into the Asa Cheney. Gus felt under his feet the ground he had travelled over so many Sundays, saw flames in the tops of pines he had thinned out and cut other trees away from that these might grow straight and true. He fought for every inch, and did not remember that he had neither eaten nor slept for two days and nights; but the fire beat him back. It was stronger than he was, stronger than his arms, or his will, or his devotion. He saw the dollar bills with their green tracery, for which he had labored and schemed through the first ten years of his married life, shrink and curl and crumble, golden-edged, into ashes; and not only that but he saw the trees taken, the life torn out of them, heard their scream as they were caught, and saw them stiffen and grow cold. He saw more than he was thought to be able to see, and felt more than it was known he could feel, but his digging never stopped, and he said nothing.

Once Ben brushed against him. It was the first time they had met here.

"I see it's got yours, father," Ben said. "It's nothing that I hoped for, but you will remember I once told you something like this might come to you. I only wish it might open your eyes."

"Fur as I can see," said Gus, "this smoke ain't no use to anybody's eyes."

And Ben went away and left him.

A little later the rain came, first in a drizzle through which the men kept on working, but at last in a steady downpour that swept even the tallest flames under and held them down to a feeble hiss. The woods were thick with smudge, and the fight was either won or lost, according as a man might look at it, depending on where his property lay, whether without the sooted circle or within. The crew felt about the swamp for the shirts left hanging on the alders, and tried to sort out their tools, but it was pitch-dark, so each one who had brought a shirt and pail and shovel took one of each and tramped homewards with them. Harvey went along at Gus's heels, and several others kept within hearing of these two, for if anyone knew his way through the woods on a rainy night, it was Gus Bragdon.

"Didn't git quite all the way acrost yourn, did it, Gus?" Harvey asked, coming up beside him as they turned into the Lane.

"No. About three-quarters," Gus answered, treading heavily.

"Some of that stuff down on the further end is pretty good stuff, ain't it?"

"Not much pine down there. Mostly hard wood. No, best of the lot was on the upper side."

"Big trees as them is, though, fire ain't to 'em what it is to little ones. They'll still sell."

"Yes, they'll sell. But not for what they'd ought to. Dealers'll know I can't hold onto 'em now. By a year the hearts'll be a-rottin'. Can't hold off for a price after fire goes through, and dealers know it. Means they've got the whip hand. Ye take what ye can get as quick as ye can."

"Yeus . . . Yeus, I guess that's right. . . . Cost ye suthin', Gus, these last two days."

"Cost me a thousand dollars anyway."

"Stinkin' shame. Stinkin' shame, that's what 'tis. . . . I s'pose there ain't no doubt Ezry and them set it, cookin' fish—"

"I don't see's they is. They was thar."

"I don't see what made 'em sech tarnal fools. Dry spell as we'd been havin'!"

"No jedgment. Never had."

"I feel like goin' over there and knockin' their heads for 'em."

"That wouldn't do no good. What's done's done."

When Gus reached his yard, Harvey turned in with him.

"I'll take a cat nap in your barn, if you don't

care, Gus. Come daylight, I'm goin' over to Jeddy's to git my clothes and be cleared out of there. I'm through with Linscotts. I never been much to 'em, and now it's come to this, I'm through. Won't none of 'em care only Jeddy; he kind of sets store by me; but I'm through. I'm goin' to git me a place to board and live decent . . . So if ye'll jist let me ketch a nap now in the barn, Gus—"

"Come in and lay on the lounge."

"No, I ain't fit." He grinned uncomfortably. "Ye needn't think I'll drop sparks in your hay, Gus. I do my smokin' outdoors. I know a little something, even if I be a Linscott!"

"Ye ain't all Linscott."

"No. I s'pose I'm part Blaine. But that ain't much neither."

"Put the two together," Gus said, "they made something! Yes, go ahead and sleep where ye want to, Harvey. I'd trust ye quicker'n any man I know on."

Kate, still sitting at her window, saw the two come through the yard, one climbing the rise of ground to the porch, the other going on to the barn. Lovice and Sarey had gone wearily to bed when the rain came, but she was still up, thinking of the trees, and of her father, of what it would have meant to her if fire had crossed her own lot which still stood so live and proud beyond the marshes. She heard Gus splashing at the sink, and his heavy footsteps through the sitting room and into his own chamber. Sarey's voice came up sleepily to Kate.

"Well, you back? It went through your lot, didn't it? There, I never see the beat. Anybody can kill themselves to get somethin' together, and then it's gone. I been about crazy thinkin' of it. It's a wonder some of ye wa'n't killed, in any such a place as that looked to be. Ain't Jeff jest about tired to death, a young one like him?"

"Jeff! What're ye talkin' about?"

"Jeff, I say. Ain't he wore out? And about starved he must be, too, the way he likes to eat. We put out supper on the table for the both of ye. Did ye see it?"

"Was Jeff to the fire?"

"To the fire! *Was* he to the fire! God in heaven, Gus Bragdon, didn't you know it? Wa'n't he with you? Why, he went over last night in the evenin' and he ain't been back! Oh, my soul and my body, *ain't he come home!*"

It was a minute before Gus answered. Then he said: "I ain't seen the boy, Sarey. I ain't seen him since I sent him home yesterday mornin' and told him to stay here. I ain't laid eyes on him, Sarey."

Kate reached the bedroom before her mother cried out again, and flung open the door. Her eyes, accustomed to the dark, made out the small figure of Sarey sitting up in bed, her face stiff with horror, and Gus's big body in a chair, bare from the waist up, and his head slumped back against the wall. She had rarely seen them in their room together, and never seen Gus as he was now. It crossed her mind that he was beginning tonight to be old.

"Jeff's all right," Kate said. She gave Sarey a shake. "Stop it, mother! Hush! Jeff's home, abed and asleep. He come in half an hour ago, and I fed him and put him to bed in the parlor, not to wake you. Jeff's all right."

"Oh, thank God," Sarey sobbed. "Thank God, thank God—"

Gus said, "Where'd you say he was?"

"In the parlor. Asleep like the rest of us ought to be. Keep quiet, mother! As if we hadn't all been through enough!"

She was going back through the front hall when she heard her father's step behind her. He came very softly.

"I thought I'd just look in at Jeff," he said. "It gave me sech a start—"

"He's all swelled up with browntail poison," Kate whispered. "I put sulphur napthol on. He'll be all right by morning."

"I told him to stay away from there. It wa'n't no place for him."

"I know, but he had to go. Everybody else was going, and he paced up and down here all the afternoon. When it looked like it was bound to get into your lot, there wasn't any holding him. He went loaded down with pails and shovels, and I guess he fought with the best of 'em twice his age. His hands are rubbed almost raw . . . Oh, he had to go. I could see that. He ain't so far from being a man now that he could stay back at such a time."

She went on upstairs, her eyes heavy with watching, but Gus stepped into the parlor and stood for some time in the dark beside Jeff's bed. This was his youngest one, the one he had kept on thinking of as a little boy in a stocking-leg cap, always wanting to climb up on the load and have a ride. But that was changed. In a few years Jeff would be twenty, a man grown, and a different kind of man than Ben had turned out to be; a big fellow, a brave one, willing to work, and with quick wits about him. This was Gus's son; he had gone alone into the woods and out again by night, and fought fire without its beating him. He was Gus Bragdon's son, and safe.

The next morning Harvey, going over to York Road for his clothes, found that the only Linscott he had hesitated to leave would not miss him now. Generally such a fire takes one life, and this time it was Jeddy's. Stumbling about on his short old legs on the hill above Ham's place, he had been surrounded by the fire, and when the rain came to make a gate through which his boys could get to him, there was little left to bring out. The rain had not come in time to save him, but, at least, the shanty, the baskets, the planted pieces and the creatures in the barn he had fought for remained unharmed.

11

Within a week Bedford C. Gibbons, Porchmuth lumber dealer, called on Gus. He came about noon, driving into the yard with a hired team from Ed McIntire's stable, a slim, high-stepping black horse and a rubber-tired top buggy, with a green felt covered cushion to sit on and a blonde plush mat for his feet. Gus looked up from his plate to see the portly figure under its white panama hat backing cautiously to the ground, and then bent again over his potatoes where they swam in thickened pork gravy. It was Sarey, with her hair hastily smoothed back and a fresh apron on, who answered Mr. Gibbons's knock.

"Oh—good day, Mr. Gibbons!"

"Hullo, hullo, Mis' Bragdon. Well. This is a nice day."

"Yes, 'tis. Real nice. Felt kind of fallish this mornin', though. I can't bear to think how fast winter's comin' on. Well, step in, Mr. Gibbons, won't ye?"

"No, no. I won't come in. Gus around, is he?"

"Yes, he's jest eatin' his dinner. He'll be right out. But ye might step in."

"No. I'll stop out here. Always like to get under the shade of these maples. Handsome trees. Means a lot to a farm to have some good shade trees in the yard, don't it?"

"Yes. Only nobody takes the good of 'em much. We're always to work."

"Yes, I suppose so. Yes, farmin' is a hard life. A dog's life, I always call it. Especially for women-folks. I know, I know. I was born on a farm. My poor old mother, she worked like a slave."

"I'll bate she did. That's the way it is. Drivin' the heart right out of ye—"

"But I'll tell you, Mis' Bragdon. I'll tell you one thing. She ain't spendin' her last days that way. No, ma'am. As quick as I was grown up, I saw to that. Before my mother was an old woman, I come into a little money, and first thing I done, I took my mother into a house in the city where she could have a few comforts. And how she does enjoy it!"

"There! I guess she does, of course. Must have been a master great change for her."

"Change? Why, for the first time in her life she's got water piped into her sink. Think of that —never to have to step outdoors. And she's got gas light. No more kerosene lamps to clean and fill every day—"

"My land, that must be awful handy!"

"Handy? Why, she don't hardly have to lift her finger. And she's got a furnace in the cellar so all five rooms of the house are every one of them just as warm as the kitchen, whatever time of year it is. But I'll tell you what pleases her most of anything, Mis' Bragdon. It's bein' where she can get into the stores every day and have a few dollars in her pocket to buy herself a little something new once in a while. She likes a new string of beads or a pair of buttoned kid boots as well as her granddaughters do, now that's a fact. Years don't change women much, you know. Their skin might get a little mite wrinkled, but their hearts are just the same whether they're eight or eighty, and a new shawl or a piece of satin for a dress will set any of 'em up, and give 'em a new lease on life. . . . Yes, my mother, she's a great gadabout these days. And my wife and I, we always put her right ahead. 'Go it, mother,' we tell her. 'By George, go it while you're young!' Does me good to see her, when I think of the way she used to have to do. She's earnt it, all right. Any woman has, that's spent her best years on a farm."

"Yes," said Sarey, staring bitterly past him. "Yes, she's earnt it, like enough—"

Her face made Mr. Gibbons uncomfortable. He looked at his watch.

"Well—Gus be through pretty soon now, will he?"

Sarey's attention came slowly back.

"Gus—why, yes. Yes, sartain he will, Mr. Gibbons. You take this chair." She dusted it with a sweep of the clean apron. "I'll go see what's keepin' of him. I'm sure he'll be right out."

She hurried through the entry.

"Gus! Gus, don't you hear? It's Mr. Gibbons, that lumber dealer. He's out there." She spoke in a whisper, fidgeting with the dishes across the table. "Gus! You can come in afterwards and eat that pie!"

Gus thrust his fork into the point of his wedge, and cut it off as if it had been meat, the knife slicing another piece while he chewed firmly and deliberately.

"Let him set," he said. "Let him set and cool his heels. Reach me a cut of that cheese, will ye?"

His meal finally finished and the plate very clean, Gus pushed back his chair. Passing the stove, he closed the draught, and took a strap from the mantelpiece.

"Your hair is standin' right up on end in the back," Sarey whispered.

Gus dropped his hat over it.

Through the screen door he could see his quiet, sunny yard, the row of maples, the woodpile and the chain pump, the fields and pastures and woods, as always. But now between him and them was the back of Bedford Gibbons, his broad, flabby girth with fine blue serge below and silk shirt and white panama above. Gus drew the strap through his hands and pushed open the door with his elbow, stepping out, still studying the strap as if to decide whether it would do, or should be longer, or must have more holes. Bedford Gibbons lurched, beaming, to his feet.

"Well! Hullo, Gus! Here you are, then!"

"How do," nodded Gus.

"Well, fine day, ain't it? Warm and nice. I notice you're goin' to have plenty of apples next winter. Trees hang full out there."

"Them ain't winter apples."

"Ain't?"

"No."

"Thought they looked like Baldwins."

"Baldwins ain't that red this time of year. Them's Astrachans."

"That so? Well, Astrachans are good apples. I always say it's a sensible man that has a good orchard. An apple a day keeps the—"

"What did you come about? That lot of mine you been hagglin' for and tryin' to beat me down on for two years?"

"Why, yes. Yes, I just thought I'd stop in as I was goin' by. They tell me the fire you had up here went through that growth of yours."

"Yes, it did. Part of the lot. Just the biggest trees."

"Too bad. That was a hard blow, Gus. Now I know it must have been. Anybody that's worked as hard as you have to get together what you've got—"

"Didn't do me no hurt. I ain't complainin'. Fire can't hurt trees the size of them."

"No, no. No, of course not. Trouble is, though, anybody that buys it has got to cut it quick. Can't hold off on cuttin' lumber that fire has been through, Gus. You know that as well as I do. Man that buys that lot of yours has got to put a mill onto it and saw like all getout, if he's goin' to get it while it's good."

"Well, nothin' to hender a man puttin' a mill onto it, as I see."

Bedford Gibbons chuckled softly, archly.

"Got to buy it first, ain't he, Gus?"

"Yes. He's got to buy it."

"Sure he has. And what's your price?"

"Five thousand dollars."

Gibbons whistled.

"Still sayin' that?" he asked softly.

"Still worth it."

"No," smiled Gibbons. "No, nor never was, Gus. Never was worth five. Now the fire's been through it."

"Sartain the fire's been through it. So ye think ye can git it for four thousand because I won't dast hold out—"

"Three, Gus. Three thousand. That's my offer—"

"You offered four!"

"Before the fire."

Gus stood looking at the lumber dealer. He was a half a head shorter than Gibbons, all bone and muscle, lean, grim, and weatherbeaten, peering under his bushy eyebrows.

"Ye think ye've got me beat!"

Gibbons chuckled, entirely good-natured and friendly, stroking his bulging stomach, with his thumbs inside his belt.

"Sure I've got ye beat, Gus. Might as well take it easy. Man that invests in lumber has got to make up his mind to some losses. This is your hard luck. Too bad. But a fire's a fire."

"Sartain," said Gus evenly. "And a skunk's a skunk."

He turned and tramped away to the barn, rolling the big door to behind him with a thud. Bedford Gibbons stood looking after, waited, finally strolled down and took a long drink at the pump. He turned the handle and drew up one small pailful, icy and dripping, let it down, and drew up another, listening to the spatter of the water against the stones of the well. But still Gus did not return, and finally there was nothing left for Mr. Gibbons but to unhitch his horse, settle himself on the felt-covered cushion, his feet on the plush rug and his head protected by the shiny leather top, and start his long ride back to the village where he could take the rocking electric car home to Porchmuth. Gus, mending harness as he sat on a sawhorse in the barn, watched him go, and regretted nothing. He poked holes with his awl and pushed the needle in and pulled it out again with patient care, though it was not a harness he would need until next spring.

But Gibbons had learned not to take a harsh word too seriously. An insult might be worth a duel, but was not worth the loss of a deal. Within two weeks he was back in Gus's yard again, and kept on coming, whatever his reception, always friendly, even genial, and full of compliments. Other dealers came, too, but none of them so persistently as Gibbons. Lunt from Somersworth could not pay cash, and so Gus had no ear for him. Samuels from Kittery liked to buy and pay so much a thousand feet as he sawed, but those who sold to him always came out on the short end. "It's four thousand dollars cash, or nothin'," Gus said many times through the summer and early fall. But Bedford Gibbons kept on saying smilingly: "Three's my offer, you know, Gus. And you know as well as I do I'm the only man in these parts can handle that lot as you want it handled." So in the end he got it.

"Well, there," Gus said suddenly one day. He

was in the field stacking corn, and Gibbons stood on the stubble beside the planted piece, watching the sickle knife sheer off the stalks and Gus's arm gather and tie them into bundles. "I've heard enough. You git it for three thousand."

"Well, now we're comin'!" Gibbons exclaimed. "Now, Gus, that's showin' judgment. That's what I've always said, Gus Bragdon up in Derwich is as quick-witted a feller as I've had any dealin's with. You can see how 'tis with me, Gus; I've got to get my mill onto that lot in such a hurry—"

"Clear out!" Gus told him, hacking savagely, with his head bent nearly to the ground. "Clear out, clear out. I tell ye, I've heard enough."

The day Gibbons came with the check Gus was at the beach gathering seaweed for fertilizer. He knew a short pebbly stretch between two rocky points at The Gunkit where seaweed rolled in during a storm as if dragged by the prongs of a horserake, and he went there every fall for three or four loads which he could bring home and stack beside his barn. By spring it would be ready to plow into the furrows, and better than any grain-store phosphate to lay the seed on.

"Gus is off somewheres jest now," said Sarey, "but I'm expectin' him most any time. Step in, Mr. Gibbons, step in. Gittin' too cold now for settin' round outdoors with any comfort."

"Much obliged, Mis' Bragdon. Think I will."

"Yes. Kitchen fire feels good, a day like this. I mistrust we're goin' to have an early winter. Nobody knows how I dread it. Sometimes snow blocks us in here for a week to a time."

"Oh, I know, I know. Always seemed to me a farmer ought to have a little place in a town somewhere that he could move his family into through the toughest months. A man can't do anything outdoors that time of year."

Kate was at school. Jeff had outgrown education and stayed out of school this year, and was away today with his father. Lovice, the only one at home, sat in the sitting room taking her last stitches; she would be married any day now; any day when Harvey, who was marking at the mill operating the Shem Joy lot, could get home in time to take her for a ride, and they found Ben at home at the Gray place when they stopped by. Ben's license to wed was only a month old, and Lovice and Harvey would be his first couple.

Sarey and Mr. Gibbons were alone in the neat kitchen, she in a rocker by the table, he in a straight chair at the end of the stove. He was more sympathetic and friendly than ever today, on the edge of complete triumph, and Sarey wore the anxious, faintly apologetic air of the country hostess. She did not often meet his eyes; her glance darted about to see no lint had been left beneath the stove, that the button was turned on the dish-cupboard door and the window glass showed clear when the sun struck it; the fingers of one small hand with its distorted joints continually stroked the red and white checked tablecloth. The yellow oak clock ticked cheerfully on the mantelpiece over her head.

"That would be a fine way," she said, "but farmers is poor people, Mr. Gibbons."

"Some of 'em." He smiled. "Not your husband, Mis' Bragdon. He's a smart man, you know. All them Bragdons have got hard heads when it comes to business. I've dealt with 'em all, and my father before me. They're hard fellows to get around, and Gus is the smartest of the bunch. I've got ahead of him a little mite this time, but it ain't often anybody can. I guess there never was a Bragdon died anything but independent, and your husband will be a long ways from there in his last years. Yes, ma'am. Gus Bragdon will live to see the day he's a rich man, and able to have anything he sees fit to buy, or I miss my guess."

"Yes," said Sarey slowly, stroking the tablecloth. "Yes, I don't doubt he will. . . . The pity of it is we can't all live that long. Take me now—"

"Oh, Mis' Bragdon, you've got a good forty years—"

"No." Sarey looked straight at him, her eyes large in her little face. "Ain't no use talkin', Mr. Gibbons. I won't be alive when Gus is in his last years. He may be the smart one, but he ain't done all the work. And he's the one to git all the benefit. That's the way it's bound to work out."

"Well, for that matter," Mr. Gibbons agreed, balancing genially on the small chair, his arms folded, "as I always say, most folks that's makin' money hold onto it too hard. Of course that's the way such ones as Gus get ahead, but still it's no way to live. There ought to be a kind of a happy medium. It's well enough to invest most of what anybody gets, but as I see it, a little slice of whatever comes along ought to go for something that's needed right then. Anyway, that's the way we do in our family. Now I've got a check for three thousand dollars right here in my pocket for Gus. If that was mine, my wife would have a dip into it before night. She'd want a trip to New York or some new piazzas on the house, and she'd get 'em. That's the way you'll have to handle Gus, Mis' Bragdon."

Sarey gave back no answering smile. She was looking at the tablecloth, stroking it.

"He ain't so easy handled."

"No," Mr. Gibbons chuckled comfortably. "No, I can see that."

"It ain't so needful to move into a village. Anybody can stick out cold weather here, one way or another, with the house banked up and the window frames stuffed around with rags, and wood enough—"

"It's a lot in bein' used to it, ain't it?"

"And I wouldn't care about no more piazzas—"

"That's what I say. One'll do. You can't sit on more than one piazza at a time."

"Nor I wouldn't want to go fur off. It would seem awful strange. I never had no experience with city places—"

" 'Tis always kind of confusin', the first time."

"What I'd want, if I could have anything,—I'd want a parlor set. One of them done up in red plush, with a sofy to it, and a table with one of them white marble tops, like my sister Roxan McIntire's got. She's got lace curtains to her windows too. I'd like best of anything to have me an organ and my front room fixed up nice to put it into. That's what I'd want. An organ—"

"You can play tunes, I s'pose?"

"I can play chords . . . Then I'd want to git marm and me suthin' nice to wear, and take her on the train to Quarterly Meetin' down to Kittery. Ain't nothin' I love to do like ridin' on the train—"

"I've took quite a shine to the electrics."

"Have ye? I do' know. I ain't never been on 'em. Seems to me they look as if they was runnin' kind of wild like a horse that's slipped his bridle. I don't believe marm would take to 'em much.

They're kind of more for younger folks, I guess. Anyhow, don't seem like it would be any proper way to go to Quarterly Meetin', bouncin' along on one of them—"

"Well, maybe you're right. Would you say it's about time now for Gus?"

"One other thing that would be a pleasure to me. If I only had a mite to do with to git Lovice suthin' real fine and pretty and have her a little weddin' here to home, with all her own folks and the neighbors in to see and eat a mouthful with us afterwards! Lovice is my second girl, that's goin' to marry Harvey Linscott—"

"Is that Gus comin' now?"

"No. No, that ain't him . . . I can't think of much of anything else I'd want, if I had all the gold there is in the Klondike. What would that much cost, would you say, Mr. Gibbons?" She looked up at him for the first time in several minutes.

"Kind of hard to tell," he told her. "Depend on how free you was—"

"Oh, I'd be keerful. I always been brought up to be keerful. I wouldn't know no other way to buy. Ain't no excuse for waste—"

"Why, you could do it for five hundred dollars, or you could spend a thousand if you was like some."

"Like some?"

"Like some women in the cities that always has to have the best there is."

"The best there is."

The room went quiet. The tick of the clock sounded very loud, and the cawing of a flock of crows pecking at the corn stacks beyond the window. Mr. Gibbons grew restless on the hard seat, bending forward every minute or two to peer up the road. Still Sarey sat stroking the tablecloth.

"I don't know but what I'll have to go, Mis' Bragdon," he said finally. "It's gettin' towards night." He drew a paper from his pocket. "Too bad this can't be fixed up and done with it. All I need's your two names on here, and I can turn over the check, and we'll be through."

Sarey looked up again.

"Have I got to sign suthin'?"

"Yes. Yes, a man can't sell property without his wife puts down she's agreeable to it. Not in this state, he can't."

"Why, I never signed nothin' of Gus's before."

"Must be he never sold any property."

"No. No, I guess this is the first time he has." Sarey fumbled for her glasses in her pocket. For all her worn and aged look there was something so childish about her that she seemed absurd with glasses on her nose, as if she were dressing up, pretending. "Let me look at your paper."

"Well, but you better not put your name to it until Gus gets here. I don't s'pose he'd take kindly to you signin' papers until they'd come to his eye. I've had trouble with different ones about that before. Men don't like to have their womenfolks signin' blind."

She read with care, her lips moving.

"Well, there," she said at last. "No, I won't. I guess ye're right. Gus wouldn't think I'd know what I was a-doin' of. Here, you can take it back." She rose suddenly, putting the glasses into her pocket. "You'd better wait, though. Gus'll be along any minute now. I'll jest step into the sinkroom and git my supper started."

She had scarcely gone when Mr. Gibbons heard wheels, and saw Bell's hind quarters arch and strain, as she hauled a big blue dump cart full of wet seaweed through the yard. Gus, walking beside her, threw the reins to Jeff who followed.

"Take her down behind the barn and onhitch," he said. "See ye rub her down well in the stall, and don't leave the window open thar behind. Give her some hay, and in an hour or so she can have some water."

He glanced at Bedford Gibbons's equipage, went to the well and pumped and drank, and came toward the house deliberately. He was some time in the entry, but entered with no change of clothing, his pale blue overalls and frock damp and stained, his feet and legs as far as his knees dripping salt water.

"Well!" Gibbons exclaimed. "I had about give you up. Thought you must have drowned yourself down there."

"No," Gus answered. "Ye ain't got me where I'm ready to drown myself yit. What ye here for?"

"Come to bring you a big check," Gibbons said, waving it. "I've made it out so it's just like money. Guess that makes me welcome, don't it? Just you sign your name right here, and get Mis' Bragdon in to put hers on too, and the check is yours."

"And the Asy Cheney lot is yours, I s'pose," said Gus.

"I s'pose 'tis."

"For three thousand dollars."

"Three thousand *cash.*"

"It ought to rot," said Gus, "before you saw a foot of it."

"Will if I don't git to sawin' pretty soon," Gibbons chuckled.

Gus took the check to the window and studied it, front and back. He took the paper and scrutinized it well. At last he tramped across the kitchen floor, took a quill and a bottle of ink from the mantelpiece behind the stove, and sat down at the table to write his name. Gibbons stood listening happily to the sputter and scratch of the quill on the paper. There was no sound in the sinkroom, nor had there been since Sarey went out.

"There," Gus said. "There you be."

"Fine. Fine. That's fine. Now we'll just have your wife in here." He stepped to the sinkroom door and knocked almost coyly. "Mis' Bragdon!"

After a minute Sarey came, wiping dry hands on her apron. Her hair had been combed back slick and she wore a fancy pin at her neck, a gold one in the shape of a violet, which had been Hannah's. She did not reach the shoulders of either of the men, but stood looking from one to the other.

"We just want you to put your John Hancock right here, Mis' Bragdon."

Sarey did not look at the paper Gibbons indicated. She was looking at Gus.

"Ye've got to write your name," Gus said shortly. "Can't ye understand?"

"Yes, I can understand," Sarey replied with glittering eyes. "But I ain't a-goin' to do it. Not till I see."

"Till you see what? It's all right. Put your name down onderneath where I writ mine."

"I know where to put it," cried Sarey hotly. "Don't you start tellin' me what to do, Gus Bragdon. I know a little suthin'. I know where to write my name as well as you do, and I can write a sight better hand. . . . But I won't do it."

"Won't do it? What's the matter with ye? Be ye out of your head?"

"No, I ain't," Sarey told him. "I *ain't* out of my head. That's just the it of it. I'm in my head for once. For once I've got my wits about me. . . . As I understand it, that lot can't be sold unless I sign my name there. And I won't sign my name there till I git things as I want 'em! Can't nobody make me! And I tell ye, I won't sign till I git things as I want 'em!"

Gus took a step toward her.

"Now you make a ruction!" he said. "*You* make a ruction, will ye!"

Sarey stood her ground. With fists dug deep into her apron pockets, the cords in her neck working, and her eyes almost black, she bent backward to look up at her husband.

"Make a ruction?" she screamed. "I guess I'll make a ruction. You'll see! I'm goin' to have a third of whatever ye git for that lot, Gus Bragdon. They's goin' to be two checks made out, instid of one, and a third of what he's goin' to pay will be give to me. Oh, yes, 'twill! Now for once *my* mind is made up, and *I*'ll stand on it like the Rock of Gibraltar. Ye can fuss and ye can fume, but ye'll never git my name onto that piece of paper till I git my check in my hand. Never if we both have to wait until Kingdom Come. Now, that's flat! . . . I s'pose ye think don't none of that lot belong to me by good rights, Gus Bragdon. Well, I'll have ye know it does. Who worked that butter and picked them hens ye sold to market for the money ye paid up your note with? Tell me that. And who dragged and slaved to fill your stomach up so ye had heart to do the work you done—"

"Hold your tongue!" shouted Gus suddenly. "Hold your tongue before I throw suthin' at ye! . . . Now not another word out of ye. Ye hear what I say."

Whatever Sarey had expected, it was not that he would shout at her. In all their years together she had never heard his voice raised in the house, and did not know it would make the windows rattle. She shrank back.

Gus turned a look at Bedford Gibbons.

"Set down there," he said. "Write out two checks. Like she said."

"Two—two checks?" Gibbons stammered. "One for—for two thousand and one for one—one thousand?"

"Like she said, I told ye!" thundered Gus. "If she's bound to git a thousand dollars out of me, she can have it, if she'll hold her tongue. It ain't but half of what you cheated me out of. Now, write it out; come."

Gibbons wrote words and figures on two blue slips. Gus took up first one and then the other, and satisfied, held out one to Sarey.

"Now will ye write yer name?" he asked her.

She looked greatly shaken. He picked up the quill and gave it to her, and she stooped and traced the letters: Sarah Emma Bragdon.

"There, as I see it, Mr. Gibbons," Gus said, "your work here is through with. Ye've done yourself proud. Want ye to know I'll never sell ye nothin' more anybody else will take—"

"At the same price or better," returned Gibbons, bowing out.

Gus did not hear the retort. He was already on his way to the barn.

Alone in the kitchen Sarey stood staring at the blue slip in her hand. "Pay to the order of Cash," it read, "two thousand dollars and no one-hundredths ($2000). Bedford C. Gibbons." And across the back it was endorsed. This was two-thirds!

Gus could not stand a woman's tongue, but he had as much respect as anybody, more than most, for a good stroke of business. And it may have been that something in the still white of Sarey's face as she shrank before his words touched a secret place in him.

In any case, here was the check. "Pay to the order . . . two thousand dollars."

Sarey went on stiff knees toward the sitting room.

"Lovice! Lovice—"

12

A year from the next spring, in May, Kate and Mindwell stood one morning just inside the parlor door. It was a spacious, pleasant room, the largest in the house, with ivory-painted panels and four deep, lace-draped windows. An ingrain carpet, gray with red diamonds, and red roses inside the diamonds, covered the floor, and the various pieces of a red plush set stood about over it, an easy-chair, a rocker, a sofa, and four straight-back chairs, each with its red plush seat and padded back and with casters on the legs. The organ filled one whole side, between the door into the entry and the corner; its top reached to the ceiling and all its filigreed crevices were occupied by Dresden figures and stuffed owls, polished shells and dried salt-marsh grass tall and feathery in luster vases; a photograph album bound in red velvet with a great silver bumblebee clinging to the nap lay on the little stand to the right of the keyboard, a lamp with a painted china shade stood on the other, and, down between, the black and white of the keys shone richly in the thin light. The organ stool was covered in brown velvet and finished with a fringe. A white china silk scarf painted with forget-me-nots covered the mantelpiece, and above it hung a framed motto worked in red: "God Bless Our Home." There were pictures, too, about the wall,

all in new frames—one of Lovice and Harvey on their wedding-day, taken in this very room, Lovice in white with a lace veil and carrying a Bible in her hands, and Harvey in a new dark suit and standup collar; one of Kate as a little girl, wearing a plaid frock and jacket and cape scalloped around with black silk and fastened down the front with many silver buttons; one of Roxan just after she went into the mill to work, her hair short and brushed into curls, long earrings in her pierced ears, and rings on three fingers of each hand, her dress heavy with shirred taffeta and the neck filled in with ruching, row upon row. The marble-topped table between the windows held another album, this one in leather, a basket of loose pictures, a volume of Tennyson bound in watered silk, and a little dish of the gold-flecked chips of stone Stephen Blaine had brought back from the Klondike. Sarey's parlor was the finest of any anywhere around.

Only one space was left vacant. The corner opposite that which held the organ had a bare look, as if just cleared, or yet to be furnished.

"I had them put the bed up in the shed chamber," Kate said. "Seems as if that's going to leave room enough, without taking out anything else."

"Yes," Mindwell answered. "I wouldn't change nothin' else. She wouldn't want ye to. It looks so handsome."

"Shall I have 'em put it there, when it comes?" Kate asked. "Would you? Or had I better move things around, and have it maybe here by the door where the organ is?"

"I wouldn't change nothin'," Mindwell repeated. "It'll be as well there as anywheres. I s'pose you picked out suthin' nice."

"Yes, it's real nice. We didn't get black. Neither Lovice nor I could stand to see the black ones. We got one finished off in a gray, a real light, nice-looking gray. And of course the inside is white, something fine and soft. I think you'll be satisfied with it when you see it."

"Well, there, I'm glad you didn't get black. Some way it don't fit her. Not the way she looks. She's done awful pretty, Kate, don't you say so?"

"Yes—yes, I thought you'd say she looked—nice."

"Well, Mr. Barrs is wonderful that way. Seems as if he always gets such a—peaceful look."

"Yes, but—that's the way she *did* look, grammum, when she went . . . I wish—you could have seen her so you'd know how—how peaceful and happy she went . . . I don't know how to put it but some way—Lovice and I both spoke of it—some way she died so—so different from the way she lived."

"That was the Lord, Kate. The Lord was closer to her—"

"She looks so young, grammum—"

"Yes, like when she was a girl. Before she left home. When she was there to home by the fire of an evenin'."

"Only not afraid—"

"No. No, the Lord—"

"Like sometimes when she was singing, grammum. That's the way she looked night before last, and does this morning too—"

"Well, Mr. Barrs is a master hand—"

"Like when we were all singing over to your house together. That's the way she looks."

Lovice came in quietly, her face mature and pale, her hands long and thin. The sun shone softly on her hair and she smiled as she put her arm around her grandmother.

"You got the baby to sleep?" Mindwell asked, smiling back.

"Yes. Sound."

"Poor little soul. How Sarey did set store by him!"

"He's wrapped up this minute in that white cashmere shawl mother brought—brought back to me time you and she went down to Porchmuth. Time she got that blue silk dress we're goin' to put on her for the—for the—"

"We picked out the organ that day too. We had an awful, awful good time."

"And after that she—oh, grammum, why

couldn't she have lived to—just to enjoy it a little longer? Only a year or two—"

"Lovice, child, the ways of the Lord are beyond—"

"I don't know," Kate said, looking at her sister. "I don't know, Lovey. She wasn't very used to being happy. I kind of think maybe she had all she wanted, all she could stand."

EARLY EVENING

1920

❧

IT was the middle of May, and lilacs were in bloom at the Elder Gray place, their purple clusters brushing the windows of the west room. Mindwell no longer lived there, but her flowers kept on blooming just the same. The evergreen trees along the back of the house had grown taller and crept closer and spread around the ends, and the clapboards had absorbed more and more weather until they were as black as ink stain would have made them; so that altogether it was a very dark little house. But it was in no way gloomy or neglected. Harvey had lately built a portico over the wide, panelled door and put in window frames and painted them all white. The chimney had a new top. Mindwell's tangled, spicy garden, in which Lovice labored helplessly but happily whenever she could get outdoors, was fenced around with white pickets. The barn was new, the shed had been shingled within the year, and barelegged Maddy and Martha were just now driving up the pasture lane the herd of four fine, fat cows and two frolicsome heifers. No, Harvey had not done badly. The place in which he kept his family had more a Gray or a Bragdon than a Linscott look, by far, though it had belonged to him for ten years now, with no one to tell him, as Mindwell while she lived had always felt she must, when and where a nail was needed, or that cold weather was coming on and he should house his wood and riggings.

The sun had barely set. The sky was still streaked with color, and it was light enough outdoors. But lamps had been lit in the house, reddening the ripples in the glass of the window panes, and shadows moved back and forth inside. The yard was warm and still; its new grass and lilacs, the pump and the elm tree and the hen houses. Nothing moved except the cows and the children.

"Hi up! Hi up in there!" cried Maddy.

"Don't screech so," Martha told her.

"Why not?"

Martha did not know. She was only five years old, very small in a pink print dress and ruffled dark blue tire.

"I'll screech if I want to," said Maddy.

But she did not even speak aloud after that. Together, brandishing their willow withes, they urged the cattle into the barnyard. Panting, Martha tugged the lowest bar across the gateway. The middle one was Maddy's task, Maddy being three years older with stout arms and legs like a boy's. But not even Maddy could handle the top one. Their father must take care of that when he came out with the milk pails. It seemed strange that he was not here already, for they were much later than usual with the cows. Everything had been strange today. They dropped their frayed sticks into the ditch when they jumped across, and Martha felt for Maddy's hand as they went through the yard.

"I don't know as we'd ought to go in," said Maddy.

"Why not? Why can't we go in?"

Maddy did not know. She paused on the door rock, studying the windows anxiously, then drew Martha with her toward a coupé which stood at the edge of the driveway. It was the doctor's car and had been there since noon. The children had seen it every time they looked toward home from Aunt Berniece's where they were spending the day. Martha wanted to get into it when they came into the yard at five o'clock, but Aunt Kate came to the door and sent them scuttling after the cows.

"Let's climb in here," Maddy said.

She went first, and Martha followed her. It was dark and they sat with their arms around each other.

"I want my supper," said Martha.

"Well, it don't do any good to want it," Maddy answered. "I guess I want mine too. Don't you s'pose anybody but you ever wanted their supper?"

"Why can't we go have our supper?"

" 'Cause we can't," said Maddy.

The rest of the world was inside the house while they were outside and dared not go in and did not know why. They sat very still, blinking.

In the West Room, Lovice Linscott lay asleep in the big brass bedstead. The smell of the lilacs did not reach her, and the lamplight did not disturb her, nor the sounds the doctor made splashing in the bowl Kate brought to him and packing away his white coat and gloves, boxes and bottles in a leather case. Harvey sat by the bed as he had been all day, not terrified now, more relaxed, but still watching Lovice's delicate, worn face as if he would never have enough of it.

"She'll be all right," the doctor said. "I'd wait until she comes around if it wasn't for their wanting me over to Amos Hamilton's. You can give me a ring there if you need me. But she'll be all right."

"Ye're sure she will, now?"

"Oh, yes. She's through again. But no more of 'em, Harvey."

"No, doc. No, there won't be no more."

Lovice stirred as the door closed. Harvey put his hand awkwardly over one of hers, and it felt cold. He crept away and piled wood on the hearth, then went back to his place. She would like the fire when she saw it. She always liked to watch an open fire. The room was beginning again to feel like home; the walnut and pine furniture from the

Elder's time looked once more familiar, and the new wicker chair, Mindwell's organ, the carved shutters and clover-leaf cupboards, and St. Francis feeding the birds inside a gilded frame. Dandelions the children had brought in the day before stood in a blue cup on the mantelpiece. There was the smell of the lilacs, and the reflection of the fire touched Lovice's face rosily as she stirred again. Harvey bent his head close to her ear.

"Lovey! Lovey, can ye hear me? . . . I want ye should know we've got us a fine little boy."

Lovice raised her eyelids but could not see. She smiled. She looked much as Sarey had in her later years, though Sarey had never taken on that pretty petulance about her mouth and that womanly confidence in the lines around her eyes; there had been no one to flatter Sarey.

"A little boy," said Lovice in an unnaturally high, sweet voice. "A little boy—a little boy—"

Kate came in quietly, with the baby in her arms, and stood across the bed from Harvey.

"You'd think to hear her that it was the first one."

"Well, 'tis the—" Harvey cleared his throat. " 'Tis the first boy in quite a spell."

It was natural then that they should think of Herman. Others might forget the war, or begin to remember that, however heroic his death, Herman had been a Linscott through and through, a simple-minded fellow, a good-natured scamp; but here a faded and streaked service flag with a gold star still hung proudly in the front entry window. Kate thought too of Clyde, Lovice's third child, who was fifteen years old but had never walked and never would, though otherwise he was strong and well and had a quick mind and was as much help as another girl in the kitchen.

"A little boy," Lovice said. "A little boy—"

Kate moved Lovice's arm and fitted the baby comfortably inside it, turning back a corner of the blanket. She had done this many times before, but never, she thought, for one with such clear skin and such wide-open eyes. She stood taking a long look at him. This was the son she might have had; not Herman, nor Clyde, but this one.

"Weighed seven pounds and over, Lovice!"

"Not—very—big."

"Big enough," said Kate. "Got nothing else to do now but fatten up. Nor you either. How do you feel?"

"I—don't know. All right—I guess. Ain't nothin' the matter with him, is—there, Kate?"

"Right as rain."

"Let me feel his—feet."

Harvey guided her hand. Lovice's fingers moved exploringly, then she sighed and smiled and made a motion as if to pull the blanket across.

"Well, there! Wasn't that—foolish? I kind of—got it into my head—he was clubfooted!"

They did not answer. It was Clyde who had a clubfoot.

Lovice spoke suddenly, herself again.

"Have you got Maddy and Martha to bed, Kate?"

"No. They're just eating their supper. They stayed late after the cows, and then got into the doctor's car and fell asleep. He had to bring 'em in one to a time before he could start for Hamilton's. We got so excited over Tiddledywinks here that we forgot all about them. But they'll get seen to all right."

"Well, you get Lillian and Clyde to see to 'em. You go along home."

"Oh, I'm not leaving this soon."

"Yes, you are, too. I'm all right. Why, I feel fine. You never got a wink's sleep last night and been drivin' all day. Now I say you go along home and get a night's rest and be there to cook father a hot breakfast in the mornin'. Evvie'll be here any minute; it's a Saturday night; and if them two girls and Harvey and Clyde can't make out until tomorrow, I'll find out the reason why. You go along, I tell you."

"Well, if that's the way you feel about it," Kate said. "I s'pose father will be wanting to hear.

I'll bake up something and bring over in the afternoon. That all right with you, Harvey?"

"Yes." Harvey nodded with his eyes on Lovice. It was wonderful to him to see her face live again. "We'll git along."

"Well, then—"

Kate bent over the baby, settling him. She straightened the covers of the bed, and shook the lamp to see how much oil it held, and brushed a few chips off the rug into the fire. The room was quiet. Lovice lay under a white spread with her son on her arm and her eyes easy, and the wall-shadows and firelight folded them in. Harvey sat by like a shaggy old dog. Everything went gentle for Lovice; whatever was small and frail and human came to her naturally; Harvey first, then seven babies, one after another, and this house, so old it seemed held up only by the invisible hands of those whom it had sheltered. Kate lingered in the warmth which surrounded Lovice.

"If you need me before then, just send. I could be here in two shakes."

"I know it." Lovice drew Kate down and kissed her, rubbing her nose childishly against Kate's cool, smooth cheek. "Tell father we're both doin' well." As Kate reached the door she added: "But don't you call this young one Tiddledywinks. We've got a better name for him than that."

"Named him already?"

"Been named for six months. Name is James Aaron."

Moving swiftly among the black pines of the pasture with the sky cloudy and heavy above her head, Kate thought about that name. Kate was in her middle age now, and had her own ideas of how to cut and stitch together again a breadth of cloth, so that, whatever the material, her clothes had always the same strange grace of line, blowing back freely from her stride. Her face was serene and aloof, her eyes placid, as if she did not fear, even liked the woods in the evening. The path was more distinct than in Mindwell's and Sarey's time, for the children used it morning, noon, and night, Lovice and Kate went back and forth often, and even Gus and Harvey paid occasional visits to each other's barns of a Sunday. Kate's feet could find their way here with no guidance, whether by daylight or by dark, and her thoughts be left to go where they would.

Aaron, she knew, was for Gus's father, and James for Sarey's; James Aaron; it made a fine name. It was the first name Lovice had used that Kate herself might have used if she had the calling of a child. Lovice had named the others as if they were dolls,—Herman, Evelyn, Lillian, Clyde, Madelaine, and Martha. Martha was a good name enough, but it meant nothing to either Grays or Bragdons. Aaron stood for a man that this child had behind him, one who was six-foot-three in his stocking feet when he was married, who reared a family of a dozen at the edge of a salt marsh and made it pay. James stood for another grandfather, as tall as Aaron but not so stout, neither wrestler nor chopper, but silver-tongued and golden-throated. It seemed to Kate that Lovice had brought these two to take up positions, one at either end of her seventh child's cradle, which was what Kate would have done in her place.

But Kate had long ago finished with thinking of Lovice's life as rich and her own as bare and solitary. That had been only the last mood of her youth. There was once when she hoped for and believed in and expected everything, when she stood ready and vibrant, waiting to be played upon. But no hand strong enough and sure enough touched her, and for a while she went dull and silent, believing in nothing. Now she was in her middle age and had been through the bad time; it was easy now; it was fine and free; she could play herself. Perhaps it was not a tune she played. Sarey had once said: "I can't play tunes. I never learnt how. But I can play chords, and if you know the right ones, all the tunes chime in with 'em." Kate's strings hummed chords with no need of fingers on them, like those of any good instrument for the ears of those who can hear.

Much else had changed while Kate was growing

older. Most of the houses along York Road had crumbled into their cellars, and of the few which remained between the end of the Lane and the salt marsh, only three were lived in, two by Linscotts and one by French woodchoppers; it was a woods road now. The river had dwindled to a brook, Captain's Eddy become a shallow pool, and the Selden Mill Dam rotted away until it was only a heap of mossy planks where men and boys sat to fish on rainy spring days. A handsome pine eight inches through grew between the split halves of Aaron Bragdon's door rock, the brown spills filling up the troughs where Charles, Edward, Jefferson, Ruel, and the others had drilled their initials and those of one another's girls. The most promising of all the young growth which Kate had bought covered a field which Moses Dockham had been trying to plow the day he died. The district system in the township passed away; there were no longer district fire wardens, road commissioners, and school committeemen. The rural school remained, but all control of it was kept in the village, and still Kate Bragdon was known as Teacher; it had been over twenty years now. Supervisors became superintendents and it was fashionable for girls to go to normal school, but Kate went on teaching without analyzing how, as she always had, ringing the same bell with the black walnut handle, applying as often as she must the ferrule her father had made for her; and not a curly-headed college boy, taking up his job of superintending, but stayed to ask her advice whenever he stopped at her school with its draughty floor and wood stove and cracked blackboards. She was Miss Bragdon of Number Nine, and knew her business.

Still the number of pupils lessened steadily. At first it was a relief, the room had been so crowded; the removal of a row of seats across the front and another along one side left space for the children to stand and take their exercises by open doors and windows; Kate could remember when all the seats had been filled and boards laid across so that others could sit in the aisles and share desks with neighbors. But now boards were needed only for Christmas concerts, and late years not more than half the desks had been used. Most young people of marrying age moved away to town or city jobs, to sidewalks and electricity and moving pictures. Those who remained bore few children and sometimes did not care whether these attended school or not. If they did see value in education, they were thinking of getting their older ones to the Academy, and it became a custom for two or three of the more prosperous farmers, Charlie Hamilton and Fred Dockham and Harvey Linscott, to move their families into the village in late fall and bring them back again in the spring. This took away the little ones, too, to the Grammar School, and left Kate's room some winter days all but deserted. These were the times when she was most likely to suddenly push aside the books and put back her head and sing; sometimes she sang for an hour or more, hymns and songs and rude folk tunes, what ever came to her tongue, while the children quivered with excitement and delight. "She sung," they would tell the others in the spring. "One day while you was gone, she sung!" It was a good deal to have missed, just to be in the village for the winter.

But the towns reached out and caught hold of strings which bound together the people from up-country and drew them gently in. The main roads were good now; the state contributed to their construction and upkeep. Nearly every family had a car, a Model T, and even those who must still depend upon horses could on these roads cover five miles in half or three-quarters of an hour. There was no longer only one day a week for going to market. Some still went every Friday to take butter and eggs to customers, but, if they forgot to buy the molasses for the beans or a cake from the bakery, could run down again the next day. All who were social went Saturday evening; the whole main street of the village was lined every Saturday night with mud-splashed or dusty vehicles in which farmers' wives and children sat as on a balcony, to watch the passing show, while the farmers themselves leaned against unused hitching posts to talk together of politics and prices and how things used to be. If they were not too late home, they might all be down again in the morning for Sunday papers or church services.

The Nubble Point Meeting-house was no longer open. Soon after Sarey went, Ben felt his power going, and opened a series of revival meetings, but at the close of the second one, where he had worked himself to a high pitch, he fell going into his grandmother's house and the spurt of his first hemorrhage stained the door rock. He could not continue the meetings, and died within a few months. It was then that Mindwell sent for Lovice and Harvey and the baby to come to stay with her. To lose the one who had lived in her house like a shadow of the Elder, and to see the shutters drawn again on the church was more than she could face alone at her age. Now, Mindwell, too, had been gone for ten years.

Then the war came. The Boston papers carried tall, black headlines: "England's Back to the Wall" and "5,000 American Troops Land in France." Stephen enlisted at the first. He sat on Gus Bragdon's step, reading Gus's paper, one Sunday evening while Kate knit quietly on khaki yarn behind him, and rising with his hands in his pockets, said he believed he should see one of these days if they would take an old fellow like him. The next morning he was gone. They took him quickly enough. He wrote Kate a letter once in a while, with the crossed flags of the Signal Corps stamped on the corner of the envelope. The food was good, he said; sometimes he slept cold at night. Kate sent him a patchwork quilt but did not hear whether he got it. He liked sentry duty in the Alabama camp; he tried to tell her something of how the peaks of the tents looked against the sky; and he wrote of buying watermelons from pickaninnies, at five cents apiece, the meat as red as blood close to the rind. After he went across he did not write much, and there was little to read in what he did write. Herman enlisted at a time when men were badly needed, and reached the shores of France within two months of the day he signed his name in the Porchmuth recruiting station; it did not take the enemy long to make an end to him. Lovice's red star, of all those in the neighborhood, was the only one which turned to gold. Charlie Hamilton's oldest boy and Fred Dockham's two were caught early in the draft and saw foreign service but escaped with their lives; Charlie's got a bad heart from being gassed, and one of Fred's lost an arm; but Floyd Dockham came off scot-free. Jeff Bragdon was called but excused because his farm was as productive as any in the town and he had two small children and Bertha was ready for another; Bertha, ill and heavy, travelled with him for four days, from Portland to Augusta and back again, explaining to the men in the brick buildings how things were with them at home; she understood that if it took words to save Jeff, she would have to be the one to speak them. Kate was hanging her washing on the line the morning the bells rang for Armistice. She stood in the crisp air and thought of Cora and Maud, to whom they would mean one thing, and of Lovice, to whom they meant another. She thought also of Stephen at the front and wondered if he felt a sense of victory; it seemed doubtful, remembering Stephen and thinking of his age; it would be more in the nature of a young man to want to crow over someone else. She did not hear until much later how, young and old alike, German and American, they scrambled out of their ditches and stretched and had a smoke together.

After the war, everything began to move much faster. Even the cloistered old families in the village put their horses out to pasture and bought electric broughams. Busses gave competition to the trolleys; no one wanted to be bound down to rail and wire. There must be more and more electricity, more and more cement, better trained teachers, better roads, new public property, a fire engine, a snow plow; the indebtedness of the town grew as fast as the years went by. At first the town officers could borrow of Gus Bragdon, but when he saw what was done with the loan, his eyelids drooped and he said he had no more money to spare, not even at the high rate the last note had carried. "Ye're gittin' in too deep," he said. "Ye can't swing it." Taxes went up to fifty dollars a thousand, and still the bonded indebtedness of the town increased. Gus said nothing more, but sold as many of his Derwich wood lots as he could let go to advantage and bought up others in more frugal places. Gus was now the richest man in his town or any round about, with many lots sold and the best still to sell, government bonds and mortgages in his chest, and a neat sum in every one of a dozen or fifteen banks; but he did not alter his house or his way of living; he scraped his plate clean and pegged his own shoes and said of Lovice's cooking that it tasted well enough but she used too many eggs and too much butter and such high flavor was not fit for the human stomach. Villagers drove out in shining cars and asked him to run for selectman, but Gus said no, the town did not want him; he was too close; they would not get along; he might as well marry himself to a woman interested in nothing but silks and satins.

So the town and the times went their way and Gus and Kate went theirs, and the way of Gus and Kate was the main track of New England farmers from the beginning. Bragdons had never been whiffle-minded, from the first one down to these;

where whiffle-mindedness was, it had come in through another strain. Bragdons knew that travelling from one place to another was only a way of spending time, of which they had none to spare. Some men would ride, whether ahorseback or by motor or on wings, and others would go afoot, whether on cement or moss, and it made little difference; everything depended on what they did when they got where they were going. When money was invested, it brought returns, but when it was spent, it was gone. They knew that life was hard, and ought to be, and did not improve with being made too easy. A war was a squabble, most likely foolish; a man did well to keep himself free of such, and attend to his own affairs. Honor and glory were baubles, self-respect the only crown worth earning. In one generation people had crowded this land and these shores until their weight might well have sunk them; now everyone was leaving on the first excuse, to crowd some other place until that sank. And all the time these were the same shores, with plenty of clams for the digging and plenty of fish on the Banks, and this the same land, some of it worn out but none of it so far gone it could not be brought back if a man set to it, and much of it still virgin, only needing a sturdy and willing arm to clear it. Stumps had too long roots for most men lately, but the roots would keep on growing longer and still there would come men who would be glad to spend their strength on them. There was land and water, sun and rain, woods and brooks and seed and natural fertilizer, as there had always been. Anyone who did not want too much could live here. Those who did want too much had gone to seek it, but it was nowhere, and they would come back. Gus and Kate waited for them as they had once awaited Sarey when she flounced away from home with her little wagonful of peas, pies, chicken and other produce of the place, a small store of luxury which could not last long. While they waited, they made themselves snug.

Passing through the dim woods, Kate now and then laid her hand on the trunk of a birch or the tassel of a pine as she might have on the shoulder of a child in her school. Once she knelt and felt among thick dark leaves for ivory plums and, finding a few, tossed them one by one into her mouth, and came on quietly, confidently up the hill, through the fence and into the yard at home.

"That you, Kate?"

It was Stephen Blaine who had spoken. He sat on the floor of the porch with his back against a post, his knees drawn up and one crossed over the other, and his hat slanted sharply over one eye. Only his white shirt and necktie and the spray of flowering almond in his hatband indicated he recognized this as an occasion.

Kate did not gasp, even though it was three years since he had last sat here, and one and over since she or anyone in Derwich had heard from him.

"Steve! For the Lord's sake! Whoever heard tell of you!"

She took him by the shoulders and shook him warmly. His hands reached up and closed hard about her waist. They beamed at each other. There was no constraint nowadays between Stephen Blaine and Kate Bragdon; they were friends.

"What's this? You still a slipperstick? Why don't you take on a little fat?"

"You're fat enough for both of us, I must say. Well, my land, where's father? He know you're back?"

"I don't know. I stepped into the kitchen and didn't see any sign of anybody, so I—"

"Likely he's gone to bed. He gets tired earlier than he used to . . . Well, I never, Stephen! Why couldn't you give anybody a little warnin'? How'd you get here? Come into Porchmuth and up on the bus?"

"Yes. Sure."

"Not very handy, now trains don't stop at the Junction any more."

She broke off and stood looking down at him. His father had died just after he went away, and Catharine, too, had gone since anyone had known where he was.

"You been home, have you, Steve?"

He bent his head a little, working with one heel to push a twig into a crack.

"Yes, I been there. Stopped in for a wash and to get some clean clothes on." He turned abruptly and sat with his knees spread wide and his elbows resting on them. "Been some changes," he said.

"We'd have sent you word if we could have, Steve," said Kate. "You know that." She did not add what everybody in the neighborhood had thought, that it was nothing short of a crime for one who was the only support of three old people to go away and leave them to shift for themselves and not even let them know where he could be reached. Gus had hauled in every stick of wood they had to burn for three winters now, and Jeff or one of the Dockhams had sawed and split it; and during the time of Catharine's sickness Kate and the Cheney girls had given her all the care she had, sitting up nights and changing her bed and getting nourishment into her whenever they could. It was a poor end for Blaines to come to, but Kate did not speak of it. "We did what there was to do as well as we could, the neighbors," was all she said. "They went easy, the both of 'em."

"So Uncle Thoc mentioned. He said they got along all right. Said it was something that was bound to come to all of us sooner or later, and no use dwelling on it until anybody had to." Stephen's face began lighting up again. "There's one nothing makes any difference to—Uncle Thoc. Don't the years rest light on him, though? Why, he must be way along into his nineties by now, but I don't believe he's forgot a minute of anything that ever happened to him or anybody ever told him about!"

"Cheeks pink as a young one's," Kate agreed. She sat down beside Stephen on the porch step and thought of Thoc, how trim and clean he still kept himself, the Lord only knew how, for the house was filth and clutter from cellar to roof every time she looked into it. "I'd have gone over and cleaned up if I'd known you was coming home, Steve. I try to get over to see to it every week or two but lately—"

"Why, I had hardly stepped through the door when he started telling me about that time Shem Joy's father rigged up in sheets and went into the graveyard one night to try to cure Shem of staying out so late. And when Shem came home, he took the old man with rocks till old Eben had to put for the house at a dead run, or Shem would have killed him, Eben said. That always tickled Uncle Thoc, to think the old man had to make back tracks. I guess it tickled Eben, too. I suppose he thought that Shem of his was quite some young fellow."

"Yes, Thoc likes that story. He tells it to me and chuckles away over it."

After a minute she said: "Am I supposed to wait until you get around to speak of where you've been and what you've been up to since all the rest of the soldiers got home? Or is it all right to ask?"

He turned his head towards her. It was so dark now that she could scarcely make out his features, and the wonder was what he could see in her face to study so long and so soberly on.

At last he said, "You can ask, but I don't know where to begin to tell you, Kate." Then he smiled suddenly and bent again over the new grass at his feet. "Why—I had a chance the very day I was mustered out to ship on a cattle boat going down to Rio. Fellow I was with was one of the crew and he heard there was a berth open, so he got me on. We took a night train to New York and shipped in the morning without time for a thing but a cup of coffee and a handful of doughnuts; even went on board in uniforms. It was a great trip. Hurricane took us, down off the Brazil coast, and put us high and dry on a reef. Boat's there yet, I suppose, but we got every head off, men and cattle both, and loaded onto another old hulk that didn't look as if it would keep afloat an hour, but it got us down to Rio and back up the west coast to San Francisco as neat as you please. Funny thing what a lot of travel that old tub had in her."

"How Thoc will love to hear all you've got to tell about!" Kate said.

"I've done some flying," Stephen said. "Not at the controls. Just with other fellows. You know that's the coming thing."

"That's what father says. He says the country is going bankrupt building roads and by the time they're all built there wouldn't anybody be seen using a road."

"He does! Why, the old geezer! I wouldn't suppose he'd look that far ahead."

"You might know he never got where he is by looking behind, Stephen!"

"All right, all right, Katie."

"Well, then! Now go along with your dyestuff. Where'd you do your flying—in France? I suppose you felt kind of afraid you might not get killed."

"I knew if I was going to, I would, and otherwise I wouldn't. Yes, I went around a little over there. But after this last trip, after I got back to California, I met up with a man that was going to buy a ranch somewhere in the Southwest and spent most of a month with him, flying a good deal of the time all around over Texas and New Mexico and Arizona."

"What did he want you for?"

"I don't know. I took it he was a stranger out there. Out for his health, I guess. Chest. Awful homesick, he was. Talked a good deal about it."

"All this time I don't suppose you was homesick any?"

"Me? Oh, yes! Yes, I was. Matter of fact, Kate, I always do a good deal of thinking about the house and things around here, when I'm off. You might be surprised. Means a whole lot to me. The place over home there. I don't know what you'll say when I tell you, but I swear it would have hit me harder to see that house burnt down when I got back than it did to find the folks gone. Now that's a fact . . . I don't know. Some way the place where you belong is part of yourself. And not many people come quite as close to you as that. If you see what I mean."

"Yes. Yes, I see it all right. I'm some the same—"

"I always wonder, what if it might have been hit by lightning—"

"Yes. I'm the same way when I'm off."

"You know, I'll tell you how it seems to me—it seems to me as if the old house is full of everybody that ever lived in it. As long as it stands they can't be dead, even if they're not there. Some way tonight, ma and pa seemed to me as if they were right around somewhere. I couldn't miss 'em out of that house. But once a house has gone—I don't know; it's foolish; but it's kind of like everybody that spent their lives there went dead all of a sudden."

"No, I don't think that."

"No. I know it's foolish—"

"What interests me, you feel that way about your

place, and still you're all for going off and leaving it!"

"It is funny, isn't it? You wouldn't understand that. The thing of it is—after I've been here awhile I kind of—well, it feels as if I was getting homesick for somewhere else, some place, likely enough, I never laid eyes on. It is funny . . . But I've got an idea I've made my last splurge, Kate. I guess this one was my last."

"That's what you said when you come back from setting up steam shovels all over the globe. In 1913."

Then Gus's voice broke in upon them through the open sitting-room window.

"Kate! Ye goin' to palaver out there all night?"

He had spoken from his bed, and sounded half asleep. Kate looked at Stephen.

"He don't know it's you," she said. "I didn't suppose we were talking loud enough for him to hear. His ears are not so quick, near, as they used to be. But I suppose that window being open—well, maybe you had better go, Steve. You need your rest, too. Come over again as soon as you can. You and Thoc come over for supper tomorrow night."

"Could do that, Katie."

"Well, it'll suit us fine. I'll be back from Lovice's in time to bake some biscuits, and maybe the young ones can find strawberries enough for a meal."

They stood together, smiling, their eyes on a level.

"Glad I'm back?"

"Awful glad, Steve. This is a different place without you dropping over."

He felt for her hand almost wistfully. He had these times when another woman would have cried over him. She gave him back a firm, warm pressure.

"Why didn't we ever get married, Katie? Was it because I was never around long enough?"

"No. It was because we're not the marrying kind."

"I suppose you're right. I think an awful lot of you, though, Kate. Don't you forget that."

"I guess that goes both ways, Steve."

"I'd like to do something for you," he cleared his throat, "any time I could."

He was always saying this when he was near her, and always meant it. The barrier between them lay in his not knowing what and how to do. She did everything so well, was so self-sufficient and so proud she never seemed in need, and he did not have eyes to see beneath the seeming.

"I know that, Steve," she said. She had long ago passed the time of struggling to tell him how she needed him, that sometimes her arms grew very tired from carrying weapons and tools a man could handle better. She had never had words for it, and he could never believe it. He would understand only if he could see for himself, and she had realized for many years now that he never would. She gave it up. What she had managed for half a lifetime she could finish out with. "I know that, Steve, and I appreciate it," she said cheerfully. "Well, good night. Keep in mind we're expecting you and Thoc for supper."

He gave her a military salute, and walked smartly away out the driveway. His walk had not changed since he was eighteen, his feet were as nimble and his back as straight as ever; one of the Brace-back Blaines, he was.

Kate felt smilingly for the doorknob and turned the key in the lock behind her. The kitchen table was littered with dishes, but she would leave them until morning, not to keep her father awake. As she went through the sitting room, past the half-open bedroom door, he spoke again.

"Who was out thar with ye?"

"Well, father, I guess you'll be surprised when I tell you. That was Stephen Blaine."

She heard a sudden movement among the corn-husks.

"Stephen Blaine!"

Laughing, she went and stood in the doorway.

A moon was coming up, and the light crept thinly across the dark blue, polka-dotted spread on the bed. Gus's knees made a hill under the covers as he lay on his back; they were too stiff to stretch flat late years. His head looked big and hairy against the pillow, all his features blotted out by the dark.

"Wouldn't you know that would be the way he'd turn up?" Kate asked. "There he was, just sitting on the porch when I got back from Lovice's, as if he'd been there at the same time last night and the night before. It gave me quite a start for a minute."

"So he's back ag'in; like enough with the soles a-flappin' on his boots."

"No. He looks real up-and-coming."

"Well, if he is, it won't last long. It's such ones as him that ends in the poorhouse. His father and mother come nigh onto it. . . . Where's he been to this time?"

"South America."

"Hm. Now I s'pose he thinks he's better off, one way or 'nother."

"I guess he's had a great time of it. Do you lay warm, father? Quite a breeze coming in that window."

"Yes. Yes, I'm warm enough. Ye might put a comforter over the bedpost thar where I can ketch holt of it without gittin' out of bed."

"This blue one?"

"No, no. That's too heavy. All anybody can do to turn over under it. One of them old ones. One of them your mother made. Thar, hang it up thar."

"I suppose you'll want to hear from Lovice."

"What say? Lovice? Well, she git along all right?"

"Yes. She was pretty sick, but she's all right now. The young one is a boy. A real nice sound one, he seems to be. They've got him named. James Aaron, they're going to call him."

Gus, who had only been half listening, stirring about and settling himself, went suddenly still.

"James Aaron?"

"I suppose it occurs to you who it's for."

"Plain enough who it's for," said Gus. After a minute he made an amused sound. "I'd give suthin' if the Elder had lived to hear that," he said. "That would have made him cuss if nothin' else ever did, thinkin' he couldn't even have a young one named after him but a Bragdon had to git in on it too, and spile it all."

Kate laughed.

"I'd better shut your door," she said. "There's such a draught."

Gus made another sound.

"I s'pose Lovice referred to all the great-grandfathers she's willin' for a young one of hern to have," he said. "But I thinks likely a couple of other ones, anyway, has stirred a little suthin' into this dish."

2

"But, faith be king, they had to sink her," Thoc Blaine said one winter night some years later.

He was about as old now as men ever live to be, but did not look it. He sat low in the arketty-vine, bending forward with his hands crossed on the gold knob of his cane, nodding emphatically at the end of every sentence. It was below zero outdoors, and the cold came up through the floor and down from chambers which were all but open to the weather; but fire sizzled over the green wood which filled the stove, and five or six men lounged around it and Thoc—Stephen and Harvey and Jeff, and Charlie Hamilton and two of Fred Dockham's boys. They were here every night, or others who took their places.

"Yes, sir," said Thoc. "You'll find there always is that kind, some way. Jeddy never could lay eye to a boat and let her ride. No, sir, by the faith, he'd got to sink her. Couldn't leave her alone; got to sink her. Sunk mine all right. Now 'twasn't he had anything against me. Jeddy and I, why, we got along like twin peas in a pod. I'd have trusted him as far as I would any of you. Unless it was a boat I wanted to keep afloat. Then seemed as if he was possessed—"

"Kind of like a taste of liquor, wa'nt it, Thoc?" asked Charlie. "I know how that is. A man that's got to drink has got to drink, that's all about it; and they can law and more law, but if a man's dry, he's goin' to git him a swaller of something some way, and nobody needn't think he ain't."

"Like old Ab Selden said, the foolish one, time he run off down to Porchmuth and watched 'em heave anchor on a boat," said Harvey. "The sailors was a-pullin' and a-haulin', and they kept yellin' 'Hey!' and 'Hy!' and 'Hey!' and 'Hy!' back and forth. And old Ab, he stood there watchin', and he says, 'Well, ye can "hey" and ye can "hy" till the day ye die, but ye'll never git *that* great long crooked piece of iron up through *that* little hole!' "

"Yes," Thoc chuckled. "Yes, sir, faith be king. Ab knew enough to know that, so he wasn't as foolish as he might have been."

"I've heard 'em say Ab was a pretty quiet feller," Jeff said, letting out a long breath of smoke and spitting into the ashes in the front of the stove. "Never one to talk much."

"Sho!" cried Thoc in delight. "Ab was quiet enough. He come pawing around the kitchen where his wife was to work one day, and then he went into the shed and she heard him hunting around; and then he come back into the kitchen, opening up all the cupboard doors, and at last she said, 'Well, Ab, *what's* got into you? What *are* you s'archin' after?' And Ab says, real pleasant and kind of absent-minded, 'That ar rope. I'm looking for a rope.' 'Well,' she says, says she, 'what have you got to have a rope for, now?' 'Why,' Ab says, real patient, 'for Ikey, mother. Ikey's fell in the well.' "

These were not new stories. They had been told in this room a thousand times. Familiarity made them all the better and the funnier.

"Harve here is kind of a slow, quiet feller, too," grinned Charlie, "but I guess you wouldn't be that long gittin' a rope down to one of your young ones at such a time, would you, Harve? Leastways, not if it was this last one!"

"Yes, how's that little wildcat of yours comin'?" Floyd Dockham asked. "Last I heard of him he was about ready to lick you, accordin' to your tell."

They all laughed. Harvey reddened, but the flush could not drown the satisfaction in his eyes.

"Well, now he's a tough little davil, just the same, for four years old," he said. "When he gits mad, he ain't nothin' for a woman to handle. You ought to lay your hand on the muscles of his legs. Now, I tell you, they lump up like a man's. Lovice, she can't keep him rigged out in clothes big enough, and that's a fact. His last coat was an eight size, and I'm tellin' you he won't be able to git it on a month from now to save his soul."

"Don't you worry about that coat, Harvey,"

Stephen said. "I've told you and you hear to it. We'll be through sawing the Plaisted lot by a week or ten days from now, and Jim and I are going to take a trip to the village and see what we can see. Jim and I, we got that all planned. He'll have a coat, and I believe there's a pair of rubber boots on order too. Hip rubber boots at that."

"They'll be long ones if they reach to his hips," said Jeff. He nodded gravely at Charlie and the Dockhams. "Big feller all right," he said. He shook his head. "Awful big feller for four years old."

"Funniest thing about that young one," said Harvey, "the ways he's got with animals. Ye know, there ain't a cutter on the place that he can't handle better than I can. Now that's a fact. I've got a horse over there that never was more than half broke and don't act as if she knowed a thing; but Jim will into the field every time he sees her grazin', and she'll come right up to him and foller him wherever he goes, if he'll let her, into the barn or anywheres else. . . . I've heard 'em say my mother was a good deal that way. Must be suthin' some folks is born with."

"Like them fellers at circuses," Charlie said. "You know they'll go right into a cage with a wild animal and make nothin' of it. Or take them women that handle snakes; wrap 'em around their necks, they will."

"But now about this little fellow of yours, Harvey." Stephen said. He paused and shook his head. "I don't know. Seems to me as if the darnedest thing about him is the music he's got in him. Why, I never heard anything like it, the voice that young one's got."

"Master pretty voice," said Thoc. "Master pretty. Clear and sweet as a harbor bell. I always get him to singing every time he comes over here. Oh, he's always running off over here to see me, you know. Yes, by the faith, he and I, we make quite a pair. I tune up my old fiddle, and he'll sing to it or he'll dance; one's just as easy as the other for him. And he can fiddle, too, if he ain't any more than a baby. Oh, mind you, that young one had never laid eyes on a fiddle the first time he came over here and before he went home that night he was a-fingering and a-scraping at a tune."

"Well, all of 'em over to the house has got music in 'em," Harvey said. He thought more of the size of this third boy and how handy he was already about the place. "It come down from the Grays to be quick at a tune."

"Yes, but now this is nothing ordinary, what this boy's got," insisted Stephen. "I've been around enough to know—"

"You know singin', don't you, Steve?" nodded Charlie. He had to break this up, about that little

Jim of Harvey's, or it would go on all night. "You're like my father. He tells how Mat and Flo Cheney went over by the house one evenin' raisin' up their voices, and he didn't know what could be makin' such an infernal racket. He says he thought for a while it was the cutters gorin' one another to death in the barn, and then it come to his mind he didn't have but one old cow, and so he knew it must be the Cheney girls."

"None of them Cheneys could ever carry a tune."

"They was all for education. Malachi, he set out to study law, but I guess he never got further than usin' some big words. I remember hearin' about somebody stoppin' to talk to him on the road one day, but he was in a great rush and couldn't linger. He told 'em he'd just recalled that he had three fleeces of wool in his woodshed chamber and he was afraid if left there longer, they would create a spontaneous combustion. And with that he marched off and left the feller standin' there in the road with his mouth hung open."

At the end of every story laughter shook the group in a kind of spasm, as if they had tried their best to keep it back, but it came rumbling out in spite of them.

"Speakin' of learnin'," Harvey said. "I s'pose you've heard we won't have no school up here after this year."

"I've heard there's talk of closin' it up," Jeff answered. "They have in mind to haul what young ones there is into the village next fall."

"Be pretty tough on 'em to go that fur through all kinds of weather."

"Yes, 'twill. You're right. 'Twill, sartain."

"Put Kate out of a job, won't it?"

"Looks like it."

"Oh, they don't intend to leave us anything up here. Them down to the village, they think they're it and all. They'll come up here to git our taxes, but anything else that's needed we can go down there for. We can't make any headway against them and they know it, because no matter how many acres a man owns he only gets one vote to cast. A feller workin' in the shoeshop and livin' in a company house can vote as heavy as we can for what is goin' to be done with our money. Now that never seemed right to me; you know it?"

"They try to make out this way of doin' about the schools will be better for the young ones."

"Sure they do. They're smooth-speakin'. Anything they want is the best way. What I say, I say a neighborhood without a school is loose hung together."

They went on from this to other matters, and other stories. There was the question of town meeting, due next month, and how it was likely that the roads would be by then. Jeff said he didn't hear anything at home but that Bertha would have to have a new hat to wear to it; Bertha was a village girl, one who had sat on her porch and smiled as wagons drove down the main street from upcountry until even Jeff took notice of her, and it was Jeff she had been aiming at especially all the time; Bertha could not go into town unless she looked just so, not even in mud time. Stephen told of the rattlesnake which had sung behind his heels as he sat on the side of his bed in Texas, putting on his shoes, and of how adventurers in the Yukon valley carried bits of their luggage over a steep and rocky path so near the edge of a cliff that it was only by digging in their fingernails that they kept from slipping off and over the side, and then left the first bit and went back for more, each traveller making the trip five or six times. Someone knew a funny story to offset every serious remark. A train whistle reminded them of Luke Butler, a man who had died long ago, but was still remembered because in his simplicity he had said, expressing some deep-seated, inherited nostalgia, when he heard the first train whistle on a winter night, "G'ove us, I wisht I was aboard of her, a-goin' to England!"

It ended as it always did, by Thoc tuning up his fiddle and playing a jig or two for these bearded men in overalls who lounged around the kitchen stove in this crumbling house which had at one time sheltered a very different company and listened to very different but never any gayer music.

3

The fall the schoolhouse did not open and the lummocking blue bus became something to be reckoned with on the highway was a new kind of fall for Kate Bragdon. She made no show of her feelings on the last day of school in June. The children were put through their recitations quickly and sent home to be dressed in their best for the speaking as usual, and though she noticed that more parents came than in many years to the exercises, she did not speak of it, but showed them quietly and pleasantly to their places. She sat serene while the small, shy voices spoke the familiar verses, and made her usual grave speech before awarding the prizes. She saw tears shed, but shed none herself, and when there was talk that the children would never get into a bus if it hung around waiting for them a hundred days, she hushed it up.

"Come, come," she said, "these young ones have no time to be taking up cudgels for the neighborhood. Getting their lessons is their business. If there's any fight put up, older ones will do it."

But she knew the elders never would; they had no cudgels to take up; they were mute before the glib tongues of the villagers. This was the end of the district school, as there had been an end to all the other district responsibilities, and it might be a good thing, but Kate did not think so, and Gus did not think so; and they were Bragdons of the Bragdons who had held the reins well from away back, and now had no reins to hold.

"Stand," said Kate, from behind the desk.

The children stood, nine of them, the little boys in short tweed pants, white blouses, and plaid ties, the little girls in flowered dresses and choice ribbons. Their faces were solemn, their eyes hanging on the Teacher.

"March," said Kate.

They passed through the entries where the caps and straw hats hung, and the round tin dinner pails and brown leather lunch boxes lined the floor, and out into the yard. It was June. The air was sunny and sweet. The garden the girls had made was on one side of the path, that of the boys on the other; the girls had a much better garden.

"Salute the flag," said Kate.

They tipped up their heads to look at it where it floated from the top of the pole. Thoc Blaine could tell a story of when that pole was cut and what had happened at the first flag-raising. Now they had had the last one. The edges of the gauze were tattered as if it had been to battle, and the ink Herman Linscott had thrown on it in spite one day still showed dark; perhaps some of these little ones thought such a blot was a part of the American flag. A soft white line ran beneath every upraised chin and along every lifted arm.

"I pledgeallegiance to my flag and to the country for which it stands, one nation indewillable with libertenjustuce for all!"

"That will do," said Kate. "Martha, it's your turn to lower."

"I want to lower it," said James Aaron.

It was the first time he had spoken all day. He was only a visitor at the exercises and stood beside his mother, a stalwart child with big, proud-setting head and firm, full mouth, a child to turn back to and watch. His words were not a request, more a remark, almost an order. Martha, a tall little girl, paused with her hand on the rope and looked in alarm from him to Kate.

"No. It's Martha's turn," said Kate. She spoke easily, as if tomorrow would bring its turn for someone else.

"When she gets it down, I'll pull it up," said James Aaron gravely. "I'd rather pull it up than pull it down. You'd have to be awful strong to pull it up."

"Yes, you would," said Kate. "All right, Martha."

Martha unwound the rope carefully from the coil, holding it firm above with her left hand. The flag could not have felt the loosening until the very end. Then she let it down slowly. All Lovice's children had a sense of the dramatic. At last the red, white and blue breadths fell billowing into her arms, and three other children came to help her fold it. Kate held the canvas bag while their small, warm hands pushed it in.

"The next time it goes up, I'm going to pull it up," said James Aaron. "I can. I'm plenty strong enough."

All the mothers were crying. The fathers who were there looked another way.

Kate got through that day very well. But when the fall came and there was no need for her to do her canning, as much of it as she could, before Labor Day, and if she rose at her usual time her days were empty after ten o'clock, then she noticed a difference and knew it was a new kind of fall. She did work about the house which had been waiting for years—sorted out old papers and magazines Hannah and Sarey had headed up in barrels, built shelves in the milkroom, and varnished all the chamber floors, made new clothes for herself and Lovice and the children and new covers for the chairs—and spent more time than ever at the Blaine place, trying to patch it up, but still there was no end to her days.

Now she found what the woods meant to her. Since she was twenty years old she had known them as a solace and an occupation; now she came to recognize them as her love. It was not a thought; it was a feeling, and began small in her, like the son she might have had, like the soft shine which spreads for a schoolgirl's eyes over everything some schoolboy's hands with their neat, clipped nails and hard young knuckles have touched, like any seed which lies trembling in an earth pocket where no one can see it, biding its time. It was something which came to Kate because so much else had been taken away from her and the soil was too rich to go sterile. She or her father already owned most of what little virgin timber was left in the country, but now lots which had been stripped in Kate's childhood were coming in thick and strong, and little pines spotted even the Aaron Bragdon fields black. Kate watched them eagerly, and bought what she could. These trees felt real to the touch. They had a rich, stout smell. They were alive and growing. Nothing but weather and fire affected them, no change in style or policy, no shift in population. Once they were hers she could hold them. She gave them her protection and they gave her theirs, which was much greater, a careless protection, kindly enough, grave, powerful, one she had to come close to and ask for humbly or would not get, one even she could feel small beside and look up to, only half understanding, content not to quite understand. Nothing conquered the woods. Men cleared a patch of land to live on, but it was never many generations before the woods took it back. Fire went through one summer, and by another spring alders and sumac and huckleberry bushes had turned the black to green again and the twin leaves of little maples broke the ground. The sawmill came, roaring, coughing, whistling, piling up red sawdust, and trees lay in tiers of boards, but the woods were not dead. They stood about like Indians with folded arms.

Sometimes it happened that Gus and Kate went onto a lot together, but more often he went his way and she went hers from the edge of the clearing where they left their team; and generally, late years, Gus did not go into the woods. He could not walk as far as he wanted to; his legs were stiff, and it took his breath; but he did not complain or seem to notice it, indicating in no way that he realized age was creeping on him. Kate knew the woods as well as he did now, was how he put it, and she had nothing else to do; let her watch the boundary lines when there was sawing going on. He had business every few days at the village, and dealers were always taking up his time. Every night there was the figuring, and every day there was the farm to see to, the plowed pieces, the mowing, the pastures, and the barn. At seventy-five he still went to market Friday mornings, climbing in and out of his wagon at the door of every customer. The doctor's wife and the Perkins girls and Old Phil Tubbs's sister noticed very little difference in him from forty years before; Mr. Bragdon had always brought the sweetest butter and the biggest, brownest eggs they could get anywhere; of course they had to pay him more, but it was worth something that his count was never short and his change did not need watching. Few in the village wondered at him. His kind of riches did not mean much to them down there; they forgot he had them. There were neither bay windows nor wooden lace trimmings on his house; he did not even own a car, but drove click-clack, click-clack behind an old horse, on steel rims, over the pavement; his coat was green across the shoulders and his shoes cracked with polish. "Too much," he told the storekeepers. "Too much. All foolishness. Keep it. I'll go without, fust." He did not mind that the small, dark-skinned boys who lived in the tenements above the stores hooted after him as he rode away. "Git along," he told his horse amiably. "Come. Git along." He was toothless now, and had never visited a dentist in his life. When a tooth ached, he pulled it out. Sometimes they came hard; then he took a chisel and a hammer, standing in the doorway to spit the blood across the porch into the grass. "Hm," he would say, coming back to put away his tools. "Must be hot today. I'm all of a sweat. Can ye see to read how much 'tis on the thermometer, Kate?" His sight was not all it had been once, and Sarey's old glasses did not help much, though he sometimes put them on for looking at his paper.

At Lovice's the young ones grew older every year. Evelyn took a vacation from her typewriting in Porchmuth and went on a visit to her great-aunt Roxan in Fall River. Ed McIntire had deserted Roxanna, stable, children, and all, long before, and left her nothing to do but marry Cyril Bannister. With his savings and the proceeds from the McIntire property they had gone into partnership with Cyril's brother in Fall River. Now both Cyril and his brother were dead, but Roxanna lived on, a magnificent ruin in her weeds and sables, with a diamond clover-leaf setting off the velvet ribbon she wore about her throat. With Minnie to keep the house and Mabel to run the shop and the other children scattered, she lived in modest luxury on the second floor of an old house with a walled-in garden, near a hospital where she could withdraw for treatments as often as she liked, and wrote home glowing, plaintive letters to Derwich. Evelyn went to visit her, found work in a law office, and stayed. Later Lillian went to visit Evelyn and met the man she was married to within six months. From then on Lovice grew more and more restless. She pitied Clyde that he must stay inside so much just because it was too hard for him to turn the wheels of his chair on rough ground. She worried about the children riding to and from the village every day through the fall and spring, and dreaded the work of moving into town every winter. But most of all, as Maddy began to grow up, she was concerned about Maddy.

"I don't know what in the world to think about that young one," Lovice cried. "She ain't a mite as ever you or I was, Kate, or Evvie and Lil either. I'm sure we was all glad enough to get what education we could. But now here's Harvey and I wearin' our fingers to the bone, tryin' to get her into the Academy and keep her there. And Evvie sends her money and Lil sews for her, so she has just as much to do with as anybody else in school. But do you think she cares a tinker's dam about it? No, she don't. She will not study and she will not try. There, I don't know, sometimes I'm ashamed to death of her. For a fact, Kate, sometimes I doubt if she's as bright as she might be."

"Bright enough when she went to school to me," Kate said.

"There!" Lovice cried. "Now was she, or did you favor her? That's what I want to know."

"I didn't favor any of my scholars," Kate said. "I couldn't afford to. I should as soon have jumped into a hornets' nest. Maddy is bright enough. Maybe she can't quite come up to Ev but she's full as bright as Lil, if not brighter."

"Then all I can say," sighed Lovice, "is she don't act like it." Rocking on the porch in the summer evening, she added suddenly, "Kate, I'll tell you. What worries me is I wonder if she don't take some after—well, her grandmother Linscott!"

Kate laughed, hugging her knees on the top step, her hair smooth and her face placid.

"Lovice, you don't really mean to say—"

"I don't mean to say anything. God knows I want to think well of her if I can. But if she ain't crazy after that Thibedeau boy over here on the Berias Blaine place, then I miss my guess, now!"

"He's ten years older than she is."

"Well, and since when has that much difference in age helped anything?"

"They're nothing but neighborly."

"That's what I hope, but think if it should go farther. A Frenchman!"

"Why not a Frenchman? He's a good, steady fellow."

"That's got nothin' to do with it. Stop and think, Kate. A Frenchman in my own family!"

"You always have to rush ahead so, Lovice, heels over head. Maddy's not old enough to marry. It never entered her head—"

"That's all you know about Maddy's kind!"

"How do *you* know so much?"

"Kate!"

"Well, don't slur out at me like that. If I

don't know anything about such things as you've got on your mind, then keep still to me about 'em."

"Kate, I didn't mean—"

"And what's more, don't be so suspicious. That'll do more harm than good. Maddy's young and full of spirits. She likes to be outdoors and on the go. That's natural enough. And Freddie's got red cheeks and blue eyes, and he's around. What can you expect?"

"I expect what I get, but that don't make me take to the idea any pleasanter," sighed Lovice. "I know it's just as you say, but it hadn't ought to be so. Maddy ought to have other ones to think of besides him." She rocked anxiously. "I shan't take it layin' down anyway. I'll fight as hard as I can. I'm goin' to get her away from here. I'll tell you what I'm goin' to do. I'm goin' to make Harvey get him a job up to Fall River, and move us up there!"

Kate straightened.

"Lovice Bragdon, you wouldn't do such a thing!"

"Well, I guess I would, too!"

"Leave your own home that you've been all these years getting together—"

"What's that compared to givin' Maddy her chance?"

"A city's no place for a man like Harvey—"

"He can fit to it."

"What can he do? How'll he keep you going?"

"He's a good hand at carpenterin'."

"You think he can go to Fall River and start right in carpentering—"

"Aunt Roxan knows folks. She could help us to get started."

"So you're veering back to Aunt Roxan, after all you've had to say about her!"

"I never said a word!"

"You might as well."

"Anyway, that's another reason I want to get up there. I want to see after my other young ones." Lovice was crying now. "You can't seem to see how 'tis with a mother."

"I can see you're bound to go," said Kate.

"You think it's for myself," sobbed Lovice. "Well, it ain't. It's for the young ones. It's for Maddy so she won't tie herself down to a foreigner with no schoolin' and all he knows is how to chop wood and dig in the ground and whistle. And it's for Evvie and Lil that's up there so far away from me into nobody knows what kind of life. And it's for Martha, to save her all this strain of gettin' back and forth to school. You know yourself she ain't never been strong. And it's for Jim; for his music. Think what it might mean to that young one, Kate, to get the right kind of teachin' for his voice."

"The rest of us have sung without teaching," Kate said.

"Well, we wasn't him and didn't have what he's got, and you know it," Lovice answered, the cords in her neck working as Sarey's had used to.

Kate knew it.

"I can see you're bound to go," she repeated bitterly.

And that fall they went.

Kate made up her mind to it before it happened. It was just one more blow to take without flinching, and she had learned how. She remembered having overheard the boys of her school explaining to one another how best to meet her black walnut ferrule. "Bend your fingers way back hard," they had said. "Make your palm just as bony as you can. Like that. Then it don't hurt a bit. Anyways, not much." They had the right idea. She was calm and very busy picking over barberries and boiling them down for sauce, going back and forth between porch and kitchen, the day Maddy and Martha and James Aaron came over to say good-by to Gus.

From the sinkroom window she watched the three emerge from the pasture pines and come single file along the path through the field. Jim first, eight years old now, with a broad stout body, looking like any healthy farmer's son from his ankles to his neck, but with light feet like—yes, like the Blaines and like Keturah, and with, to top him off, a big head, long and narrow, such a head as would have overbalanced him, despite his breadth of shoulders, except that he carried it so well and proudly; there was something about this boy; no one knew what, but its presence was unmistakable, even a field's width away. Maddy came next, a long, lanky girl with prominent bones and no flesh to speak of, her face lean and burnt almost black from the summer, her fair hair in a shock; she rolled along behind Jim's stride like a colt behind a young master. Martha was last, never so strong as the other two, dainty in her ways; Jim was in overalls and nothing else and still looked the prince, and Maddy had pulled on an all-over apron and a pair of sneakers, but it was like Martha to have, even on moving day, a white dress with a red sash and red kid slippers where she could put her hands on them and come fluttering across the yellow stubble. Kate had stood at this window to watch them running along that path a thousand afternoons before, and before their time it had been something to stir a quick, warm joy in her that Lovice was coming this way, pushing a carriage or pulling a wagon with one or two babies in it, to let them play about the floor here while the sisters sewed or talked or had a cup of tea together. Still earlier there had been Mindwell. Kate could remember the soft, squat figure appearing unexpectedly out of the woods on a winter day when it had not been reasonable to suppose anything could happen but more wind and more snow and night; and how all Sarey's children would crowd this window in breathless eager welcome, fearing for the peppermints in Mindwell's pockets as her skirts whipped about her, and wondering what she carried in the blue-banded lard pail which glittered so when the sun struck it. Sarey and Mindwell had taken a good many steps to lay the course of that path, and for years Ben had spent a day every fall cutting away branches which threatened to join hands across it. Now its use was about over.

"Well," said Kate. "Here you are. How's your mother getting along? Most ready?"

Only the girls came in. Jim had stopped outside where Gus sat on a bench by the door with his stick between his knees and the visor of his black felt cap pulled down over his eyes.

Kate heard Gus say, "So ye're goin' off and leave grandpa, be ye?"

She had never before known her father to mention his relationship to anyone.

"Most," Martha answered. "She and daddy stayed up working hours after you left last night, Aunt Kate, and today we've all been into it. I guess everything will be ready by morning. I packed all my own clothes and a whole barrelful of dishes."

"I don't see why she's in such a rush on that packing," Kate said, "when she's going into a place that's all furnished, as the girls say that one is they've picked out for her."

"Well, she says she might want to send for 'em any time, and she don't want to think of you having to get 'em ready."

"Of course that's thoughtful of her," Kate admitted, "but nobody wants her to get herself down sick before she starts."

"And besides, when Mr. Burton gets a buyer for the place, our stuff will have to be cleared out quick."

"Yes, that's so, too," Kate agreed, settling a cover over her kettle of sauce and laying the wooden stirring spoon on the shelf of the stove. "Mr. Burton come with the new sign yet? Your mother said he didn't think the one you had was big enough."

"Yes, he came with it. He came and put it up this morning, between the parlor windows, right where it would show between the lilac bushes. He says he's sure to get a buyer. He says an old house like that is just what a lot of city folks are looking for, for a summer place. Of course it *is* awful nice in summer—"

"How does the sign look to you, Maddy?" Kate asked. "You seem kind of quiet today. What's the matter? Don't you realize that you're about to shake the dust of Derwich off your feet? You ought to be standing on a chair singing."

"Maybe I ought to be," said Maddy, "but I'm not."

Maddy stood with her arms folded on the middle sash of the back kitchen window, looking down along the Lane. Her chin rested on her wrist, making her head jerk as she spoke. Her shoulder blades thrust out the faded, yellow-brown print of her apron.

"No," said Martha. "She's not a bit glad. She's sulky. That's what mama says. She says Maddy don't know when she's well off. All she does is crab around and spoil everything. She don't care if we *are* going to take dancing lessons, and she don't care if we *can* go to picture shows, and she don't care if we *do* have a bathroom, and she don't care this and she don't care that. But mama says just not to pay any attention to her; she's got to go where the rest of us goes, and that's an end to it."

"If she told you not to pay any attention, why don't you do what she told you?" asked Maddy calmly. "You're such a well behaved little girl yourself . . . Sure I have to go, but I don't have to like it." An instant later she whirled from the window and bent on Martha a look as hot as any her Uncle Ben had ever worn. "You get out of here, Martha Linscott," she said thickly. "You get out of this room before I get hold of you, for if you don't I'll give you a slap, and if I do, you'll feel it, and I don't care who knows it! Now *get out!*"

Martha backed in terror through the doorway.

"When did you take up slappin' folks that didn't act to suit you?" asked Kate.

Maddy let out her breath slowly through her teeth.

"You have to slap Martha lately to live with her at all. You can't take it out in talk because she can talk better, and everything she says is right and everything you say is wrong, no matter what 'tis. That is, if it's she and I."

Kate picked over several handfuls of the barberries, letting them run red into the pan. Maddy watched her dolefully.

"I see myself where it would come natural enough," Kate said at last.

Maddy reached into the basket. The berries felt hard and cool to her fingers.

"It's going to be awful for me up there in Fall River. There won't be *anybody* to see where anything *I* do or want is natural. Nobody but dad, and you know as well as I do how he'll be squelched. Why, in a year's time, in a city place, he won't know his soul's his own. He's already getting a kind of a rabbity look around his nose and mouth, and we haven't even started."

"He may stand up to it better than you think. You've both of you got to stand up to it. If living here when they didn't want to didn't take the spirit out of the rest of the family, then living there hadn't ought to take it out of you."

"I don't believe it's the same thing."

Kate did not believe so, either.

"I believe that's what cities do to everybody. They all go soft."

Kate thought so, too.

"But I won't, Aunt Kate. Not if I can help it."

"Of course you won't."

"Nor Jim either."

Kate laughed.

"Nothing could soften that boy. Only thing will be, Maddy, if he don't get to thinking too much of himself. You'll have to watch that because your father and mother are not the kind to. He's pretty hard-headed and strong-willed for a little boy, and that's fine, if it don't go too far. You'll have to watch it."

"I know it. I know what you mean, Aunt Kate."

"That's why I'm glad you're going too, as long as he is. For anything else, I'd have worked to try to keep you here with us. . . . But it wouldn't have done any good. Your mother's got her heart set on putting you in a city high school."

"That's not what she's got her heart set on."

Kate poured water over the barberries and drained it off. Maddy stood against the wall with her hands behind her.

"She's got her heart set on getting me away from here because I like it, and getting me away from Freddie Thibedeau because I like him. . . . You don't s'pose I don't know that. . . . You don't s'pose I can't read what's held right up in front of me. . . . Well, I'll show her something. . . . I'll let her take me away, but I'll make her wish she hadn't. I hadn't thought much about marrying Freddie, but I'll do it now. I'll marry Freddie Thibedeau the minute I'm eighteen, if it kills me, and come right back here to live."

"Seems to me if it kills you, you'll get the worst of the bargain."

"Sure." Maddy smiled suddenly, brilliantly. "But I don't think 'twill!"

Jim came in, banging the door, strewing grass roots across the floor, and stood beside the sink where Kate was at work. Perspiration stood on his upper lip and under his eyes and on his forehead. His hair was very thick and wavy.

"Well, I come to say good-by to you, Aunt Kate."

"You did? Well, you needn't have. I'll be over to see you off in the morning."

"It was grandpa you came to say good-by to, silly," Martha told him, venturing in again in his wake.

"Yes, but while I'm here," Jim answered, "I

might as well say it to 'em both. We'll be in an awful hurry in the morning."

He put out his hand. Kate dried hers on her apron and took it.

"Well, then, good-by, Jim. You come back and see us when you can."

"Yes, I will. You come up there and see us."

"Yes, I will."

"I don't s'pose grandpa can. I s'pose he's too old. That's what he said. He said he was getting too old to travel so far off."

So Gus had at last spoken of his age.

"All the more reason why you'll have to come often to see him. He thinks a lot of you, Jim. He'll miss seeing you around."

"I s'pose he will, won't he?"

"Oh, yes!"

"I s'pose he'll miss having me pick off the potato bugs and count the eggs for him. He says I'm awful handy now to get the cows up, now his legs are giving out."

"Yes. Yes, you are."

"He says I'm the best boy he's got."

"Did he say that?"

"Yes. I s'pose he will miss me. I s'pose you will, too, won't you?"

"My goodness, yes—a dozen ways."

"And Thoc and Steve'll miss me all right. I said good-by to them last night. They'll miss me singing and playing. They like to have me read their books, too. Steve says he's going to send me a lot of Enoch's books. . . . When I said good-by to Thoc and Steve, they cried."

Kate laughed.

"Well, if you're expecting me to carry on as they begun, young man, you'll get your expectations stepped on!" She seized him almost roughly by the shoulders, rumpling his hair, and was amazed to find his head suddenly pushed hard against her and his tears wetting her dress. "Why, Jim! Why, Jamie—Jamie Aaron!"

He stood away from her, unashamed of the tears. They ran fast down his cheeks, and his voice shook, but emotion did not weaken him. His young strength filled the room.

"I won't live up there," he said. "I'll *stay* up there, but I won't *live* up there. I live here. Wherever I go, I'll still live here."

"Why, Jim!" Kate repeated, staring at him. "Why, Jim, I think that's—that's a fine way to do!" Suddenly she saw herself revealed in him, her pride, her power, her independence, her hidden sentiment and need, saw all she was repeated in him and deepened, and saw much which she had never had, for there was no gentle blood in her, no lingering feel of velvet and gleam of china, and no wild, sweet, childish strain of Linscott. All his life this boy had been a wonder to her; now she saw him clear. He was something left of all that had gone to make York Road and the Lane, product of lives without which he could not be what he was, and which, but for him, would soon be dead. He was the last furrow Bragdon, Blaine, Gray, and Linscott had turned or ever would turn, and perhaps the best. She put her hand on his shoulder. "It's—pretty lucky for us that you feel that way. So don't you forget it, Jim. It's a promise."

She urged him ahead of her, with the girls following, through the doorway to the porch where Gus still sat. First one and then another of the three stepped up timidly and kissed him on the cheek. It was, as a matter of fact, the first time they had ever deliberately touched him, or he them. He inclined his head slightly to each one, and when it came James Aaron's turn, fumbled for the boy's stout knee to close his big, stiff fingers on it. Then he pushed back his chair quickly and stood up, peering out under his visor at the sky and fields.

"Well. Got to be gittin' them cows up. Chore time."

They watched him go across the yard and roll open the barn door. He stood in it briefly with his back to them. When he faced about, he swung his stick.

"Take keer of yourself, all of ye," he said. "You

tell your mother. And come home as often as ye can."

A minute later they heard him calling the cattle.

"Co, boss, co; co, co, co."

4

Fall blew away, winter melted, and it was spring again. The real estate agent, Mr. Burton, stopped in one day to ask Kate for Lovice's address, and said he had a buyer for the Gray place, a professor and his wife from Boston; they had grown up in the country and enjoyed spending their vacations there; they liked the woodshed at the Gray place and the good, musty smell of the cellar, the fireplaces and the brick oven, the clover-leaf cupboards, the high baseboards, and the lilac bushes.

"How much will they pay?" asked Kate.

"They say two thousand. Your sister's price was three. I guess I can get the difference split."

Kate had thirty-five hundred dollars in the bank. She sat down that night and wrote Lovice a letter. An answer came within a week, and when Mr. Burton drove by the next time, with a little Polish man he was trying to interest in the Charles Bragdon house, which had been closed up for ten years now, Kate went out to the road and hailed him.

"My sister wants me to tell you she's decided

not to sell," she said. "She and her husband think wise to hold onto it a while longer. Some of the young ones might want a place to come to. . . . But she'd like to rent through the summer. You might take that up with the professor."

"I don't think that would suit him. He wants to own."

"Then he can go somewhere else," said Kate, walking away.

"Just like ones up in here," muttered Mr. Burton. "Awful hard ones to do business with. Never know their own minds." Then he caught himself up and turned genially to little Mr. Chernock. "Of course in the case of this place I'm going to show you, sir, it's altogether different. The Charles Bragdon heirs sold out some years ago and the ones that own it now are Massachusetts people, good, sensible folks that know something about business. As I always say, I'd rather do business with somebody that's got a business head, every time. Now I'll say to *you,* I could tell the minute you stepped off the train this morning that you and I would get some place together right off quick. You'll look at this place, and you'll want it or you won't, and if you want it, you'll make terms and we'll have the whole thing settled in time for you to get your seed into the ground right along with the rest of your neighbors. You know, to be perfectly frank with you, Chernock, there's nothing that does so much for a man's contentment and peace of mind as having space around him and some ground to dig in. I don't know, it sure does something for you. Yes, sir, it's great stuff. . . . There now, here we are. House set right in the fork of the roads—roof in fine shape—all the barn needs is a brace or two until you can get around to do more to it—sixty acres of land, including the pasture—on a rise of ground, fine and free—Lord, the air smells sweet out here, don't it?"

Little Mr. Chernock, forever smiling, trod around and around this set of buildings with its broken windows and rotten underpinning, and back and forth across this barren land which would in two months be feathery with wolf grass, the child of pauper fields. Mr. Burton never left him, never stopped talking and gustily breathing in the good air.

Lovice's letter to Kate had read:

It does seem to me you're very foolish to want to put your money into that place, but I know you've got a better business head than ever I had, and if you want to buy it, you must have some good scheme up your sleeve. The more I think of it I don't doubt it is to anybody's advantage to hold onto property now if they can, the way prices are and going up all the time, but I feel as though I've got to have ready money, so if my need can be to your advantage I'll be glad of it. I never was one to begrudge anybody anything, you know that. It is not my way. Even if I can't have anything I am glad if somebody can.

It seems as if things will never straighten out for me. If it ain't one thing it is another. I thought my work would be so nice and handy in a flat, and of course it is in some ways, but I have to lug everything up and down that great long flight of stairs and it does seem sometimes as if my back will break. And I guess I shan't ever get used to so much dirt. I dig from morning until night and still it don't seem to me my house ever looks clean. You ought to see the wash I put on the line twice a week. Of course I have an electric machine and I need it. Lil's got a job now doing substitute teaching and it keeps her busy most of the time so I do her wash and Evvie's, as long as I've got the machine. The machine can't do it all, though, and don't seem as if they realized that. Seems as if this generation of young folks had grown up awful selfish.

I still have that trouble with my back. Aunt Roxan says I ought to have it exrayed and I guess I will as soon as I get the money for the place. It worries me dreadfully, though, for fear of what they may find. Aunt Roxan has been over to the hospital having treatments now for most two weeks and don't know when she will get home, but, as Harvey says, she looks real chipper. It's fine she can afford to pamper herself so. The rest of her family is well as far as we know. We don't see much of them lately. They are having one of their spells of thinking we are from the country and kind of beneath their notice, and I'm sure they are welcome to feel so for all we care.

Jim is doing wonderful with his music. It seems as if it is all he is interested in and he goes right ahead. His teacher says we ought to get him into Boston for lessons, and if he can have a chance, he will be taking care of all of us in fine shape before he's grown up. What do you suppose grammum would have said to hear that? Well, everybody always said the Grays had music born right in them. It looks as if it is coming out in Jim in a big way. I can stand right at my sink and laugh and cry both just to hear him practicing. Then I think about that it is my own young one, and I go kind of weak. I'd give the world and all if you could hear him the way he can do now. Maybe we can get home for a visit this summer. I hope so. But Jim's lessons is going to come first. I've made up my mind to that. Just as soon as you send the money for the place, I'm going to see about him starting in to take in Boston.

Once I start thinking that we are going to sell our house, sell the roof right off from over our heads, as you might say, it seems as if I can't stand it. That kitchen where we all used to set with grammum—do you remember the night Ben got so mad and told how the Bragdons was killing mother? And my parlor that I worked so hard to get and keep looking nice. That was the hardest room to clean the paint in I ever tried. And when I think of strangers digging in my flower garden it seems as if my heart would break. But then, I know I'm that way, one to make an awful fuss over anything I love as I do that place, and I suppose I am foolish. It's a good deal better to be sensible, the way you are, if anybody can. You and father never could see what it was mother and me made such a piece of work about, lots of times, and I've never expected anybody to understand it since she died. I just try to keep my chin up, as Herman told me in that letter he wrote to me, the only one I ever had from him. You have to take life as it comes, and nobody knows that any better than I do, and when it's a choice between Jim's future and anything I own it don't take me long to make up my mind. As I tell Harvey, we got him here and now we've got to do well by him. You can't turn your back on a gift like Jim's, I tell Harvey, just so as you can have a chance to keep your own cow.

Of course we would do just as much for any of the rest of the young ones, but the way it seems right now, it seems as if Jim comes before any of them because he can't wait and they can. Now sometimes we have an awful time with Martha because she has to stop her dancing lessons while he keeps right on with his music. And then she will take on awfully about her clothes sometimes because we can't dress her as well as the best in school in a place this size and it's no use trying. And it don't seem as if Evvie and Lil took as much notice of us now we're here as they did when we was to home. As I say, young folks nowadays are awful selfish. Evvie and Lil seem to need about all they can get their hands on for themselves. (Don't breathe a word of this, but, between you and me, Lil's in the family way. She don't say anything yet but it won't be long before she'll have to. Poor young one, I'm afraid she'll have it awful hard, being as she's so small built. But there, it's no use crossing bridges ahead of time.) As I was saying, when Martha gets on a rampage, I tell her if she'll just hold her horses, Jim will see she don't lose by it in the end. When he's twenty years old, she'll only be twenty-five and she'll like wristwatches and silk stockings as well then as she would now. Besides, it may not be that long. His teacher here says he might get into concert work any time, especially if he gets in with the right ones in Boston. And I say the same to Harvey, too, when he gets blue. I tell them all that this is the time to get behind Jim and, if we do, we won't any of us be the losers.

I don't know about Maddy. She just about drives me crazy. She can't get along with anybody and nobody can't get along with her. She's got the darkest outlook of anybody of her age I ever see. She won't go anywheres and she can't take any comfort to home nor let anybody else. She's just passing at the high school and that's all. She wants to go down and spend the summer with you. That's all she talks about. But I tell her you don't want a Gloomy Gus like her around. I don't suppose you would, would you? Of course she could be of a good deal of help to you. You must have to do most of the work around the place with father his age and his legs giving out so, and more and more of it will come on you, of course, as time goes on. There! There I go again. I never mean to write such blue letters. I declare, they remind me of Aunt Roxan's that you and I used to get into such a gale over every time one come. And how mad that would make mother. The only time she ever hit me in her life, I was laughing at Aunt

Roxan's string of symptoms; I was a big girl too, but I didn't know then what trouble was. Of course it's no use to dwell on it, though.

Clyde's the contentedest here that I ever see him. He loves to go to the moving-pictures. We had him to the Clinic but they don't see much they can do, now he's so old. If they'd had him as a baby it would have been altogether different.

How are you anyway, and all the folks around home? Have the Cheney girls decided to try to sell their place? How's Lucy Hamilton holding out? I said to myself the last time I see her that she would never be out of her bed again. It must come awful hard on Cora to have her sick so long. I only hope when my time comes I'll go quick. How's Jeff's family? I suppose he's working hard as ever. If Bertha was as careful as some, he would get ahead fast. I thought the baby was a darling the last time I see her. Give her a squeeze for me. Every once in a while I come to with an awful jolt to think I don't have a baby in the house any more. You get so used to doing for them that you miss it when you don't have it to do.

Write when you can. We all love to get your letters. And if you see fit to send a down payment on the place I'll see that Harvey has the deed made out to you right off and then you can pay the rest of it when you've got the deed in your possession. I hope you'll make a good deal on the place when you come to sell it. I don't doubt you can get a big price for it, with all that panel work and the wide boards in the floor; they say them old square bricks are awful sought after, too. Likely enough you may get five or six thousand dollars for it. Of course anything old and historic like that takes on value every year. Well, I'm glad you thought of getting in on it for somebody was going to profit by me having to sell and it's nice it's you. I hope you get nice people in, that's all; I should hate to think of foreigners or like that in there.

Now you be sure to write soon. And let me know what you think about Maddy. I don't want you to take her as a favor but if you would have any use for her, I do think a change may be what she needs. She may be just homesick.

I hope this finds you both well, as it leaves us.

Jim wants to be remembered to Thoc and Stephen.

Early that evening as Kate sat in her rocker by the back kitchen window and Gus lay on the lounge and Stephen, at the end of the stove, whittled a small boat from a piece of white pine, Kate said: "I had a letter from Lovice. Jim wanted to be remembered to you, Stephen, and to Thoc."

"He did, eh? Hm. I'd like to see that little fellow. Does he keep at his playing?"

"Yes. And his singing. I guess he's doing fine."

"I'll bet. . . . I'll bet he figures he'd like to get back around here, though."

"I guess he does. They can't transplant him so easy."

"Rest of 'em all satisfied up there, I suppose?"

"Satisfied enough, I guess. As much as anybody expects to be anywhere. All but Maddy. She's restless. I think likely she'll be back to spend the summer with us. Lovice was all high to get her away from here and now she's forgot what it was for. That's just like Lovice. If Jim come into her head, Maddy would have to get out. But I guess Maddy don't mind that."

"Why don't she bring Jim along?"

"He'll have to be at his music. It takes learning to do it right, like anything else. He's got a hard row ahead of him, it looks to me."

"He'll hoe it though. You leave it to him. Now you mark my words. There's nothing that little fellow will stop at, once he's going good. I know. It's just like horseflesh in the races at the fair. I can pick a winner every time. And he's one. Don't you say so, Gus?"

"What's that?"

"Jim. Lovice's boy. I say he's a winner."

"Oh, him," said Gus. He cleared his throat. "Yes. He'll git along."

"Burton got a buyer for the Gray place yet?" Stephen asked, rolling the little boat in the palm of his hand.

"Yes." Kate laughed ruefully. "He's got one all right. It's me. I bought it."

Gus turned on his back with a thump.

"Foolishest thing," he said, "ye ever done in

your life. Poor land and always was, and who is there to bring it back or keep it up? Ye'd ought to knowed better."

"I didn't buy it for the land," said Kate. Bitter amusement marked her face, but her voice was quiet. "Bought it for the panelwork and floor boards and square bricks. Summer folks will be willing to pay a good price in a few years for an old, historic place like that."

"She's right there, Gus," Stephen agreed quickly. "This old stuff is doubling in value every year or two. Why, you wouldn't believe it if you was to take a look at some of the old places down through Kittery and Wells and hear the prices they brought. And if people don't want or can't get the place, they'll pay you a mint for what they can rip out of it. There's men rapping at my door every day or two, trying to buy the house, or the furniture, or even the handles on the chest of drawers and the legs right off the chairs. Why, Uncle Thoc has to keep his feet on the floor and his back against the baseboards every minute or they'd have 'em out of that kitchen before he knew it. Yank the beams out of the ceiling, they would, and walk right off with 'em, any time we said the word. Why, we've been offered five hundred dollars just for the stairs."

"Then why the Sam Hill ain't ye took it?" demanded Gus.

"Holding out for a thousand," answered Stephen promptly. "Besides, Uncle Thoc and I kind of think we want to keep them stairs so we could get up chamber if we should ever need to. Where else would they ever be any more good than right where they set?"

Gus pushed himself to a sitting position and swung first one foot and then the other to the floor. He sat rubbing his knees gently, looking around him. This was the kitchen of his house. He remembered building it. He remembered hauling his trees to mill to be made into lumber. He had put this finish on by night, every foot of it, with Sarey holding the lantern; had to; it was planting time before he got to the finish and he was needed outdoors by daylight. That was the only reason some of the pairs of nailheads were not quite even; he could not see them lately but he knew how they were, and it had happened so because the light was bad, no other reason. He bought that stove for a dollar; no, not that one, but one just as good; there had been no need for a new stove, no need at all; more waste; there was always waste where women held forth and had the say. Most of this furniture he had built himself, the two tables and the chairs; not those chairs, though, at that—why, what in tarnation, had Kate gone and bought new chairs?

"Where'd them chairs come from?"

"They're the ones mother bought as long ago as before she died," Kate answered.

She did not say they had stood in this room ever since. She let him think they had been stored away and just brought out.

Well, there had been no need of them. The old chairs were good enough, good stout chairs made out of hard pine. It had been no small job to get them ready to sit in. He had found no time of evenings to whittle out toys, like Stephen here. When the rest was done, this lounge had to be made. He and Sarey had had quite a tussel with it. He remembered they carried it into the yard to finish it up by sunset light one night, but Sarey had to go in after the lantern and it was ten o'clock before it was done. Then—how was it now?—for some reason they dropped down and slept on it there until morning. It must have been a narrow bed; their bones must have been cramped and chilled before daylight; but young folks take no notice of such small matters. Those were the times when, if he and Sarey walked to or from the Aaron Bragdon place of a Sunday or a Wednesday night, they might as likely as not hear the folks in the church praying for them, maybe in loud voices and maybe with sobs. Well, they might have saved their strength and spent it on themselves. Gus Bragdon was all right. Gus Bragdon was minding his own business, doing his own work and doing it as well as he could; he was safe enough; he had taken a drink out of old Jeddy's jug and left the church, and he had taken other drinks from time to time for one reason or another, but—what was it somebody had shrieked after him? Old Mose Dockham, it was. "Drink makes a devil or a dunce out of every man that puts his mouth to it"—that was what Mose said. Well, it had not made either out of Gus Bragdon. He had shown them. He had proved a man could go his own way and use his own judgment, and if he was all he ought to be, the Lord would have no complaint to make of him. The Elder and Mose Dockham had not known it was no way to get one like Gus Bragdon to go along with them—to try to scare him into it, and thunder out, and threaten. One like Gus Bragdon would not be interfered with; he could take his own chances, and come through clean. The Elder and Mose Dockham had not known that. How would they? But it was likely the Lord did. Anyway, he had been allowed to prosper.

"Now ain't the time to buy," he said. "Now's the time to sell."

"I'll bet that's where you're wrong, Gus," Stephen spoke up to him. "Prices are high, but they're going higher. Especially on what can't be duplicated, like old-fashioned stuff. Anything that's rare is getting rarer all the time. You know that."

Gus paid no more attention than he would have to the twittering of a bird. He unlaced his shoes and pulled them off, grunting, and set them under the side of the lounge. His toes spread comfortably inside his brown stockings. He took out his handkerchief and wiped his face, and heaved his weight to his feet with the strength of the knuckles in his right hand. He was ready for bed.

"Now's the time to sell," he said again, going through the dark sitting room.

Kate and Stephen heard his overalls drop to the floor, the rustle of his harsh mattress, and the squeak of the rope of his bed. He cleared his throat several times, and was silent.

"Signal for me to go, I guess," said Stephen, smiling.

Kate creased the letter which she had been holding thoughtfully, slid it into its envelope, and stood up to tuck it behind the clock.

"Maybe you had better. He gets his best sleep the early part of the night."

Stephen snapped his knife shut and looked about for his hat. She followed him to the door. The sky was clear and full of stars, the air warm. A slight wind stirred the branches of the maples, making wavy shadows on Stephen's face.

"You made me laugh," he said, "talking about buying that Gray place for what it would bring as an antique."

"I made you laugh?"

"Yes. Needn't tell me you'd sell out the Grays to a souvenir hunter. Any more than I would the Blaines."

"You're well known for a sentimental old fool, Steve. I'm a business woman."

"Yes, you're all Bragdon, ain't you?"

"That's it."

"Yes. Like hell you are."

For the first time he had seen through. It was the first time anyone had seen through. Her throat went suddenly husky and her eyes stung. Her hand tried to go out to Stephen. She looked down at him as he stood below her, she on the top step and he on the bottom; his merry, boyish, confident eyes, his wide, warm grin, the bunch of lilies of the valley pinned on his coat lapel. Kate-and-Steve. But that was years ago. He was nearly sixty now, the flesh softening along his cheekbones, his shoulders too well padded. It was too late. She would have the best—the tallest, the straightest, the hardest, the strongest—or nothing. There was ahead for Stephen only to be another Thoc in a house which trembled more and more with every wind that blew.

"You must be a mind-reader."

"Well, I can read yours, Katie."

"We know each other pretty well, don't we, Steve?"

"We ought to."

"That's right. Well, don't you forget to give Thoc Jim's message."

Stephen chuckled.

"No. Say, I'd sure like to see that little fellow. I've got something for him. A couple of rabbits, young ones, I picked up in the woods. I'm tending them till he gets down here some time."

"He'll like that."

"Yes. He's great for pets . . . Well—so long, Kate."

"Good night."

She watched him tenderly as he went, stepping so neat and light, like a soldier to fife and drum. After the dark had shut him off, she could still hear his trim Blaine tread and knew the angle at which he would have tilted his hat.

Left alone, she sat down on the step, hugging her knees and studying the line the woods drew against the sky. Pride went quietly out of her dark face, and humility came in. No human being had ever seen her so; but against the trees, the sky, and the wind she did not need protection, and from them she had nothing to hide.

The woods were the love of Kate Bragdon's life. They were a man who asked no favors but took what he wanted, and did not explain himself. All day, though she did his service about his rooms, she never saw him. It was only at night that he came inside, and even then she did not often catch sight of his face. He sat at a desk with his back turned, his coat still smelling of the outdoors. Sometimes she finished all she could find to do and went away without his having spoken to her. At other times he said from above his papers, "I shall want you tonight." These nights she stayed, and waited for him in another room.

She never saw him in his house by daylight, but there was a sunny slope above the pasture brook where he knew he might find her any morning. Sometimes he came there, and she lay watching him moving toward her, a deep shadow striding across the bright grass.

"You're afraid," he sometimes said, gently.

"No—"

But she was, always, wonderfully afraid.

5

That summer was full of many things.

Thoc Blaine had a stroke and went completely helpless, his mind turned as childish as his face. He felt strange and frightened in the bedroom where the stroke took him, so Stephen brought a small bed from upstairs into the kitchen and laid Thoc on it. He was happy there. Kate came every day and kept him very clean, and Maddy and the Thibedeau girls were always running in with flowers, shells they had found on the beach, or branches of huckleberries for him to pick off. He did not know who they were, but he liked to have them come. He called Kate Catharine and called Maddy Keturah, and sometimes chuckled, asking how they got along now living in the same house. Stephen cooked the meals and fed them to him, and men wandering from habit near the Blaine place at night often heard Stephen's voice singing sea and war songs at the soft pitch of a lullaby. It was a hot summer, and the kitchen windows always stood open, with the old-maid's-pinks and hundred-leaf rosebushes looking in.

"Wonder is he's lived this long," said Gus.

Gus at eighty was older than Thoc had ever been. Sixty years of plowing had bent his back until he could raise his eyes from the ground only by stretching his neck and thrusting his head upwards. He did not often need to. The ground was what he wanted to see. His legs were so stiff that they could barely drag his feet about. Sixty years of figuring had laid deep, sprangled creases in his leatherlike skin; and the drooping of the outer corners of his eyelids now covered half the steel-blue pupils. His hair stood straight up, crisp and gray, above a face well scarred by a long struggle with odds he had never once admitted himself unequal to, and did not yet.

He sat on the porch in the sun when lumber

dealers came, sometimes with a horse blanket across his knees. He felt the cold more and more, even in the summer time. From under the visor of the black felt cap he watched them driving into the yard in their big, glittering automobiles painted up like floats in a parade. He said nothing and made no motion. Even when they called, "Good morning, Mr. Bragdon!", getting out, he still said nothing. He sat watching every movement as they backed around, slammed doors, felt in their pockets, settled their hats, and came sauntering up to him. He offered them no chairs and had none available. They could sit on the steps or they could stand and save the seats of their pants. It was one and the same to him.

Buyers talked more than ever, late years.

"Well, Mr. Bragdon! How goes it? Great old day, isn't it? Pretty hot, though. I'm soaked right through with sweat. Been hiking around the Fad Cheney lot all the forenoon. Awful hike for a hot day. Been into blackberry vines up to my waist. Quite a job for a fat man, getting around a lot as big as that. How far around do you call it, anyway, Mr. Bragdon, around that Fad Cheney lot?"

"Four miles. Maybe five. 'Tain't fur."

" 'Tain't, huh? Well, felt like it to me before I got back to the car. Of course I don't suppose you thought much of it in your day. Folks are softer late years, Gus. Softer. There's been a change in the strain. Now you don't suppose there's a young man alive today that could start in as you did and get to where you've got to, do you? Why, I should say not. No, sir. You took a piece of raw land here, got the lumber off it to house yourself, got food off it to feed yourself and family—and besides that saved up to buy enough property to give you as big holdings as any man in the county. Now that took muscle, Mr. Bragdon, and that took brains. They don't come like you any more. Look at me now. Forty years old and one foot in the grave. Bright's disease. I've had too much meat and sweet stuff to eat. That's what's done for me. Drunk too much bootleg. That's what I've done. In your day a man could make his own cider and drink it whenever he felt thirsty. Back there they didn't have any law a man had to poison himself."

"There was them as would do it, though," said Gus. "Well, what did you make up your mind? Want that Fad Cheney lot?"

"Want to sell?"

"Yes."

This was a new reply from Gus. Always before he had answered he could sell it or keep it, either way. It made the dealer stop in his pacing up and down and shoot a sharp glance at the figure huddled under the blanket. So the old fellow *wanted* to sell!

"Yes, I'm ready to sell," said Gus. "I'm gittin' along in years. I want to clean everything up and leave it neat."

"Well, now, I don't blame you. I don't blame you a bit. That's sensible. Your boy, now, he's never paid much attention to the lumber, has he? They say he's all for farming; good farmer, too, first rate, making it pay even in these times. But no hand for lumber. And the daughters—well, of course, they're womenfolks and you can't get away from it. Take my wife. She and her mother. They don't have any more idea about an investment than you and I would about trimming a hat, not a mite more—"

Gus was not listening, nor pretending to listen. This was the porch he had built as a young man; he sat on it now, an old one, ready to die. Those were the maples he had set out as withes, when Benjamin was a little boy; now they stood forty feet tall and a foot and a half through, holding the house in their shade. He had no time to waste. He had never had, but less than ever now. York Road was a woods road; the end of the Lane, once a gathering place, had become only the corner where the mailboxes stood, seven of them on one board nailed between two posts; seven families on both York Road and the Lane,—two Bragdons, a Blaine, a Cheney, a Hamilton, a Polish Chernock, a French Thibedeau; all the Linscotts had gone to the other side of the Hill. The Aaron Bragdon place was now thirty acres of good growth above the salt marsh, and of all his children only Gus was left. Of all who had known Grou'nut Hill and Claypit, Rolling Rock, The Sands, and Dockham's Bridge as definite points between the highway to the beach and the road to the village, who had surveyed the woods and fought the fires and run the schools and picnicked on Mount Assabenbeduc in crowds of a hundred and more, only Gus was still alive and aware. He did not have much time, and there was a good deal to see to. He had taken sixty years to buy what ought to be sold in one, at the longest. He would clean up everything that was ready. This was the time to sell. Even if he were twenty years younger, he would still want to sell this year. The time was ripe. Prices were high enough, higher than there was any reason in. He would sell.

"I've got one daughter," he said, "could handle my business if she had to. She ain't no figurehead." He chuckled. "You fellers'll be havin' your hands full with her long after I'm gone. She's harder-headed than I be, now I'm gittin' old. Won't nobody take no advantage of her."

"Oh, I don't doubt she's learnt a good deal from you, Mr. Bragdon. But as you and I know, a woman is a woman. And don't you lose courage. You're man enough yet to finish up the handling of your property. You're just right about it, to plan to get it all straightened up right away this fall, and off your mind. Now let's you and I get together on it. I'll make it just as easy for you as I can. This Fad Cheney lot now—what'll you take for it, Gus?"

The dealer dropped down on the step, pulling out a pad and settling it cozily on his knee, his pen poised above. Gus recalled Sarey and her slate as she had sat winter evenings long ago, figuring her egg and butter money.

"What's yere offer?"

"Well, now, that's good lumber, Gus, but of course there's some scrub pine there, under the —"

"I know thar's scrub pine. You and I both know what's on that lot. Now what's yere offer?"

"Ten dollars a thousand on the stump."

"Twelve's my price."

"Oh, now, Gus, you can't get twelve dollars for that Fad Cheney lot. Now some of your lots you might. I'll grant you that. I'm no sharper. I'm a fair-dealing man, and any of them will tell you so. I'll grant you some of your lots might bring you in twelve dollars, but not the Fad Cheney. Ten is top for the Fad Cheney, situated as it is, and with all that scrub pine under the hill."

"Twelve's my price. Take it or leave it."

"Thought you wanted to sell, Gus."

"Do. That ain't to say give it away."

The buyer rose and resumed his earlier walking up and down. The pad went back into his pocket. He would have no use for it today. This deal would not move as fast as he had hoped it would, for all the old man was on his last legs and in a hurry.

Gus sat motionless, his square hands with their thick, ribbed nails folded on the blanket which covered his swollen knees. His face was slightly sad, faintly drawn, but altogether grim with the intent, pleasurable grimness of a fisherman pulling in his line. His eyes stared out across the yard, glinting blue under his bushy eyebrows.

"I'm willing to go with you as far as I can, Gus. I see how you feel about this business, and I'd like to work in with you. I'd sure like to do it, and put you easy in your mind. But if you're going to ask such prices as twelve dollars a thousand for a lot like that Fad Cheney, I can't do it, that's all."

"Can't pay twelve dollars this year to get fourteen next? Hard up, ain't ye? Ye wouldn't cut that lot this year if ye got it, and ye know it. Ye'd hold it for higher rates on lumber."

"Lumber may not go up."

"Ye know lumber's goin' up. Ain't everything goin' up? And you ain't so old but ye've got time to profit by it."

"Likely I haven't got any more time than you have. This Bright's disease that I've got coming on me—"

Gus jerked his head.

"Well. There's them that will have time. Can't ye make up your mind if ye're fittin' to do business, or ain't?"

"You're a hard man, Mr. Bragdon."

Gus said nothing. He studied the trunks of the maples and beyond.

"Now, me, I've got respect for death, and if a man's day is about done I've got a kind of special respect for him. This isn't the time for you and me to put up a bluff, Mr. Bragdon. You and I ought to understand each other, and we ought to put through the fairest deal either one of us ever made. It's something to think of that we may be held to account before long for the way we see this through. It's a solemn matter, standing where we do, Gus. We ought to feel some respect—"

" 'Tain't respect you feel," Gus said. "You're afeard."

He lunged suddenly to his feet, and stood braced against the doorframe, his eyes narrowed until the color of them scarcely showed between the slanting eyelids, his head thrust upward so that he looked full in the dealer's face.

"Ye're as good as dead now," Gus said. "Ye're dead with breath still in ye. But I ain't. I may be gittin' towards the end, but I ain't dead yet; and as long as I'm sellin' lumber, I'm sellin' lumber. Ye hear to that."

He scuffed heavily into the house and shut the door.

Kate heard it go on, week after week. There were a dozen different dealers coming and going, among them Bedford Gibbons, who had bought the Asa Cheney lot after the fire went through it, now a prosperous elderly man, thinner than he had been, with offices in Portland and Bangor and mills all over the State of Maine. It was with Mr. Gibbons that Gus made his final stand, early in September.

"That Nathan Holt lot in Kittery ain't for sale alone," Gus said. "Ye all want that, and ye all want the Simes lot and the Woodbury Dean in Buxton, but ye won't git 'em. Not alone, nor separate. Man that buys the Nathan Holt will buy the Simes and the Woodbury Dean, and the Plaisted up back of the Horse Hills and about five other smaller ones scattered around the woods. They're all goin' to once, or none of 'em is goin' at all."

"Too big a lump, Gus."

"Then let 'em alone."

"You want to sell."

"That's what I say."

"You'll wait ten years before you find anybody ready to—"

"No, I won't. I won't wait ten years for nothin'. . . . But if I can't settle it, Kate will. At the rate lumber's been goin' up the last three years, she'll git half again its present value, too. She won't lose nothin' by it."

"Still you want to sell."

"I aim to clean up my business. She's got enough of her own."

"Well, as I say, it's too big a lump."

"Take it or leave it. That's the way it's goin'."

"What are the small lots?"

Gus named them over.

"Got a price on them?"

"Got a price on the whole. So much a thousand."

"What is it?"

"You name it."

"Set your price, Gus."

"Make an offer."

Inside Kate and Maddy, peeling apples and baking pies, making over dresses and crocheting lace carried on their own conversation in low voices. Maddy was taller than she had been the fall before, but not so thin as when she had come down from Fall River. Her body was still lean, but her face had filled out, her arms were softer, almost round under the silvery film of fine hairs which gleamed when the sun shone across them. She smiled readily, a broad, bright grin, showing her big teeth. She was still careless about her clothes, did not mind that her fair locks blew rough over her head, or there was a smudge on her cheek, or a hole in the heel of her stocking; but unkempt as she was, she had always the clean, almost sleek look of wild birds and squirrels, as if the dew bathed her every night and the sun dried her off in the morning. This was a trait of personality which she shared with Kate, though Kate added to her natural neatness all that she could gain by her own efforts. But Kate could never again have skin quite so gleaming as Maddy's, or eyes so clear blue-white around the dark pupils. There was a difference of nearly forty years.

"I wish he'd go along with his dyestuff. Your grandfather must be tired to death."

"Grandpa'll come in when he feels like it."

"He don't realize how tired he is."

"Well, it's no use to worry, you always say."

"There, I know it."

"Isn't it great, what mother wrote? About Jim."

"Well, I should say it was. But nothing more than we all expected."

"I never s'posed choir boys got such pay as that, though, did you? But, of course, in a place like Fenway Temple—"

"We've got to get up to Boston some Sunday and see and hear him, Maddy. If only it wasn't for leaving your grandfather all alone so—"

"Uncle Jeff and his folks could come over."

"Yes, I suppose they could. But your grandfather

wouldn't like it a mite to find out we thought he needed watching—"

"Wasn't it just like mother to break down and cry when Jim came in, and keep on crying all through the service? Now wasn't that just like her? Everybody must have thought she was crazy."

"I don't know. A lot of people must feel kind of the same way when they see little boys' faces above the white surplices. And if one of 'em was your own—one like Jim—"

"He would look awful handsome, wouldn't he? When you think how he looks in nothing better than an outing flannel nightgown, starting upstairs to bed—"

"Well, we'll have to find some way, as I say, to get up there to Boston."

Sunday after Sunday went by, and on each one James Aaron Linscott, nine years old, sang in the Fenway Temple boys' choir, and soon the Sunday came when he stood alone behind the dark oak chancel and sang a solo, as James Gray and Mindwell Joy had both done from the wooden benches of their time, and Sarey at sixteen, and Kate and Lovice from below Ben's pulpit. All these earlier ones had sung in Nubble Point Meeting-house, now closed; Jim sang in Fenway Temple. But still Kate and Maddy did not go to hear him. With every week it became more plain that Gus must not be left, and that his need might not be mentioned to him. Chairs had to be kept out of his accustomed paths through the house, and rugs cleared away, and canes nearby wherever he was likely to sit down. Only Kate's hand knew how to arrange the cornhusks of his mattress. There was only one angle at which his bedstead might be placed if he was to be able to climb into it and out again. He lived mostly on graham bread, a fresh loaf baked every morning, and hot herb tea. Other excuses than his age and health had continually to be found to prevent his overdoing. Jeff came every other day to work at the harvest and every time Gus showed surprise at seeing him. "Well, Jeff, ye got some spare time ag'in? Why, I s'pose ye can dig some of them potaters, if ye want to. I meant to git after 'em today, myself, but there's somebody 'r other comin' to see about a lot." Every Friday morning Gus said: "S'pose ye can take the stuff to market today, Kate? There's things I got to see to 'round here." Sometimes he added, but not often, "I'm gittin' too crippled up to use a horse and wagon as handy as I used to." Kate might go to market in the morning, and Maddy to the moving pictures with Fred Thibedeau in the evening, and once in a while they went out together for a few hours, barberrying or cranberrying, but usually one or the other of them was at home, and neither was ever away for long. Of all Gus's canes, they were his stoutest, and he never knew it.

One morning in October, Bedford Gibbons drove into the yard soon after eight o'clock. Gus had just come in from the barn and sat by the stove, his arms hugging the heat. He turned stiffly in his chair and peered out at the familiar green and chromium car.

"Good land!" said Kate. "He's around betimes."

Gus opened the small door in the front of the stove and spat into the ashes, then felt about behind him for his hickory stick. Maddy slid it within reach of his hand.

"Now, father," Kate said, "I hope you don't think to go outdoors to listen to him as early as this, this time of year. You'd be chilled through in five minutes. Now you set still and let me bring him in here. Maddy and I can keep out of your way."

Gus did not answer. He took down his fleece-lined coat from the nail, his cap and mittens from the mantelpiece. They were clothes he had worn hauling logs out of snowy woods ten years before; now he needed them for a sunny morning in October. He pulled them on jerkily, breathing short, stopping between times to rest his weight on the back of the chair. Mr. Gibbons had knocked a second time, but Gus gave no sign to Maddy that she might go to the door. His hands, inside the mittens Sarey had knit and Kate had patched with canvas until none of the yarn was left, felt clumsily for the knob. The house was meant for eating and sleeping and women's affairs. A man did his business outdoors.

"Well, here you are. Thought I'd caught you napping for once. Well, nice snappy morning, isn't it?"

"Good mornin' enough."

"How you feeling, Gus? Had you ought to be outdoors?"

"Feelin' all right. What ye here after?"

"Well, Gus, I'm here after wood lots. I'm here to come to an understanding with you. I'm all ready to do business. If you and I can get together, I'll take you right down to the village in my car and we'll have it all signed and settled before noontime."

Kate and Maddy at the window saw the two standing side by side, Bedford Gibbons pompous and easy, soft and pink-skinned in his loose-cut tweeds, his pale gray felt hat, his shiny russet shoes, Gus's body stooped and shrunken, his legs swollen, his clothes poor and streaked from much washing, but his eyes looking out hard and sure from his old brown face. The glittering car beyond them belonged to Gibbons, and everything else belonged to Gus: the floor they stood on, he had built; the shed, the barn, the trees were his, the woodpile, the pump, the cornstacks and the pumpkins, the very dirt and little stones and the water in the marshes, even thirty acres of sky. He felt for his chair and let himself down until he sat in it, and pulled the horseblanket across his knees.

"Well, what's yere offer?" he asked. "Shut that door thar, ye might."

Kate and Maddy heard nothing further except an occasional word or two, not enough to tell them what was going on; but both understood that it was something more than usual. Bedford Gibbons told no long stories. He sometimes sat on the step and sometimes stood, but never moved far from the one spot, and his words came as short and sharp as Gus's own. His eyes did not leave Gus's face. He was like a doctor, alert to the slightest reaction. But there was none. Gus sat immovable, implacable, staring at the hills and pastures; he had only to hold on, and could afford to; he alone was ready to sell, with everyone else in a frenzy for buying. His remarks were the same, over and over. Maddy, glancing out as often as she would allow herself, knew this from the motion of his mustache and of the firm, bare chin between his shaggy whiskers. To her he was a wall which stood around her, around the whole family, never human but sometimes warm when the sun had beat down on it for a long time, and always strong for them all to creep inside of if they ever needed to. As a child she had lain in bed here and thought how safe she was, that as long as her grandfather lay in his bed below, no tramp, no Indian, no wolf, no witch, no genie, no unnamable horror of any kind could pass him to climb the stairs, and she could go to sleep as sweetly as if she lay cradled in the new moon. She felt the same now. Out there, old as he was, he held the future of the Bragdons and the Grays in the safest hands she knew. She was not worried.

It was Kate who showed the strain.

"It takes them so long," she said. "It's been two hours. I don't see how he stands it. I think about his heart—if he should get a heavy cold onto him—"

"He's all bundled up," Maddy said, "and the thermometer is almost up to sixty—"

"Yes, but there's that chill in the air—"

It was eleven o'clock when at last Mr. Gibbons sprang up and bent over Gus, smiling, speaking rapidly. Maddy saw the lines of Gus's back give a little, saw him jerk his head, and clear his throat, and say, "Well." He took the cane from between his knees and with the help of that and the chair got to his feet. He stood for a minute, bowed over the cane, and then started almost briskly into the house. Mr. Gibbons held open the door, and the pound of the stick and the shuffle of feet came through the entry. Maddy saw Gus's face. Kate saw it, too, though she appeared to be intent on stirring the barberry sauce. It was suddenly younger, dully red as much from triumph as from the crisp air.

"Kin one of ye find my good hat?" he asked. "I've got to git down to the village right off."

Maddy brought his hat, brushing it with her sleeve, slapping it with the corner of her apron. Kate brought his other shoes, and knelt and changed them for him; his feet were so swollen the length of the laces was soon exhausted.

"Thar," Gus said. "That'll do. Let 'em go. Tie 'em thar to the ankles. It's well enough."

He suffered Kate to put a muffler around his neck and Maddy to tuck a white handkerchief into his pocket in place of his blue bandanna. He scarcely noticed what they were doing. There were important matters for him to keep track of. He went into the bedroom and came out with his pockets bulging.

"I don't know when I'll git back," he said. "Got to see to . . . And them things is always likely to break down on the road."

"Well, we'll expect you when we see you," Kate answered cheerfully.

"Yes," Maddy agreed. "We'll have you something to eat whenever you get around."

They did not say not to stay too long and get tired out, nor ask if he was sure he felt able. They let him go as he was, his face still ruddy and his step brisk.

When the two came back, late in the afternoon, Mr. Gibbons said to Kate, from the patch of grass before the steps, "Well, your father's done a big stroke of business today." He chuckled genially. "Made a big turnover."

"That so," said Kate, in the doorway.

Gus chuckled too, a short sound. He looked worn, but his face lit up. He turned and surveyed Mr. Gibbons.

"Yeus," he said. "I guess we put through our last deal, Gibbons. And I thinks likely *you're* the one that got soaked *this* time—"

"Oh, I'll make out all right, Gus. As I've said, I couldn't make anything, sawing this winter, at the price I paid, but if I can hold onto it a year or two—"

Gus looked him up and down once more, and laughed again before he shuffled into the house.

"Humph," he said. "You got my Asy Cheney lot for next to nothin' once. Now you can hold onto this for all ye're worth. You'll *still* find I've soaked ye!"

In the kitchen he said to Maddy, fumbling to pull a slip of paper from his soft old pouch bag. "Ye'd better take a look at this here. Taint likely ye'll ever see another one this big. Not many does."

The check was for forty thousand dollars.

Well enough that Sarey had had her little fortune to fritter away.

Forty thousand dollars, and still there were many lots left growing, and there were mortgages, and bonds, and notes, and a good deal more money in the bank. Not bad, to have been dug by one pair of hands out of twenty acres of thin and rocky Maine soil. Not bad, what the Bragdons, yeoman farmers from the north of England, had accumulated since leaving the old country. The first Gus, looking ahead, had been satisfied. The last, looking back, was no less so. Workers, both of them.

6

"You still think this is the best place to keep it, do you, Aunt Kate?"

"Well, there, if we had it way off in the sitting-room or parlor somewhere, who would be in there to hear it? Here in the kitchen is where we take the good of anything."

"But I keep thinking what if, dropping wood into the wood box or banging the stove door, we might jiggle some of the wires loose. Like just now when I dropped the tank cover. Don't you believe I'd better stop and see if it still works?"

"Well, perhaps you had better. It's got to work today, of all days."

"That's what I mean. And if anything should

be wrong, Freddie would have time now to get over here and fix it."

"I don't know whether he would or not. It's 'most eleven o'clock."

"Oh, they can't get here much before noontime, coming all that ways."

Maddy took off the sweater she had worn to the well after water, washed her hands at the sink, and seated herself before the dials of the radio, which set like a sewing box on the table between the windows, with a disk-shaped loud-speaker on top and a dozen or more wires hanging to connect with the batteries which filled the shelf underneath. Her lean fingers moved with delicacy and precision, her head inclined to catch the first sound. It came creeping into the room, the deep voice of a minister in the midst of his Thanksgiving service.

"—has come a financial crisis in the industrial life of this great nation. It is, after all, a small matter, but there are those in whose eyes it looms large. There are men, strong and wise men, who in the last few week have lost whole properties and to them this loss made life seem not worth living, and they have by their own hands cut it off. This type of tragedy, repeated in each morning's paper, is to me, my friends, a greater cause for concern than anything which could happen to our economic set-up. Are our strongest indeed so weak that they cannot face hardship after ease, privation after luxury? Are we so well trained in victory that we have no courage with which to accept defeat and start at once to build upon it? If so, what fatal training we have had! Are our wisest indeed of so little wisdom that they do not know how much stronger God is than they, how puny are all these little matters of poverty and wealth, success and failure in His sight, in comparison with the eternal verities? Are we as a people so entangled, so enmeshed in ticker tape—"

"That's certainly all right," said Kate. "Comes through fine."

She had stood for a minute, listening, her hands on her hips and her face proud of what her polished box could produce. Now she turned again to the stove. There was a popping sound as she dipped up gravy and poured it over the crisp brown breast of the roasting chicken. The rich smell filled the room. The floorboards, those which Sarey had scrubbed, the doorframes with their uneven nailheads, the tables and chairs, the littered mantelpiece, the yellow oak clock with the brass face, all breathed it in gratefully, making it part of themselves, one of many Thanksgivings they had known. Only the radio was new, and seemed reluctant to exchange its shine for homeliness.

"Sounds good, don't it?" Maddy asked.

"Oh, it's got a fine tone. There wasn't another one in the whole of Porchmuth—"

"I meant the sermon," Maddy said, tying on an apron thoughtfully. "That's all I miss since I came home. I always liked going to church."

"Well, I've kind of got used to it, it's been so long since I had one to go to," Kate answered. "I don't know. I liked the singing, and it meant a lot to get together, but the sermon—I don't know—all that runnin' on about being damned if you didn't believe things you couldn't believe—I never got very far with that. It never made any sense to me. As father says, religion is all right, but I can't hold with all of it, the way you have to—"

It was time for the potatoes. Kate stood peeling them. Maddy stood beside her, peeling onions. Both wiped the sting from their eyes every minute or two.

"You don't have to," Maddy said. "Churches must be different now. We didn't in Fall River. The minister up there talked about the way anybody ought to live, not what they had to believe."

A step fell on the porch. It was Stephen. Since Thoc had gone, Stephen spent here part of every day the sawmill did not run, and he was coming now for dinner. He brought a box in his arms, a wooden box with chicken wire fastened across the top. When he put it down on the foot of the lounge, Maddy could see the half-grown rabbit, sharp-eyed and sleek, which lay very still in the corner. Kate, too, stepped across and looked in.

"Well, come, come," said Stephen. "Come, Tango. Come to, and do your hopping. You're not hurt by a little trip like this. Not a mite."

Stephen was smiling broadly into the box. His shirt crackled with starch, his suit was pressed into knifelike creases, and his thinning hair had been wet and combed so smooth that the pink of his head showed through. He gave Maddy a pat on her upper arm, and beamed at Kate.

"Thought I'd bring her over to have a visit with her young master. I didn't know how long they'd be here, whether he'd have time to get over to the house or not. I'm in hopes he will. Uncle Thoc left a box of things for him to look over and take what he wants—the fiddle and a set of ship's compasses and some stripes and buttons off old uniforms. But he can see them when he has time. Tango, here, can't wait. She's growing up fast, and I was bound he should get acquainted with her—"

"Well, it's too bad, Steve," Kate said. "It's too bad, but Jim ain't coming today."

"Ain't coming—"

Stephen's face changed. Kate did not watch it. She turned back to the stove and reached in to baste the chicken once more.

"I would have got word to you," she said, "but we didn't hear until the mailman got around late yesterday, and the Thibedeaus were in and spent the evening."

Stephen said, "Hmm." He stood looking down into the box. Tango was beginning to stir with the warmth.

"There's an awful good reason why he isn't, though," said Maddy cheerfully. "A great thing has happened to Jim. Wonderful news!"

"That so," Stephen said, brightening a little. "What's going on?"

"A concert," Maddy cried. She stood triumphantly before him with her feet wide apart, her hands behind her back, her face lifted. "This afternoon, I'll have you to know, sir, James Aaron Linscott, no less, will sing a solo with the Boston Philharmonic Symphony Orchestra, over the national network, and we'll all sit right here in this kitchen and listen to him!"

Stephen looked at Kate.

"That young one going to broadcast?"

"That's what they say," Kate answered, spearing the potatoes and pulling them back where they would cook more slowly.

"My soul," said Stephen softly, his eyes shining, "my soul, my soul, my soul!"

"And he's getting five hundred dollars for it, Steve," Maddy cried, shaking him by the shoulders. "Five hundred dollars, and it is a test, a try-out! If he does as well as they think he will, they'll take him on a tour in his Christmas vacation! And the leader—he's an Italian, he's wonderful, he's known all over the world—he says it isn't just Jim's voice; it's the music in him. He says lots of child voices are true and sweet, but most children don't have music enough to handle 'em. He says Jim won't just sing until his voice changes and then fade out, like most of 'em. He says it's only Jim's way of beginning, and by the time he's through singing soprano, he'll be ready to play the piano before as critical an audience as this country can produce! What do you say to that? *Jim!* If only he does as well as they think he will—"

"Huh," Steve growled. "Whatever they think, he'll surprise 'em! He's got more than any of 'em knows for yet. Now you mark my words!" He bent again over the box and wagged his finger through the wire. "Don't you say so, Tango! . . . My soul, my soul, that little tyke!"

"Well, here they come!" Kate exclaimed. "Maddy! Here they are, driving right in. My land, yes, the yard is full of Linscotts. Here, you put this sweater onto you. There . . . Well, hul*lo,* you folks! Hul*lo,* Harvey! There, Lovey, you old nuisance, you, come along in here! And all you young ones. Well, Lil, you with a baby! Let me get a hold of him. My, what a lump! . . . And here's all Jeff's folks right behind you! . . . Father! Father! *They've come!*"

They made this house of Gus and Sarey Bragdon seem suddenly small. They overran the kitchen, flowed into the sitting room. Here was Lovice, delicate and pretty in her fifties, with a permanent wave in her whitening hair and a dust of pink powder on her cheeks, her dress a heavy blue crêpe with white, ruffled silk organdie collar and cuffs, and her small feet very trim in high-heeled, patent leather pumps. There was something absurd about her, something precious; she grew less like Sarey as the years passed and her condition changed, more like Roxanna. She made Kate want to laugh and cry. They brushed against each other, moving about. Here was Harvey, too, growing stout, looking excited and happy, but uncertain; he watched Lovice closely, taking all his cues from her; his suit seemed new and a little tight for him; he stretched his neck to free it of the collar, and his glance kept running eagerly out of the window to the hills he knew, the marsh, the banks of the Lane, the fence between Gus's and what had been his pasture. Evelyn had not come; she was with Jim; there was talk that Evelyn would soon give up her job and devote her whole time to managing the business of her little brother. Not that he would need her many years, for he was already remarkably canny about money matters: the Bragdon in him. Lillian, her figure much thickened, never a pretty girl, now very plain, like Roxanna's Minnie, had something strong and fine in her face as she handled her baby; her way with him was deft and jolly. Her husband—Raymond, his name was—still a boy, watched her and all the rest self-consciously, as if he vaguely felt how many separate desires of men for women were represented in this milling group, and his own, his for this short, round, laughing young woman, one of them. Raymond's face was white from being always under cover, his hands clear red, and veined, with bitten nails. Clyde clumped about, older than when he went away, looking as much as thirty; as soon as one cigarette went out he lit another; he laughed with a curled lip, bitter, hard, knowing, or pretending to be; no one could say which. Martha was a beauty; small, frail, fine-featured, and yet a beauty in a deep and startling sense; she knew how to walk, how to laugh, how to tilt her head; you thought, without meaning to, of moving pictures, those she had seen and those she might one day make. Maddy strode about among them all like a stable boy, glad to see them, acutely aware of the changes in them, proud of them, ashamed of them, not the same girl as when she sat here alone with Kate and Gus, or when she went out with her whistling Frenchman, light and free.

Here, too, were Jeff and his family. Jeff himself, in overalls and a checked shirt, felt dressed up enough, a big man, quiet, withdrawn, saying little, never speaking the name of those he did make a remark to, not looking directly at any of the women or children, or his father, if he could help it, but not looking at the floor, either, looking off, thinking of impersonal things. Harvey was a godsend to Jeff; these two kept disappearing into the shed or barn, standing bareheaded on the porch to point and nod and shake their heads. Bertha in her old brown taffeta with georgette sleeves felt inferior to these others, especially to Lovice and Martha; she put up her hands often to the pins in her straight hair, and twisted her feet to hide them under the lounge because her shoes were scuffed, and it was not that Jeff could not afford to buy shoes for his wife either; he was an old skinflint, like all the Bragdons; her pretty mouth sagged at the corners and her voice had a plaintive note even when she laughed. At least her children were better-looking and better-behaved than this one of Lil's. Why, she could put her baby down anywhere, and he was asleep without a whimper. The three older ones, Mary Louise and Sally and Frank, sat quietly beside her and caused no one any trouble, until Maddy had to get them off into a corner and start them playing Old Woman's Soup; then of course they made a racket, young-one-like.

Gus came in slowly from the barn and stood and looked from one to another.

"So ye got here, did ye? No—got to wash. . . . Been gittin' down some hay."

He washed, and shook hands around. There was no telling whether he thought of Sarey and their nights on the cornhusk mattress; no telling what he thought; no telling whether he remembered that this prinking little woman in the blue silk dress was the life Sarey had borne alone, while he sat waiting for the train to move along from across the road. He looked mildly pleased, hospitable.

"Well, so ye got here all right—"

Suddenly he was puzzled, having dropped grunting into his chair which, though the room was crowded, had been left vacant. He glanced from face to face, and at last at Kate.

"There is another one."

"You mean James Aaron."

"Yes. The boy."

"He couldn't come, you know, father. We got the letter yesterday. He's going to sing up there to Boston this afternoon. We'll hear him over the radio."

Gus looked surprised. He struck the polished box with the back of his hand.

"Hear him over this, kin we?"

"Oh, yes! At four o'clock."

"Hm," Gus said. "Have to keep it in mind. Four o'clock, ye say." He did not know he had heard of it before, or what it meant. He jerked his head in the direction of the box and made a friendly motion of his hand toward Harvey. "Quite a thing, ain't it, radio?"

They were at table, eating heartily of roast chicken, fricasseed chicken, roast pork, and all kinds of vegetables, hot biscuits and cranberry sauce and sweet pickles, mince pie and apple and pumpkin pie and plum duff: ten grown-ups at one table, three children at another, and the two babies asleep on the lounge. The kitchen was full and warm and snug. Outdoors the sky was lead-colored, the grass pale yellow, the woods dark almost to black. It was two o'clock. They were talking.

"The papers is full every day of what happened in Wall Street last month."

"Well, what do you make of it, Harvey?"

"I don't know what it's all about. They say it means a hard winter, though. Feller like me is lucky to have the janitor work to do in a school. Schools is the last thing they'll close down."

"Father of a boy like yours hadn't ought to have to do janitor work—"

"Well, I'll do what I can. He'll have enough to lean on him, if he ever gits to earnin' more'n he needs."

"What're you hintin' at, Harvey?"

"Nothin'."

"Harvey don't think we ought to spend a cent of Jim's money for ourselves. I suppose he thinks we can travel around with a boy like that looking as if we had come out of the ragbag—"

"Well, you don't, anyway, Lovice. My, that's a handsome dress!"

"I don't s'pose we'll ever see you folks back here to live."

"Well, I don't know. It don't look like it now. Harvey would like to. Maybe some time. I don't know where we'd come to, though. Have you sold the house yet, Kate?"

"No."

"No offers?"

"None high enough."

"There will be next summer, if business picks up."

"I'm thinking now of renting."

"Oh, Kate, anybody that rents a farm will let it go to seed and get the house into dreadful shape—"

"Well, this will be a nice family."

"How do you know?"

"Oh, I know 'em well. It's a young couple. Nice, clean, ambitious folks."

"Who in the world—Oh, Ma-addy!"

"Now, Aunt Kate!"

"Well, didn't you say you wanted me to help you tell it?"

"Well, she told it herself all right. What a face!"

"Now, Madelaine Linscott, if you think I'll stand for that! After I thought you was old enough to have some sense! I s'pose it *is* that Frenchman—"

"Yes, Lovice, it's Fred Thibedeau, and he's as fine a boy as ever grew up in this place. Now you sent Maddy down here to me, and you'll have to leave this to us. He'll be over here after dinner, and you treat him decent, and leave them alone. They're going to be married Christmas Day and stay here until spring and then move into the old place."

"Well, there, I—"

"We're going to be married in the meeting-house, ma!"

"Why, I thought he'd have to have a priest!"

"No. Happens they're Methodists. We're going to have it right here, and Elder Milton from the village will come up. We've already spoken to him. You'll all have to make plans to come and stay two or three days and help decorate the meeting-house with evergreens. Oh, ma, if only it will work out so Jim can come and play the march for me! Of course I don't want him to miss going on that tour, but if it should come right! And Martha will stand up with me, won't you, Martha?"

"Oh, Mad, I'd *love* to!"

"I knew you would. And ma and Aunt Kate and Clyde and Stephen will have to sing."

"Me, sing? Makes me think of an old story Uncle Thoc used to tell about hearing the Cheney girls go by singing at night. He always said he thought it was the cattle loose in the barn and goring one another to death. It wasn't until he had rushed out into the tie-up that he recalled he hadn't but one old cow on the place at the time. So then he knew it must have been the Cheneys."

"Well, it needn't make you think of any such thing. You've got a good voice, and I love to hear you. I guess you'll sing at my wedding if I ask you to, won't you, Steve?"

"Oh, I guess I can make a stab at it, Maddy. But if I do, I'll tell you what you'll have to do after you get spliced. You and Fred will have to bring your crowd over to my place for the wedding dance. Them old floors ain't had any tapping for a good while and they need it. Now is it a bargain?"

"It's a bargain, Stephen."

"Good. Shake. I'll be tuning up the fiddle."

"My, it sounds like old times around here, don't it, Kate? Weddings and dances—"

"Well, it's not old times. It's new times. Ain't it, Maddy?"

They were in the parlor, crowding around the organ, filling the room. Kate's feet pressed the pedals, Kate's hands stroked the keys, playing chords. It was three o'clock. They sang the gospel hymns, the Civil War tunes.

"Aunt Roxan would like to be here," said Lovice. "You'd be surprised how strong and clear her voice still is. You wouldn't believe it. She often speaks of how we used to sing right through the book, over there to grammum's."

Fred came in, was introduced around, and stood holding Maddy's hand; it amused him that she was shy; he kept laughing and drawing her closer. "What is the matter with her?" he asked Lil. "Have you been telling her it's no fun to be married?" They sang "Carry Me Back to Old Virginny," "Blest Be the Stars," and "Hear Dem Bells."

"Heard about the merger of the banks round here?" Gus broke in suddenly upon a chorus. "Derwich bank is j'inin' up with a trust company down to Portland. It ain't no way. It's resky doin'. What will them off down to Portland know about investments folks up here is interested in? Too much runnin' everything from afur off. Too much of it. They'll find it don't pay. Too much combinin'. Ain't no few men fit to run everybody's business."

They were out in the kitchen, sitting very still. It was four o'clock. Maddy's fingers trembled on the dials.

The music came faintly, louder, louder still,

burst into a tumult, and finally ended in a crash. The rows of faces were polite, waiting. They did not understand Chaykovski.

"KCKF brings you now a solo, 'Sanctus,' from Gounod, sung by James Aaron Linscott, boy soprano, accompanied by the Boston Symphony Orchestra."

The music came softly, beating like the hearts in the room. Jim's voice stole into it, a wraith, a small silver thing carried on wings, riding high and gliding down. It came in out of the dull Thanksgiving sky, across the yellow fields and black woods, and filled the house Gus Bragdon had built. It did all the Italian director had expected of it. It did more. It caught what the voices of the Grays, through many generations, had been reaching for. Jim was not here, but he would always live here on York Road and the Lane. Someone had once written, "Thou art come of great things, and great things shall come of thee." No one in the room knew these lines; but Enoch Blaine would have known them, and Enoch Blaine was in this boy.

The voice was still. The music went on, but no one heard it. Lovice sat crying into her hands. All the others were as quiet as in the beginning.

Gus said suddenly: "Kate! Who was that singing?"

"That was James Aaron, father."

"Who?"

"Jim. Lovice's boy."

"Hm . . . Sounded like your mother."

7

The last week in February, Gus did not leave his bed. His room was small; the gray-painted post bedstead and black chest of three drawers very nearly filled it; a brass-bound trunk in a corner and the picture of a spray of goldenrod above the mantelpiece completed the furnishings. The floor was bare. There was only one window. Gus, lying in his flannel workshirt, with a quilt pulled up to his waist, loomed large in the small dim space. His flesh had wasted away, his cheeks looked sunken and dead, his forehead was a strange, gleaming white, but the framework remained, he was still a big man, and he lay like a fallen tree, unable to turn, his colorless eyes quick and grim in their deep sockets.

Kate kept the door open and a hot fire burning in the sitting-room stove. She looked in every little while. There was not much else which could be done. Bertha sent over a note every day or two, saying that Lovice had just telephoned from Fall River to ask when the doctor had been and what he said, wanting to send up a nurse and a wheelchair; and Kate knew Bertha was making talk in the neighborhood that the doctor was not called as often as he should be, Gus did not take his medicine regularly, no one sat up with him at night, and, poor old man, somebody should do for him what needed doing, whether he wanted it done or not, but she, Bertha, was only an in-law with no authority, and it seemed as if Lovice would have to come up here herself, badly off as she was with rheumatism, to see that all was being done for her father that might be, for Kate meant well, of course, but was as hard and unfeeling as a man.

"I could choke Aunt Bert," Maddy muttered to Fred Thibedeau when the door of what had once been Hannah Bragdon's door closed behind them for the night. "And mother, too! Of all the mean-minded—and neither one of them coming near, you'll notice! If they knew anything about the way grandpa is, or ever had been with him enough to know how he *would* be at a time like this! And if they knew Aunt Kate—the least little bit—what she's going through—"

It did not matter to Kate what Lovice and Bertha thought and said. All she wanted just now was for them both to stay away, if only a few days longer, for everybody to stay away except those who belonged here, Maddy and Fred, and Stephen to call in at night. These few days were all Gus had, and she wanted them spent in his own way. He was used now to the steps of Maddy and Fred, and no longer noticed their quiet voices in the room adjoining his, but only Kate ever went in to him; she was the only one he needed, and he did not need her often. He lay secure in the possession of this house, the house he had built, of the snowy yard and fields; he had acquired it all, watched and handled it all, and now, at the end, the walls he had raised closed him in, the shingles he had laid sheltered him, and his own birch sticks crackled in the stove; he could feel the warmth of the fire on his hands and see the ruddy reflection on the panels of the open door. His thoughts ran like those of a contented child, only half awake, asking for nothing, wishing for nothing, touching lightly here and there. He wanted only to be let alone, and this Kate intended he should be. Drawn and pale, she worked about the kitchen all day, and lay on the couch in the sitting room at night, waiting, ready. She knew what was coming, but did not feel afraid except that strangers (all outside the house were strangers now) might try to come in, jabbering, crying, arguing that changes must be made which never would be made as long as Gus had breath to make his wishes known and Kate had strength to see they were carried out. She never heard a wheel turn on the road but what it filled her with apprehension. Other than that the days were peaceful. The wind blew hard outside; but the windows were well stuffed with rags, and not much of the cold crept in. The sun shone nearly every morning, and every afternoon the sky was thin and alive with rolling clouds. Fred knew how to work. He took good care of the barn and the creatures, and hauled two or three loads of timber from the woods every day. Kate and Maddy kept the rooms clean, cleaner than was necessary; their hands had to be doing; but they knew how to manage without making much sound. The house was very quiet, so that whenever Gus spoke Kate could hear him.

Sometimes she went in carrying a cup and spoon.

"Drink a little of this, father, can't you?"

"What ye got thar?"

"Jamaica ginger. It'll warm you up."

"Well. If ye kin rise my head."

He drank in good, stout draughts, like a horse at the end of the day's work, and dropped back.

"Could you take another cupful?"

"No. No, had enough."

"I've got some beef tea made—"

"No. Nothin' more. Not now."

"The doctor said to keep your strength. That's the main thing."

Gus did not answer. So the doctor said an old man had to keep his strength. Quite an idea, that. So strength was the main thing. Now the doctor was a smart one, to know so much. Certain it was the main thing, but it got away from a man in time, as the doctor would find out for himself if he lived long enough, and then he was better off underground. It would take a richer tea than any yet discovered to put Gus Bragdon on his feet.

"Kate. You thar?"

"Yes."

"Don't ye have the doctor here again. Ye hark what I tell ye."

"They all think you ought to let him see you, father."

"I tell ye, keep him out. Doctors can't do nothin' for me. I won't have 'em here, runnin' up bills."

"Well, it'll be as you say, father."

Sometimes there were hours when he neither spoke nor stirred. Then he would call out peremptorily, whether it was night or day. Dark and daylight were much the same to him. Through both he could see the fire reflected on his door. He heard the clock strike, but did not count the strokes. It made no difference. It only meant another hour had gone by.

"Kate. Git me a drink of water. Git it fresh from the well. . . . Ah-h-h, good water. None better. Dug that well myself. Fall of '75. Sarey didn't want the young ones fallin' into the open spring, so I dug down and stoned it up and covered it over. . . . Put it fifteen feet deeper in '97. . . . Won't never lack water in that well."

Sarey had once been envious that his body troubled him so little he could put it in a chair and leave it there, not thinking of it, until he needed to take it to another place. It must trouble him now; it was heavy and leaden and cold; but still it seemed that he had laid it on the bed and did not think of it, even to wonder what would become of it. Gus himself stood free, considering what he had owned, work he had done, all he had assembled in this place in eighty years, and by what means he had accomplished so much.

"Kate. Don't ye let 'em bring no flowers here."

"Flowers?"

"Funeral flowers. I won't have 'em. Wasted money, every cent. Anybody that wants that bad to be red of it can burn it. Wouldn't smell the house up so, neither. Now ye keep 'em out of here, mind."

"I'll do what I can, father."

"Well, ye keep 'em out of here, that's all. And don't ye go buyin' no fancy casket. Now ye hear me. I ain't leavin' hard-earnt money to be spent in no sech way."

"What do you want I should do, father?"

"Want ye should do? Git a pine box. A good pine box. Ain't nothin' better. . . . And if it looks bare to ye, wrop it up in some pine branches."

"Well—"

"Now go 'long about your work. Got your butter made out?"

"Yes."

"Eggs packed?"

"They will be when it's time."

"You goin' to market?"

"No. Fred will."

"Well. See ye figger up when he gits back. Ye hadn't ought to leave it to him so much. There's times he don't come out jest right. It's the small change counts in farmin'."

Once about midnight he said:

"Kate. Ye'll have enough to do with. Ye ain't no need to worry. Everything is straightened out. I ain't left no loose ends."

"I'm not worried. Any way you wanted to do will be all right for me."

"I got it all fixed back last fall. One day Gibbons took me to the village in his automobile, and another time I rid down with Jeff."

Kate remembered both days very well, how long he had been gone, and how she had watched the road, waiting for him to come back. Red and yellow leaves, ripening crab apples, engine smoke over back of the Pond, and flurries of dust after every passing car. Now there was nothing to see but snow, nothing to hear but the wind and Gus's voice, nothing to do but stand in her outing flannel nightgown just inside the bedroom door, hugging her own elbows.

"I didn't make no will. It's costly. Inheritance

taxes is awful steep. I had this house and all the lots deeded to you."

"You needn't have done that, father—"

"Needn't? Who else is there to see after 'em? . . . I had your name put on one of my bank books, and Lovice's on three, and Jeff's on five. . . . There was one other one. The Porchmuth bank. Around $21,000. That one I made over to Lawyer Barney. He's got it in charge for the—that young one."

"Jim?"

"Say out his whole name."

"James Aaron."

"Yeus. That one. . . . It's writ down it ain't to be used for nothin' else but gittin' him ahead. He ain't to have the spendin' of it. It's to be spent before he gits of age, and not by his folks on foolishness; by Lawyer Barney, to git him ready to go to work at—whatever he's fittin' to work at. . . . Quite a sum, but I guess he's good for it."

"I guess he is, too, father. I'm glad you did it. I'm glad you fixed it just that way."

"Oh, I ain't so fur gone yet that I don't know what'll become of whatever Lovice and Harvey gits their hands on."

"They mean to be saving, father—"

"I know it, I know it. Mean well enough. But some folks ain't capable of holdin' onto anything.

. . . Oh, you can't tell me. I know Grays and I know Linscotts and I know Blaines. I know 'em, know all about 'em."

Then came a time when Gus talked a night through. His mind was clear. He was wholly himself, but in his weakness of body he lost consciousness that there were ears to hear, or indeed that words were generally intended to be heard, and spoke as his thoughts came, of matters he would never have wasted voice on when he had more important things to do. Lying big on the bed, in the close, dark room, he listened to his own sounds with a kind of simple pride, a pleasure that he could still make them, could still feel his chest heave and his pulse beating in his throat, and see the firelight on the door. He was Gus Bragdon, old, almost gone, entirely alone, entirely secure, running over for his entertainment the life he had lived.

"Fust one I bought myself was that Asy Cheney. Good lot, that was. Within a mile of whar the railroad was bound to go through. Good buy. Come hard, right then, but it wa'n't the time to hold off. Sarey see with me on that, too. 'Twa'n't till long afterwards Sarey got off on the wrong foot. Not till she got started ag'in goin' over to the Gray place. Roxan; that cutter was a troublemaker, dyed in the wool. . . . Mother, how she stood up to Mindwell that night in the meetin'-

house! What a rinktum thar was! They thought they'd got me roped and hogtied up thar, but they found they hadn't. Drink would make a devil or a dunce out of every man that put his mouth up to it, would it? Well, I told 'em. I told 'em it wouldn't never make a devil nor a dunce out of me. Take more then one drink to do that to anybody; ye got to have suthin' to start with. I ain't drunk enough to hurt me. I ain't had neither time nor money to spend a-standin' with my foot on a brass rail. . . . I guess thar wa'n't none of 'em as was thar that night has done fur better than I have. I ain't done much prayin'. I been workin'. But I've read the kivers off my Bible, and I know what's in it, and what it means, as I see it. That church wa'n't no place for me. I didn't see with 'em. . . . What harm has poor Ketury ever done, buried down on my hill, or would she 'a' done buried anywhars? Nothin' but a crazy young one, all she was. If it wa'n't right for her to lay with Enoch Blaine up on the aidge of the Black Swamp, she paid fur it, full; and so did he, that night he set a-listenin' to Jeddy car'in' on so, and for forty years afterwards, with Catharine; wa'n't no need of the Elder a-pilin' of it on. . . . Huckleberries growed awful big and thick up in the Black Swamp. I mind pickin' 'em with mother when I wa'n't more'n five or six years old, and a-beatin' off the minges. Minges was awful thick in thar, a low'ry day. I mind the time she strayed in and got lost amongst the alders and I had to go after her. . . . I allus knowed the woods. I wa'n't more'n eight the day Cap'n David Blaine and some fine ladies that was a-visitin' thar to Blaines went up on the mountain and got lost a-comin' down. I was drivin' my cows out, 'round dark, when I heard 'em yellin', and walked three miles to find 'em and git 'em out to the road. It had come on to rain, and they was soaked, and I took 'em to the house and mother dried 'em off and dosed 'em with sassafras tea. The Cap'n, he give me ten cents. I'd 'a' throwed it at him if it hadn't been for mother. S'I to myself, 'Next time ye git lost in the woods, ye kin stay thar.' . . . I wisht I had a plate of beans, hot out of the pot. Mother allus made bannock to go with 'em, the print of her three fingers baked into every slice of it. I allus liked pepper on my beans, same as father. Kate, when she got along, she allus shook pepper onto hern, too, I noticed. Grays, they was all for sugar on their beans, and sweet apple instead of punkin in their barb'ry sauce. Now for me, barb'ry sauce ain't barb'ry sauce without thar's punkin in it. . . . Sarey would take bones out of fish when she made a chowder, every chance she got. Wa'n't no way. Backbone of a fish cooked in a chowder makes all the difference; I don't know; it's got a salt-water tang. . . . One. Two. Three. Four. Five. Six.

Seven. Eight. . . . Fust they went afoot or ahorseback. Mother rid me all the way to Waterbury on a sorrel mare before I was a year old, I've hearn tell. Round about '80 I got the fust wagon we had. A man come by with one to sell, and I give him my note for ten dollars, and he went along the road and sold the note to Charles for eight. Kind of went ag'inst the grain, that did. But I got ahead of Charles before the end of it. Charles didn't leave much over $10,000, once his bills was paid. . . . Then they got the trains to runnin', and that was suthin' great until the automobiles went to rockin' through the ruts everywhars, and now it's airships. . . . Blaines allus thought thar was treasure hid around that house somewhars. Thought the womenfolks buried money and silver pieces and other stuff durin' the Revolution. Last thing Enoch ever done, helped Thoc rip up the floor of the kitchen thar. That was like Blaines. Trouble with Blaines. Lived just like young ones. . . . Got that stove for a dollar. Good stove. Good enough for anybody. . . . Way you've got to farm in this country, way you've got to do, got to have a little mite of everything; not too much; too much is worse than nothin'. Twenty-five hens is enough; 'bout four cows and two pigs; orchard is a good thing; got to know your weather ahead, to tell when to plant. Have to keep diggin', and got to have suthin' else, some other line; farmin' ain't enough to git anywhars with, nor never was. . . . Squirrels will never take a poor nut. Never find a bad one in their holes, nor in hollow trees or niches in a stone wall where they hide 'em. Ye can't fool a squirrel. Nuts that's left where they fell is always false. . . . One. Two. Three. Four. Five. . . . The Lord is my shepherd. . . . Time Sarey went off, that time, she took twenty-four silver dollars out of my chist. Twenty-four dollars. Counted wrong, must have. . . . Too much combinin'. Gittin' too fur away from everything nowadays. Like tryin' to drive a horse while ye set in the house with the reins through a winder. Won't work. Won't work, and they'll find it out so. . . . Lumber's dropped two dollars on a thousand. Quite a drop. Mounts up. Told him I'd soaked him. Hah! Told him I'd soaked him. . . . Got to watch yere lines. Have to keep in mind ye've got to watch yere lines whar thar's cuttin' goin' on. Can't be too car'ful. . . . Father was eighty when he went out. 'Bout long enough. Y've cut yere figger by then. . . . Never see no fire like that went through the Asy Cheney lot and over the Horse Hills. That was in '98. Woods was all afire that summer. Linscotts, 'twas, got it a-goin'. Allus awful handy with matches, them Linscotts. . . . Even Jeff, he put into the woods to go to fightin' fire. Nothin' but a young one. . . . Fust schoolbook I ever had I chopped a cord of hard pine for. . . . Seems as if I smell beans a-bakin'—"

He did. It was only two o'clock in the morning, but Kate had a potful picked over and parboiled and in to bake. All the rest of the night she tended them, sitting close to the sitting-room door to listen to Gus, but going every little while to keep the fire box full and the pot bubbling with water. Unless she needed light from the lamp she left it turned low, not to attract the notice of the neighbors, and the kitchen was full of shadows. There was no sound except Gus's voice and the fires in the two stoves and the yellow oak clock ticking. Outside, the wind had gone down and the moon was out; it shone pale across the snow; Kate could make out the familiar points of the horizon against the clear sky as she stood by the window. At daybreak she stirred up hot-water bannock and set it in beside the beans to bake. The rich, grainy smell of both stole sweetly through the rooms. By sunup she had a plate of food to take in to Gus; beans and bannock and barberry sauce.

"What ye got thar? Beans?"

"Yes. Beans and bannock."

"Well. Rise up my head."

He took each mouthful hungrily as she held it to him, and did not lie back until the plate was clean.

"Put pepper on 'em, didn't ye?"

"Yes. I sprinkled it on thick."

"Thought I tasted it. Good pork, ain't it?"

"Yes, it's nice pork."

"Was it last fall I butchered?"

"Fall before last."

"Enough left in the barrel to git ye through?"

"Yes. Plenty."

"Hmm. Good pork as ever we had."

"Could you eat any more of anything, father?"

"What? More? No. No, had enough."

"Then couldn't you get to sleep?"

"Sleep? Well. Maybe so."

He slept nearly all day. Kate and Maddy moved about the house more quietly than ever. Another storm was growing outside, but Gus did not know it. He snored faintly. Kate heard his breathing come and go. A little before dark she stepped out of the bedroom to say Fred had better start now after Jeff; then she went back again and stood beside the bed.

There was no light except the reflection of the fire when Gus stirred, but Kate knew his eyes were turned on her. There was no sound except the wind, but he must have thought he heard the whistle of a train.

"I wish I was aboard of her," he said, "a-bound for England."

Kate took his hand and held it very hard. A few minutes later she slid down beside the bed and laid her face against it. She was still there when Maddy came on tiptoe, and, without looking up, she made room for Madddy next to her. They were not frightened. This was Gus's body which he had left lying here because he no longer had any use for it. It was something for them to lean against until they learned how to stand up by themselves. This was his room. His overalls still hung on the post where he had put them. His boots stood under the bed. These were the walls he had built and the roof he had shingled, and the rosy light from the burning of his birch wood still shone warm on the door.

8

"Frogs are going it lively tonight," Stephen said.

"Yes, ain't they?"

"When I was a young one, Thoc used to say that noise was the wheels of gypsies' wagons creaking over Rocky Hills."

"I like to hear 'em."

"They give me kind of a lonesome feeling."

Kate shook her head.

"They don't me. I always feel when I first hear the frogs as if everything has been over for a long time and now it is about ready to start again. I don't know what it'll be, but I look ahead to it."

It was very dark on the steps. The moon was

not yet up and the few stars were hid every minute or two behind rambling clouds. The only light came through the window from the kitchen lamp which Maddy and Fred had turned down when they went to bed. The branches of the maples tossed about in this pale radiance, beaten by a springlike wind on which the frog song rode, and which also brought proof that water ran free in the marsh once more and Mayflowers were turning out their pink underlips in the woods. Kate and Stephen sat quietly, letting the season bear down upon them.

"Don't forget you're going to give me that letter of Lovice's. My ears don't catch up everything you say lately. When I read it over to myself, I get the full gist of it."

Kate handed him the letter from the folds of her shawl.

"When was it, now, she said they would have to leave?"

"The first of June, about."

"I don't suppose he'll get down here."

"I guess they'll have to bring him down. He wouldn't start off without making us a visit, I don't believe."

"I'll have his things ready for him. What Thoc left. The brass buttons and like that. He'll be surprised to see how fat a rabbit can get if it's kept fed. . . . It's quite a thing for him, ain't it?"

"I suppose it is. All the great ones seems to have to study over there somewheres. Most of 'em go onto the Continent, they say. France and Italy. I'm glad this teacher he's going to is in England. It don't seem so strange to think of. Some way England is kind of home. Like a house where anybody's great-grandmother lived. Even if you hadn't ever been into it before, whenever you did go, it would feel natural to you."

"Yes. That's so. I feel the same."

"Lovice is cut up, not to be going."

"I suppose she would be. She couldn't stand to miss out."

"But Evvie wouldn't have it. Ev wrote Maddy she was glad Jim would be away from Lovice for a while. I guess she wears on him."

"She'd wear on anybody."

"Lots of Aunt Roxan to her. More than we ever thought until late years. That same way of always wanting more than there is. It's a good thing Jim has got Ev. She'll see after him."

"Capable girl, I guess."

"Bragdon, through and through."

A little later Stephen spoke of the Blaine place.

"When you coming over to clean up my ranch for me? Or are you sick of the job?"

"No, I'm not sick of it, but I won't lift a hand till you get them shingles on. Now I sent them over to you two months ago, ones father had stored in the barn cellar, and you ain't drove a nail into one of 'em yet. What's the use of me putting paper on them upstairs rooms when I can see daylight through the roof if I get into the attic?"

"You're a nagger, Kate," chuckled Stephen. "I guess I'm well off I never married you."

"Sure you are. But if you don't look out, you'll be living with me yet, because you won't have any other place to go."

"Oh, now, I'm not that bad off, Kate. That house will stand as long as I need one."

"Maybe. Maybe not. You Blaines are long-lived. . . . Come, Steve, now say—when will you have them shingles on?"

Stephen straightened with a long breath.

"Before the last day of the month!"

"What month?"

"This month!"

"Good. That's the talk. . . . I won't be long getting the cleanin' and papering done after that. I'm through here now. I started right after funeral, to have something to do. Of course I knew Maddy would need some help with her settling about this time."

"How soon will they get moved in over there?"

"In a couple of weeks now, I thinks likely. Fred wants to be there ready for the planting."

"Be kind of empty-feeling here for you, till you get used to it."

"Yes. I don't know, though. It'll be a satisfaction to me to have grammum's house open again. I'd as soon Maddy and I'd be running back and forth as to have her here. Maybe rather."

There was a slight change in the wind. The lamp went out. The smell of the Mayflowers and of the moss they grew among was richer than before, thick in the foggy dark.

"I don't have any objection to living alone," Stephen said. "Now some can't bear to eat and sleep without somebody always around. But I don't have any objection."

"No," Kate agreed. "No; you get used to it."

"I don't say I'd like it in a new house. But in an old one, well, I'll tell you how I feel—feel as if all them that ever lived in it was right around somewhere."

"Yes, I know what you mean. Always seems to me as if mother and granny was in the next room here. And Jeff, too, not so hard and close-mouthed as he is now, and Lovice before she turned so much like Aunt Roxan."

Stephen assented, and cleared his throat.

"Feel that way about your father?"

After a minute Kate answered: "Yes. He's here, at the table having his dinner, or in the bedroom. Or he may be out on the porch with a lumber dealer, or down in the field hoeing. Or else he's to market, or up in the woods after a load of limbs. He's not confined to the house like the rest of 'em. He's somewhere else from right where I am. That's all."

She let it rest at that. She did not go on about it. She did not try to explain that she did not believe Gus Bragdon was dead. He had grown old, and wasted away, and stopped breathing, and been buried in his pine box down on the hill, but it would take more than that to kill Gus Bragdon. He was too strong for death. As long as his house stood, as long as his land was cultivated, as long as his trees grew and his lumber went into building, as long as his blood ran in any man's veins, he would be alive.

"Well," Stephen said, yawning and stretching, "I suppose I've got to be getting along up the line."

Kate turned her head. She had been leaning forward with her elbows on her knees and her chin in her hands. Now it was her cheek her fingers supported, so that she could look at Stephen.

"What'll you be up to tomorrow?"

"I've got a little job fencing for the Cheney girls."

"You ought to be fencing for yourself."

"Always ladies first with me, Kate! You know that!"

"Oh, go on! It's anything first with you, ahead of your own work. . . . I never see the beat of you, Steve; I never did. . . . They'll pay you a little something for that fencing, and I'll bet ten to one you'll spend it on a new hat or a necktie."

"No, I shan't either. Hat and necktie's good enough. I'm going to get me some flower seeds. We haven't had a decent garden over there for ten years. I've got me a catalogue and marked 'em all down, what I want. My soul, some of them pictures is the handsomest of anything I ever saw in my life. They've got some giant sweet peas pictured out—"

"There, now, Stephen!"

"All right, all right. You'll like the sweet peas, though, when they get to blooming."

She smiled, shaking her head a little.

"I suppose I will, at that."

He rose suddenly to his feet, nimble as a cat, for all he was fast growing into a heavy man.

"Well, I've got to be going. It's a dark walk by night, late years, with nobody to light a lamp anywheres around. Nothing but a cemetery to go by."

"Well, we're not afraid of ghosts, Steve."

"No. If I see one, I'll take him with rocks, the way Shem Joy did his father the time he rigged up in sheets to try to scare him." Stephen chuckled. "Old Eben said if he hadn't put for the house for all he was worth, Shem would have killed him."

Kate laughed too.

"I guess you can take care of yourself. Come over again whenever you get around to it."

"Yes, I will. And you come over to the house."

"I will—when you get it shingled."

"I told you I'll have that roof shingled by the end of the month."

"That's what you said."

They both laughed. Stephen tapped away smartly into the dark with his quick, springing step. Kate could hear him leave the old grass of the yard for the gravelled road and then wade, a little later, into the dry husks of a field which had not been mowed last summer. The sound of him died away into the night, but she still sat on, wrapped in her shawl.

Kate Bragdon had always been a trifle strange. It was too cold yet for birth, but she felt life stirring. It was too early for the moon, but she saw its promise along the horizon. The sun was as far away as it ever went, and still it shone bright, and the warmth of it came up through the earth to her. She sat unthinking, contented, her chin in her hands, studying the toes of her shoes and the cracks in the board of the lower step on which her feet rested.